I0612955

Poppy's Choice

by

Elisabeth Rose

Poppy's Choice

Cover Art by *Tina Lynn Stout*

The Wild Rose Press, Inc.
PO Box 708
Adams Basin, NY 14410-0708
Visit us at www.thewildrosepress.com

Publishing History
First Edition, 2024
Trade Paperback ISBN 978-1-5092-5320-3
Digital ISBN 978-1-5092-5321-0

Published in the United States of America

She looked up as footsteps sounded on the wooden floor. Duncan? What did he want? Why wouldn't he keep away from her? Perspiration prickled her neck and her fingers fumbled closing the catch on her briefcase.

"Good morning." There was the smile that twisted her heart.

"Hello," she said with as little as enthusiasm as she could given something deep inside her insisted it was pleased and excited by his appearance.

Before she could organize a question he said, "What are you doing for lunch?"

"No idea. I've only just had breakfast." A stretch, breakfast had been over two hours ago.

"Would you like to have lunch with me at the pub? Or somewhere else?"

The sane part of her screamed no, she was supposed to be avoiding him, protecting herself and Jessie, but the stupidly reckless part, the part that had got her pregnant to this man in the first place, insisted yes.

"My work time is limited." She kept her tone cool.

"Oh right. Can you spare an hour?" He gave her an icy stare in return. "Don't feel you have to if you're too busy."

"Why?" His attitude made it easier to hold out against that relentless force that drew her to him.

"Why do I want to have lunch with you?"

"Yes."

"I thought it might be nice to get to know you better and…" He sighed and glanced around the room as if embarrassed to give her the real reason. "I'd like some company."

Praise

Poppy's Choice is my fourth book with TWRP, my seventh romantic suspense and my twenty third book overall.

Dedication

As always to my support network, my family: Colin, Carla, Nick, and Paige.

Chapter 1

The band was pumping out the decibels when Poppy reluctantly pushed open the door to the Royal Hotel. The unique pub pong hit her on the nose. Old pubs were like schools; they all had a distinctive smell that lingered down the decades, with the years of now banned smoking, beer, spillages, customers, kitchen offerings, cleaning products, and struggling air con combining in a familiar blend that oozed from the furnishings and carpets.

A good-sized crowd had turned up despite it being mid-week and more would come later. Mainly the student age group, most likely from the agricultural college just out of town but a few older rockers were enjoying the sounds produced by four energetic musos. It was early so the audience hadn't warmed up, content to listen and drink, not yet lubricated enough for the dance floor, although feet were tapping and heads nodding.

Poppy scanned the room for George, but he must have been watching for her because he was already by her side, leaning in to shout, "Hi," in her ear because any normal level of conversation was doomed.

"Hi," she yelled.

He wore jeans and a black shirt with the sleeves half rolled and looked subtly different in a way she couldn't pinpoint even though she'd seen him in nonschool teacher attire before.

"What?" He was in her ear again.

"Nothing. It's loud." One of the reasons she hadn't been keen on coming along.

He grinned. "Drink?"

"Beer, please." She pointed to a couple of empty stools at a high table by the wall and he nodded and headed for the bar. Poppy claimed the table and scanned the crowd. Most faces were familiar, but she couldn't see Steph or any of her other friends. She hadn't been to a rock gig for ages. Deafening head-banging music had never really been her thing, and she wouldn't be here tonight if George hadn't invited her and said he'd played in a band with one of the musicians. She'd seen the posters around town but hadn't taken much notice.

Who knew George had been in a band? She certainly didn't. She couldn't imagine anyone less likely than the slightly pudgy fifth grade teacher at the Currong Primary School. Although come to think of it, physically and apart from the teacher bit that also described one of the Blues Brothers.

George put her beer on the table along with a couple of packets of salt and vinegar chips. From across the room with the intervening moving heads and bodies it was hard to see any of the band members properly but the singer had a shaved head, a silver earring which glinted in the lights, and a top half enclosed in an unbuttoned red shirt. The band finished the song to a ripple of applause.

In the moment of silence Poppy asked, "Which one's your friend?"

"The singer. Kyle."

"Good voice." Surprisingly good. So was the band. Much better than she'd expected and not so heavy metal. More melodic but already dialed up to ear ringing level.

"Yes. He was a great front man for the soul band."

"Why did you stop playing?"

"Too hard to fit with the day job."

"Late nights?"

"And traveling. I could only do that at weekends or holidays. It was exhausting—a lot of late night driving and crappy take away food eaten at weird hours."

"But Kyle still likes it, obviously."

George picked up his beer and took a drink but before he could reply the drummer whacked out an intro riff and they were off again. Four or five tunes later they took a break. The more melodic song she'd walked in on must have been their low-key number because the tempo had picked up and the crowd filled the dance floor. Many of them knew the songs and yelled the choruses along with Kyle. Poppy excused herself to go to the Ladies stopping along the way to chat to Fran from the Community Center who'd come in with a group of friends. Still no sign of Steph who'd said she was coming. When she returned to the table George's mate was on her stool, downing a drink with him.

George smiled and stood up, indicating she should take his seat.

"Kyle, this is Poppy, my friend and next door neighbor."

Kyle stuck out a hand. An exotic looking silver ring adorned his middle finger. "A pleasure to meet you."

Hooded eyes scanned her body, rested on her breasts for too long then traveled to her face, meeting her eyes for a moment while his sweaty fingers squeezed hers. Those eyes were a surprisingly bright blue… Something clicked in Poppy's brain and shut down her breathing for a long moment. She knew this guy.

It was him.

Her lungs protested and she sucked in air. Neurons fired, her brain kicked back in, analyzed, overcame the panic with logical thought. Blue eyes, yes. The same ones, no. This guy was shorter, thinner faced. Wrong tatts. Not him. She didn't know him. He didn't know her. Breathe. Breathe.

"Georgie said you have your own business." He picked up a glass of what looked like vodka or gin and something with ice and eyed her as he drank. Probably thought her freak-out was due to his charisma.

"Yes, I offer proofreading and academic editing services." Georgie?

"Sounds boring as batshit." Kyle pulled a face then grinned at her and winked. "Whatever floats your boat. I'm not the academic type. Left school as soon as I could."

Stuff him. It wasn't what she'd set out to do in life, not that she had any idea what that was, but a single mother with an Arts degree majoring in English she'd worked hard to get had limited options when working from home in a country town, and it kept her and Jessie functioning.

"How's the tour going?"

"Touring's always a blast." He smiled and winked at George. "I won't give any secrets away, though."

"Secrets?" Poppy glanced at George who caught her eye and shrugged, but his eyes narrowed slightly.

"No names to protect the innocent." He picked up his glass and just before drinking sent another sly grin George's way, this one bordering on a threat.

By the look on his face, George wasn't happy with this pointed reminiscing. Just how much of a friend was this guy? And how could she ever have mistaken Kyle for someone she knew? No way would she have hooked up with him however briefly and however out of it she was.

The least she could do was try to distract him from poking at George by making conversation, when really she wanted to throw her beer in his smirking face.

"How long has the band been together?"

"This is our second year. We've just released an album but three singles are available to download." He rattled off the titles which she promptly forgot.

"Where else are you going?"

"Here you go, gorgeous." He fished a crumpled flyer from his hip pocket and gave it to her. She shoved it into her bag. She was fast running out of questions.

"So how was working with George?" she asked then could have kicked herself for bringing him back into the firing line.

"He was solid on bass," Kyle said with unexpected seriousness. "Pity he gave it away."

"Couldn't do both," said George.

"It must be really tiring touring all the time," said Poppy.

"It's a good way to meet chicks," Kyle said.

"Does it work?"

"Yeah?" He leaned forward. "I've met you tonight,

5

haven't I?"

Couldn't tell him to get lost the way she really wanted to—he was George's friend, although by the look on George's face the relationship was deteriorating rapidly. She tried again.

"Have you always wanted to sing?"

Maybe it was her tone or her expression but he finally got the message she wasn't on the menu, wouldn't be tonight's special.

"I played drums a bit when I was a kid but I liked singing. It was hard to do both but I like being out front better, you know?"

"To impress the chicks," she said, nodding.

"You got it, sweetheart. We're back on now. Can't keep the fans waiting. Catch you later."

Kyle drained his glass and threaded through the crowd to the band, acknowledging comments as he went, and stopping to chat up a group of giggling young women, his hand casually resting around one slim blonde's waist, fingers straying to her jeans clad bum.

"Georgie? Does anyone else call you that?" she said.

"No, just Kyle," he said tersely.

"Do you mind? Does it bother you?" Kyle hadn't used it in an affectionate way. There'd been an unmistakable edge of derision.

"It's not worth objecting. That's what he's like," said George. "I haven't seen him for a few years. Sorry. He's always been a bit..."

Didn't answer the question. Why?

"Don't apologize for him," she said. "I'm sorry if he really is a friend, but why did you say he could stay with you?"

"I couldn't think of a fast enough excuse. It's only two nights then he goes to Goulburn."

"You're way too nice." She downed some beer. "Has he always been a muso?"

"Yes, he's mostly freelanced and been in a lot of bands. He and his brother co-wrote most of those songs."

"Is the brother in the band?"

"No. Apparently they had a massive fight and haven't spoken for ages."

"Where are they from?"

"Sydney."

"What about you? Did you really want to be a musician full-time?"

"Not really. I knew I wasn't good enough to cut it as a freelance pro and I didn't want to be doing weddings and pub and club gigs, driving thousands of miles round the country till I was too old to lug my gear around."

"Teaching is your vocation, isn't it?"

Warm brown eyes met hers. "Yes. And I can teach kids to love music along the way. You never know. One of my students might make it to the world stage."

Poppy smiled. George gave lessons after school and the sounds carried easily across through the trees and over the garden and dividing hedge. It wouldn't be today's little virtuoso performing on the world stage, the one making the moose sounds on sax this afternoon.

"So no regrets when you meet an old friend who's still playing full time?"

He hesitated before replying and she looked up. "There are regrets?" she asked, surprised. She'd thought it was a rhetorical question. A joke of sorts.

"No, not that. No regrets. It was the old friend bit. Seeing Kyle again I realize he wasn't ever a friend, not really."

"People change."

"He hasn't. I think it's me who's changed. He was always a manipulative, self-centered, rude bastard but people put up with him because he's such a good singer."

Much as she'd have liked to, she couldn't follow that up because the band roared into life again.

A familiar redhead appeared briefly between the moving bodies. Steph.

"Come and dance," she yelled but George shook his head. She pointed at Steph who was threading her way to the dance floor. No doubt Lindy would be somewhere in the crowd as well.

"Go," he mouthed and flapped a hand.

She slid off the stool and went to surprise Steph, enjoying herself up front near the little stage, who greeted her with a shriek of delight. Lindy and boyfriend Joey waved but kept dancing. Kyle gyrated toward her, beckoning with one hand as he belted out the lyrics, much to Steph's surprise. Fortunately his blonde fan from before intervened and Poppy edged away into the throng of dancers, letting the heavy beat invade her body and take over.

At the end of the set Steph said, "You sure made a hit with the lead singer."

"Anyone want a drink?" Joey asked. Lindy and Steph placed their orders, and he went off to the bar.

"That guy's a real pain in the bum. George knows him," said Poppy.

"George? How?" asked Lindy. "Is he here? He

doesn't seem like the type."

Poppy gave them a brief rundown of the conversation.

"I have a whole new appreciation of him now," said Steph. "Who'd have thought it?"

"Kind of like unmasking a superhero," said Lindy.

"No," said Steph and pulled a face. "But it's a surprise. He looks so…I don't know…dull."

"I'd better go back to him. He invited me and I can't stay too late," said Poppy.

"A date?" Steph and Lindy asked in unison.

"Not really." Was it though? Not in her mind.

"Poor George," said Lindy. "He's dull but he is nice. Can't take his eyes off you."

"What?"

"Haven't you noticed?" Lindy grinned and shared a glance with Steph.

"No, and you haven't either because that's crap."

"If you say so. How's gorgeous Jessie?"

"She's fine and sweet as ever. Loving school."

"Give her my love," said Steph.

Poppy rejoined George. Lindy might have nailed the problem with him. Dull but nice. Was exciting but not nice better? That pair were teasing her yet again. He wasn't interested in her that way any more than she was interested in him. They were neighbors, friends.

"That was fun, thanks for telling me to come along."

"My pleasure," he said. "I'm glad you enjoyed yourself."

"I did but unfortunately I'll have to go soon. Nikki from up the road is babysitting and I told her I wouldn't be late."

"I'll walk with you."

"You don't need to. Stay."

He shook his head. "It's fine. Some fresh air will be good. And my ears need a rest. I'm not used to loud music anymore."

The huddle of smokers outside looked up as Poppy stepped onto the footpath, George close behind. A breeze had come up, shifting the warm air about and with it the cigarette smoke.

"Hey, Poppy, you're leaving early," said a voice. Sam, who owned the organic vegetable farm just out of town. "Too loud for you?"

"Too late for me. Got a babysitter to pay and work to do tomorrow," she said with a smile. "No fun for me these days."

"Didn't think this was your sort of gig, George." Sam's daughters were at the school. Older than Jessie in kindy.

"I know the singer," George said.

"They were in a band together," Poppy added. "George played bass."

"Cool. You should get the kids playing some metal. That'd give the school concerts a boost." A chorus of agreement greeted that remark.

"Good idea." George laughed. "We'll start with Metallica or AC/DC. We'll have to make do with our recorders, two flutes, a beginner sax, a trumpet, drums, and a couple of ukuleles."

"See you later." Poppy started toward home. George fell into step beside her.

"You realize people are now going to assume we're on a date," she said with a sideways glance.

"Is that bad?"

"I know it isn't, so I don't care one way or the other," she said. "Do you?"

George didn't answer for a moment or two.

Did he think it was a date? Was that pair right? Not that she went on dates these days which was why they were on her case tonight. It was a novelty to see her out with a man. Steph and Lindy were her companions on any outings that weren't someone's wedding or birthday, when half the town was invited.

She'd lost the inclination for socializing amidst the single parent exhaustion and mayhem but had discovered one of the joys of being a single mother was having a readymade excuse at home for cutting short anything she wasn't enjoying, or refusing any invitation she wanted to avoid. Curiosity got the better of her tonight, but it would be a real pain if it backfired by giving George the wrong idea.

"It depends on your definition of a date," he said eventually. "It's natural to go to something together when we're neighbors."

"I guess it's in the eye, no, the mind of the beholder."

"The locals certainly take a lot of interest in a newcomer," he said. "But I thought it was welcoming rather than intrusive. I haven't lived in a country town before but now I'd never live anywhere else."

"I love it," she said.

But she couldn't wait to get away from home when she was a teenager. Different town, though. Much smaller than Currong. Three houses and a dog pretty much summed it up. Even without the weight of her parents' disapproving eyes judging her every move Wilson's Creek was the pits. A girl who wanted more than life on a sheep station was not only a traitor but an immense disappointment in their jaundiced opinion. University in Sydney or Melbourne offered far more enticing prospects. Any university, anywhere. She applied to them all.

"What made you come here?" she asked.

She'd never specifically asked him before. When he became her neighbor she couldn't, and wouldn't, gossip about him at the school gate. He'd arrived in January ready to start the school year. Everyone liked him and he fitted in unobtrusively and quietly.

"I wanted a complete change, and this job came up at the right time."

"Change from what?"

"The high school I was at was tough. A lot of kids had problems. It was very stressful."

"But you're so good with kids. I would have thought you could help even the most difficult ones."

"There were other factors involved." His tone suggested she shouldn't probe.

What factors? The other staff or headmaster? Parents? Personal things like a woman or illness?

"I've been thinking of buying a house," he said a few minutes later.

"I doubt the Prestons will sell." Her previous neighbors had moved to Queensland but kept the house as a rental. "There's that new estate on the Bathurst road."

"Nah. I want one of these old houses. They have character."

"Along with a host of things to repair," she said. Aunty Evie hadn't got around to repairs, Poppy discovered when she'd inherited the beautiful old house.

"As long as it's habitable that's okay. I like being able to walk or cycle wherever I want to go in town."

"Me too." She and Jessie had bikes in the shed.

Five minutes later the porch light glowed a welcome.

"See you tomorrow. Thanks for walking with me."

"No worries. Kyle will be at my place, remember, if you hear any noises, but he won't wake up till about midday."

"Thanks." She turned to go down the path but stopped. "George, does Kyle know something about you? Did something happen when you knew each other before?"

"Why do you ask?" His smile faded and an odd expression flitted across his face so quickly she could have imagined it, but she put it down to the shadowy light and the darkness.

"It's his manner, he seems…I don't know…he said he wouldn't tell any secrets."

"As I said, that's what he's like." He flicked a smile on and off. Mechanical and unlike his usual open smile. "Please don't repeat anything I told you…about my other school or the personal stuff."

"Of course I won't. I promise. But people already know you used to play in a band with Kyle."

"Yes, that's okay, thanks. Good night."

He strode away. Poppy watched him for a moment then went inside.

What was that about, George?

Chapter 2

Poppy had always loved the house she now lived in, even as a child visiting Aunty Evie during those long lazy summers. Along with the solid stone construction, high ceilings, large cool rooms, and Aunty's flourishing garden, the sense of security, permanence, and love which seemed to impregnate the walls had always been the biggest attraction, even more so in her recent, unstable situation.

Physically, the house sat close to the center of town in a quiet street lined with beautiful old deciduous trees that turned brilliant reds and yellows every autumn but hadn't begun to turn yet. The land rose gently giving the house a view of the surrounding hills and if she looked the right way and stood in the right spot, a glimpse on a clear day of one corner of the lake, Currong's year-round playground and scene of many a picnic and swimming outing. Summer was lingering into autumn this year and the sun still packed some heat so Poppy was even more pleased to have the arching branches to provide shade as she walked to collect Jessie from school the following afternoon.

Being Aunty Evie's sole heir had been a shock, mostly because at forty-nine Evie had been far too young to die, but cancer didn't play favorites. Her father had, predictably, been angry at his sister's choice of heir and as usual made his opinion clear but Poppy had no intention of selling and made her opinion just as clear. There was nothing he could do.

When Jessie made her presence felt, retreating to the familiar house which always felt more like home than her parents' house did despite its emptiness was obvious, and she had no regrets.

And she'd been lucky with her neighbors. Across the road were relative newcomers, the Ayrtons, here for Nigel's job at the agricultural college while wife Amy was a community nurse. They were rarely at home. On one side, as ever, there was spry, elderly, now widowed Helen Chapman who headed north each winter to stay with a friend in Coffs Harbour and on the other, replacing the Prestons, George. She smiled to herself. What exactly had George got up to before he arrived in Currong masquerading as a mild-mannered primary school teacher? Nasty as Kyle may be he was referring to something George didn't want mentioned. Something illegal? Could she prise it out of him?

Jessie chattered nonstop on the walk home. Most of the chatter was one way and barely needed more than a "yes" or a "my goodness" to keep her happy but suddenly a question landed like a stink bomb with equally staggering effect. One she hadn't had to answer for some time.

"Why did my daddy go away and not come back?"

She'd asked before, of course, but had accepted the reply that her daddy had gone to live in another city when she was very small.

"You know why," Poppy said.

"Why didn't he want to see me? Not even when I was a baby?"

"I don't know." Mainly because he had no idea she

15

existed.

"Bethany said he mustn't have wanted me and he didn't care about me at all."

"That's a mean thing to say."

Where had that come from? Not from Bethany's mother Ellen, an earth mother type and the last to criticize anyone's lifestyle, let alone a single mother.

"She's mean."

"Maybe you should keep away from her for a while. Did you know Mr. Caramani used to play in a band?"

"Yes, he told us when we did singing."

"You didn't tell me." Jessie was a little songbird with a sweet, clear voice. That musical talent must have come from somewhere else; it certainly wasn't from her mother or her grandparents.

"I forgot. Can we have pizza for dinner? That's what Amber is having."

"Not tonight. We're having your favorite. Macaroni cheese and salad."

No doubt the father question would reappear. Her darling little girl wouldn't outgrow that. Was it fair to keep the truth from her? At the moment, yes. Later? That was in the future, at a time when Jessie would be able to cope with and hopefully understand the truth— that her mother had been a complete mess when she'd spent a few hours with a stranger she'd met at a party, both off their heads, and she had no idea who or where he was. Not even a name to go with the hazy memory of a devastatingly attractive man, a lean body, a Celtic tattoo, blue eyes, and an encounter that left her physically shaken and emotionally shocked, deeply ashamed, and pregnant.

"Should we stop off in the bakery?" she asked as they walked up the main street. "For an afternoon tea treat?"

"Yes! I want a face bickie."

Poppy had work to finish so after her favorite chocolate milk and two of the iced shortbread biscuits Jessie sat on the front veranda in Evie's old, green-painted cane chair and did coloring in, singing softly to herself. Poppy glanced out the open window occasionally and smiled to see the dark curly head bent over the coloring book, intent on the project.

A ute drew up outside George's house. She didn't see who was driving, but shortly after angry voices erupted from next door coupled with a thud and a crash that sounded like breaking furniture. Poppy sprang to her feet as Jessie came bursting into the house.

"Someone's fighting at George's house," she cried. "Mummy, I'm scared."

Little arms clung around her waist. Poppy knelt and hugged her. "It's okay, sweet pea. No one's going to come to our house."

"But what about George?"

"I'll go and see if he's all right. You stay here in the house and watch TV. I'll lock the door but I'll only be a minute, I promise."

Poppy kissed the damp cheek and settled Jessie on the couch. Then she hurried next door with pulse racing. A red station wagon, presumably Kyle's, was parked in the driveway in front of George's white four-wheel drive. Who owned the ute in the street?

Kyle swore loudly inside, and a couple of heavy thuds sounded as though he'd knocked something over. What the hell was he doing in there? Was he drunk?

High? Was George home yet? She hadn't seen him at school but that didn't mean anything. He could have had a staff meeting and later she'd been intent on her work.

The front door was open. All was quiet now. Unsure whether to call out, Poppy opened the screen door and stepped into the entry foyer cautiously to peep through into the open plan living and kitchen area.

Kyle lay slumped against the wall by the bookcase, fists raised in ineffective defense, a trickle of blood coming from a rapidly swelling lip. A large red-haired man, his back to the door, breath snorting from his lungs like a charging bull, took a step forward. If he connected with Kyle's face again something would break.

"What the hell's happening?" Poppy said loudly. "Who are you? Where's George?"

The stranger turned, fury twisting his features. "Are you in it too with this shithead?"

"In what? Kyle, what's going on?"

"This maniac burst in and started threatening me, then he punched me."

The furious red face swung toward Kyle but before anyone could speak the screen door banged and George appeared.

"Tell him, Georgie," said Kyle, straightening up and lowering his fists now the cavalry had arrived.

"Tell him what? Poppy? What *is* this?"

"I don't know. I heard fighting so I came over."

"Who was with him?" snarled the man.

George stared at him. "I don't know. What's this about? Who are you?"

"Name's Ralph." He raised a massive fist again

and Kyle cowered against the wall.

"It wasn't me. Tell him, George."

"Tell him what?"

"That I came here after the gig and went to bed."

Ralph glared at George. "Don't lie. I know he was with Sarah. She told me."

"I didn't see him after the gig. I was home by ten thirty and already asleep when he got in," said George.

"I was alone," said Kyle. "I don't know any Sarah."

"But she was here, wasn't she?" Ralph grabbed the newspaper from the table and waved it under Kyle's nose. "She wrote her name and number on here."

"What?" shrieked Kyle. "You stupid fucker, Georgie." He snatched the paper and threw it on the floor.

"You're frightening my daughter with all this yelling," Poppy said loudly. "If this doesn't stop I'll call the police."

"Thank God you're here, darling," said Kyle. He used his shirt tail to wipe the blood from his lip.

"Don't darling me. What's this about?"

And why was this woman's phone number written on that paper? Was George involved?

"He screwed my fiancée." A beefy sausage finger pointed at Kyle and then swung to George. "And he was in on it, I reckon."

Poppy looked at George, eyebrows raised. Was this the sort of thing Kyle was referring to last night?

"It's nothing to do with me. I only just got home," he said.

"You're not local are you, Ralph?" asked Poppy in an attempt to defuse the situation.

"Got a property out Crookwell way."

"I reckon this is between you and your fiancée," she said. "This guy isn't worth getting yourself into trouble over. He's a gutter crawler." Her mouth twisted with contempt. "And don't go home and start belting into her either because word gets around fast, and you'll find yourself at the police station."

"I'd never hit a woman," Ralph said, in what sounded like genuine horror. "I'd never hurt Sarah. I love her."

"Doesn't sound like she feels the same, mate," said Kyle with a smirk.

"Shut up," snapped George in unison with Poppy.

"Just saying…if you were satisfying her why's she hooking up with me?"

George grabbed Kyle by the arm. "Keep your mouth shut, pack your bag, and go. Don't come back."

He marched him across the hallway and into a bedroom then slammed the door before Kyle could respond.

Poppy moved over to poor Ralph who was now standing bewildered and deflated in the center of the room. Kyle did have a point and by the look of Ralph he might have hit a nerve.

"I'm sorry, Ralph," Poppy said.

George said, "He's leaving, and no way is he coming here again."

"I'll kill him if he goes anywhere near Sarah." Ralph glared in the direction of the closed bedroom door. "Maggot."

"Don't believe what he said," Poppy said firmly. "He was winding you up. Sarah probably got carried away and drank too much."

"You reckon he raped her?"

"Did she say that?" asked George quickly. "His morals are pretty much at rock-bottom but rape? No."

Ralph shook his head. "She said she got pissed and her mates dared her, said it was her last chance to have a fling before the wedding. She was going to stay the night with a girlfriend after the gig rather than drive home."

"Is she blonde?" asked Poppy.

"Yes."

She sighed. "That's what it looked like last night at the gig. They were out to have fun. They were all pretty out of it and she went too far."

"Why did she leave her phone number?" The belligerence returned as Ralph spotted the crumpled newspaper at his feet.

"She lost her jacket. I said I'd call if I found it," George said.

"You saw her?" asked Poppy. If she'd been raped she definitely should report it.

"Briefly. When she was leaving this morning."

"How did she look?"

"Hung over, very embarrassed and ashamed but otherwise okay."

"So she bloody well should." Ralph rubbed his hands over his face. "Well that's that, I guess. It's over."

"The engagement?" asked George.

"Damn right! I'm not marrying her now and be the laughingstock." He looked at Poppy. "Sorry. I didn't know about your kid next door."

Then to George. "Mate, you need better friends."

He turned and stomped out. The door banged

behind him and his heavy tread sounded on the veranda steps.

Poppy shook her head. "What a mess. I'd better go. Jessie's waiting."

"I hope she's okay."

"She'll be fine. The shouting and that thudding worried her, but we couldn't hear the words, luckily."

Kyle stuck his head out of the spare room. "Has he gone?"

"Yes," said George.

"That was a close one. Good thing you showed up when you did or I'd be mincemeat. I'm a lover not a fighter."

"Are you packed?"

"You're kidding."

"I'm not."

"Come on, Georgie." His expression hardened. "You don't want me to share your dirty little secrets, do you?" He winked at Poppy. "You'll regret that."

"Good luck." She grimaced and escaped but not before she heard the final exchange as she was opening the door.

"I don't care anymore what you do or say as long as you don't do it near me. I meant it, Kyle. Get out."

"Don't say I didn't warn you, Georgie. When your smartarse girlfriend and your boss find out what I know you'll be the one leaving town in a hurry and your teaching career will be in the garbage."

****

Back at home Poppy hugged Jessie who had turned off the TV and was hovering by the window in Poppy's office watching anxiously.

"All good. George's visitor knocked a chair over."

22

"Was George cross with him? Is that why he shouted?"

"Yep."

Jessie settled herself in the yellow bean bag Poppy had put in the office for her, with a book on her lap. Sometimes she liked to be close by while Poppy worked and today was understandable. Raised voices and harsh words upset her. She liked people to be nice to each other and her teacher reported she was a natural peacemaker.

Twenty or thirty minutes later a car engine started up next door. Not George's—she knew that sound. This one roared and revved and a moment later appeared on the road outside in a brief blur of dark red as it accelerated away. With any luck that would be the last they'd see of Kyle. She got up and closed the window. A cooler wind had come up bringing with it a bank of clouds from the south. Rain was on the way and already a few stray drops had landed on the glass.

Poppy carefully proofread the pages and made some adjustments. She pressed send and closed down the computer when the files had gone. Done before her client's deadline—just. Not bad. It was over to him now she'd managed to wrangle it into a form that was clear, logical, and made sense. No doubt he'd come back with a raft of objections to her work but until he stopped paying her she'd keep working on his presentation.

"Okay. Work is finished for today. I don't think we'll be able to do our gardening though. It's starting to rain."

"Was Aunty Evie a good gardener like us?"

Jessie loved the stories about holidays with Aunty Evie and how she owned their house and gave it to

23

Poppy before she died, and the fact that her own middle name was Eve.

"Yes, she was even better. She loved planting flowers, and I helped her plant the lemon tree when I was smaller than you."

Poppy pulled the blinds closed and checked everything was switched off.

"It's raining big fat drops," said Jessie from the living room.

Poppy joined her, scanning the sky hoping this was a shower but by the look of the unbroken, sullen grayness overhead it was here to stay. She'd grossly underestimated those gathering clouds on the walk home from school with Jessie.

"No gardening today."

The bulbs and spring flowering seeds would have to wait. A massive crack of thunder made Jessie squeal.

"It's okay. It's just the clouds bumping into each other."

"I don't like thunder." Her lower lip trembled as more rumbles and grumbles rolled around overhead.

"I know but we're safe and dry in our house. Let's sit on the couch and watch your TV programs. It's almost time."

Jessie switched on the TV and scrambled onto the couch. Poppy sat with her, snuggled up close while the Play School presenters sang and told stories and after they'd finished cartoon characters did silly things and made her laugh. Every now and then another big bang of thunder made her squeak and cuddle even closer and suddenly the screen went black.

"What happened?" Jessie sat up in alarm.

"Just a blackout from the storm. It happens

sometimes. Don't worry. The electricians will fix it soon. Good thing it's not dark yet or we'd need candles. Run and get a story."

Jessie scampered away and came back with a pile of books but a few minutes into the third, the TV burst back into life and the fridge started up. Thunder still rolled about but gradually the storm moved on leaving rain drumming steadily on the roof and gurgling in the gutters.

Poppy stood up and switched off the TV. "Time to start our macaroni and cheese. Come and help with the salad."

Later, when Jessie was asleep and Poppy was cleaning up in the kitchen, the doorbell rang. George stood on the porch holding a dripping umbrella.

"Hello," she said, surprised. George never came to visit in the evening. She usually saw him on the way to and from school, and twice he'd walked Jessie home for her when she was caught out, or on rare occasions over the weekend. The outing to the pub together was a first.

"Sorry to bother you, I just wanted to apologize for Kyle this afternoon."

"Come in."

"I don't want to intrude." He seemed flustered, speaking quickly and fidgeting with the umbrella handle. Embarrassed about earlier or nervous about visiting her at night? Surely not.

"It's okay. Come in."

He propped the umbrella against the wall by the door. "I'll take my shoes off," he said. They were soaked and mud had splashed up the sides.

"Gosh, did you get caught out in this?" Surely he didn't get that wet walking from next door.

"Uh, yes. I stepped in a few puddles."

He followed her to the kitchen in black socks and hovered awkwardly while she finished wiping down the benches.

"That was a big storm," she said. "The thunder was right overhead. Jessie is frightened of thunder. I'm glad the power wasn't off for long."

"The power?" A look of surprise crossed his face. "Oh. Yes. About Kyle…"

"I'm glad he's gone," Poppy said. "He's a deeply unpleasant person."

"I know and I'm really sorry about earlier. I should never have agreed to let him stay." He kept his voice low, a worried frown creasing his brow.

She touched his arm lightly. "It's okay. You couldn't have known what would happen, that Ralph would turn up. Maybe I should have let him swing a few more punches before I stopped him."

He didn't laugh the way she expected. Instead he shook his head, still frowning. "Having you and Jessie involved is bad enough. I didn't want an ambulance or the police turning up."

"I suppose not," she said. "Ralph could have done some serious damage. I'll make coffee or would you prefer wine?"

"No, thanks. I don't drink much these days."

"Me neither."

"Used you drink a lot?" he asked.

"That and the rest. I was pretty wild at one stage," she said. "I've grown up a lot since Jessie arrived. Had to."

"Some women don't. They just continue on regardless of their responsibilities as a mother. I've seen the results firsthand at schools."

"I couldn't do that. I've never loved anyone the way I love her. As soon as I realized I was pregnant there was no doubt about it. I'd do anything to protect her, and I knew if I didn't change I might lose her—one way or another."

"Did you have a strong support base? That helps a lot."

"I imagine it would but no. I was always happy here, so it was the obvious place to come. To restart my life. Our lives. It's almost as if my aunt is here watching over us."

She stopped abruptly. George was standing there with his sympathetic, interested expression, making her feel she was the only person in the world right at that moment, that every word she uttered was important to him. Not in a creepy, prying way but the way a friend does. Non-judgmental and supportive. Caring. Maybe it was something to do with his brown eyes.

"But you're on solid ground now," he said.

"Yes, I am. What about you, George? Where's your family?"

"Mum and my stepfather live in Sydney, Haberfield. I have two sisters, both married with children. My grandparents and more cousins are in Italy. Naples area."

Something akin to envy stirred deep inside. George had a safety net of a thousand hands all ready to support any family member in trouble. Her safety net had died years ago. There'd been no love lost between her father and his younger sister, Evie. Poppy's parents washed their hands of their difficult disappointment of a daughter when she left home and the rift deepened after

27

Evie's death, but oddly enough they dutifully sent birthday and Christmas gifts. They'd only seen Jessie once, when she was born.

"Do you have siblings?" he asked.

"No. Only child." It sounded abrupt. She wondered sometimes how on earth her parents had managed to have her. Or rather, why. They didn't seem to like each other very much. Aunty Evie told her once in a candid moment that her father had married her mother on the rebound from a Hungarian woman called Sylvana who'd dumped him.

Sylvana sounded exotic and mysterious to Poppy. A woman who chose not to spend her days on a sheep farm when life had better things on offer. A woman who didn't accept second best. The sort of woman Poppy strove to be but hadn't quite managed it.

She jerked herself away from the pathetic slide into self-pity. She was fine and so was Jessie.

Chapter 3

Duncan Barnett tried calling Kyle again.

When Lloyd had rung at around three in a panic asking if he could sub for Kyle on the Goulburn gig if he hadn't shown up by four thirty, Duncan had been mildly puzzled but not enough to really care. Kyle was probably with some woman or asleep and would roll into the venue still drunk or hung over. The thought of driving for a couple of hours for nothing wasn't appealing even though he didn't need to load up all his gear, although he never went anywhere without his electric guitar and the acoustic.

When Lloyd called a second time, sounding really desperate and said he'd cover his expenses, book him a room, and pay him extra, Duncan figured what the hell. He didn't have anything else on so he might as well. A gig was a gig. And when Kyle found out his detested brother had taken his place, the satisfaction would be immense. More than enough compensation for the inconvenience of the drive.

The call went to voicemail. It was nearly six o'clock. What the hell was Kyle playing at? No matter what Duncan thought of the self-centered bastard, he wouldn't go on a bender with gigs coming up even if he did have a few days off in between. That band was too important to him, and Kyle was a pro.

He took a swig of the coffee he'd picked up at the

Pheasant's Nest truck stop and pressed play on the car stereo system. Filling in at the last minute for his no-hoper of a brother was a big ask, especially as it entailed a two-hour drive. Lloyd and the other guys didn't want to cancel the gig and although Duncan didn't have Kyle's raw soulful voice, he knew could do an adequate job. Good enough for a pissed crowd of head bangers in a country town pub.

He'd filled in before but now they had a few new songs, ones Duncan hadn't written before he and Kyle had what is tactfully called "a falling out due to artistic differences" in the media when some celebrity team breaks up, but in reality was a blistering great fight full of venom and insults and the airing of festering grudges held since childhood, resulting in no contact for nearly two years.

Lloyd had emailed the set lists. None of the tunes were sophisticated harmonically or melodically—after all, Kyle had written them—but he was singing along and learning the lyrics as he drove. They were hardly complex or profound either. Cliché ridden drivel summed them up.

"Queen of spades, queen of death," he sang as the chorus came round again.

He pressed forward and jumped to the next track, "Overnight Sensation." He'd written it years ago, a ballad with what he regarded as one of his best melodies. He was pleased the band still played it. It wasn't quite their style, but Kyle had always liked the song because of the soul elements and it suited his voice.

"We were an overnight sensation," Duncan sang. "That should have lasted all our lives."

He didn't need to practice it but he sang it through anyway, enjoying the harmonies and Phil's guitar solo at the bridge. Nice.

An hour later there was still no word from Lloyd so Kyle hadn't appeared. Road works had slowed him down several times. There was nothing more infuriating than Road Work signs and crawl pace speed limits with not a worker in sight but the last thing he wanted was to be busted for speeding. Even so he'd get to Goulburn well before eight and the gig wasn't till nine so there'd be time for a meal and a change of clothes. As for the gig, no time to rehearse so he'd wing it.

There was a motel just down the road from the venue according to Lloyd, where he'd booked Duncan a room. The rest of them were staying with friends. Good. He didn't want to be sharing a room with any of those guys or being polite to some friend of theirs with a house and a spare inflatable mattress or worse, a saggy, lumpy couch that would be too short for his long legs. And to have to stay up drinking and reminiscing all night.

He went to the motel first, called Lloyd to say he'd arrived, washed and changed then, with his guitar and small backpack with leads and his mike, sauntered along to the pub where the others were having dinner in the bistro. He scanned the room and found them sitting at a table in the corner looking glum and eating burgers and chips—the usual cheap meal venues offer the bands who play. That or steak. He'd asked for something lighter.

Lloyd sprang to his feet as he approached. The other two turned with big relieved smiles.

"Mate, great to see you. Thanks for coming." He

pumped Duncan's hand with both his.

Duncan shook hands with Phil and Marco, the bass player. He sat down and poured himself water from the bottle on the table.

"I ordered grilled fish for you. The kitchen closes at nine so we eat now or starve. Nothing else will be open after the gig," said Lloyd. "Like a beer?"

"Thanks for that. I'm starving. Beer sounds good, thanks." Nerves were starting to stir. The lead singer was the focus, and any fans out there would be here to hear Kyle not his brother.

Lloyd went to the bar.

"No word from Kyle?" Duncan asked.

"No," said Marco. "It's weird. He was staying with that friend, you know him, don't you? George something. Played bass?"

"Italian George from the soul band? Yeah, haven't seen him for years."

"He's a schoolteacher at Currong. It's a hick town about forty-five minutes away. We played there on Wednesday. Anyway, George kicked him out because he screwed a chick in the spare room." Marco grinned then frowned. "No one's seen him since he left George's place."

Lloyd placed a beer in front of him.

Duncan glanced up. "Thanks, mate. When was that?" he asked.

"About five yesterday," said Lloyd.

"So George says," said Marco. He took a bite of his burger. Bits of fried onion sprang loose and hung suspended from his mouth.

"What do you mean?" Duncan waited while Marco retrieved the onion, chewed, and swallowed.

"Nothing. No one else saw him leave, that's all. George could have hit him when they argued about the chick and accidentally killed him and said he'd left."

He picked up a few chips and shoved them into his mouth while Duncan stared in astonishment. What the hell?

"Don't talk shit, man," said Phil while Lloyd said, "You watch too much TV. It's not Midsomer Murders."

"Killed him?" Duncan laughed. "George? Have you met him? The guy's Mr. Meek and Mild. If he did that he'd be straight round to the cops reporting it." He downed some of the beer. "Nah. Kyle's probably on a bender."

"That hot blonde was all over him and maybe they took off together," said Phil.

"Yeah well, that's more likely but he's cutting it bloody fine," growled Lloyd. "How do you feel about doing tomorrow night as well?" he asked Duncan.

"See how it goes tonight first. But I guess if you need me, I'm here now, so sure. Why not?"

****

Poppy took Jessie to her friend Willa's birthday party on Saturday morning. Luckily the rain had moved on because it was a barbeque lunch for ten children and sundry relatives and already looked like chaos in the making with lots of excited kids running about. She refused an invitation to stay but joined some of the other parents talking intently on the footpath outside the house.

Bearded dad Thomas, the baby on his back in a carry pouch turned to her and said, "Weird about that car they found, isn't it?"

"What car?"

"Near the lake, belonged to a guy from that rock band that was at the Royal the other night."

"Just the car? What about the guy?"

Kyle's car? Was he missing? Did George know? He must, the police would have been around to see him.

"No sign of him," said Thomas. "Someone reported it yesterday, I think. They're doing a search of the area. Called in the local volunteer Fire Brigade and SES."

"He's George the teacher's friend, isn't he?" Beth said. She'd dropped her granddaughter at the party and was always ready for a gossip. "George will be worried. I wonder what's happened…maybe he went for a swim and got into trouble."

"Strange time to go swimming, especially in that storm," said Thomas. "Does George know anything, Poppy?"

"No idea. I haven't spoken to anyone except Jessie since yesterday morning." Poppy smiled. *Not getting drawn into that speculation.* "See you all later."

She headed for home, debating whether to call in on George. He'd have to be worried. Maybe she should go to the police and tell them what she knew. She and George could be the last people to see him. The thought sent a chill through her body.

Why on earth was Kyle at the lake in a storm? Where had he gone after he'd left on Thursday afternoon? She'd assumed Goulburn to join the guys in the band but if his car was still in this area where was he? Had he played the Friday night gig and come back? Where had he spent Thursday and Friday nights? Maybe he'd met up with Sarah. So many questions but not really her concern. Intriguing though.

She turned into George's front gate and down the path. Knocked. George was surprised to see her but pleased too. His face went from one expression to the other in rapid succession but finished up in a wide smile. He stepped back and extended his arm.

"Come in."

She followed him to the living area, the scene of the incident.

"No Jessie?"

"She's at Willa Wright's birthday party. It's a lunch. You must have heard about Kyle's car. Someone told me just now."

He nodded. "A policeman was here a while ago."

"Did he tell you they're doing a search?"

"Yes. He wanted to talk to you but you weren't there, of course."

"I'll go to the police station."

"He's tracking down Sarah and Ralph. I had to tell him they were here."

"Of course. Why wouldn't you?" She looked at him, surprised by his reticence. He barely knew those two.

"I don't know. It sort of puts them in a bad light. Especially if something bad has happened to Kyle." He shrugged and sat down on the couch but didn't relax back.

She sat opposite on one of the two matching armchairs.

"Don't be so nice. For all you know they might be involved."

He looked at her quickly. "Do you think they are?"

"I don't know and neither do you. We don't even know what's happened. What did the cop tell you?"

"That someone found his car near the swimming hole early this morning. He asked me about damage to it. Dents and so on, and when I last saw Kyle. Also if I noticed anyone threatening him at the gig or hanging around the band."

So the car was found early today not yesterday. Not for the first time the gossip was wrong. Poppy sat up straight.

"Did you see anyone odd?" she asked. "I didn't but it was only early in the night."

"No. Sarah was the most obvious, wasn't she? Her friends have a bit to answer for. Fancy pushing her into going home with Kyle."

"She can't blame them. She didn't have to go," said Poppy.

"Maybe Ralph's done the right thing by calling off the wedding."

"Maybe. If you're getting married, what are you doing sleeping with some random guy like Kyle? Why get married anyway?" Not for her, marriage.

"If I find someone I want to marry no way would I jeopardize that," he said. "And I can't imagine why I would want to sleep with someone else in that situation."

"You're a romantic, that's why." She laughed but his words touched a place deep inside. He was a romantic and he was an optimist. She was a cynic and a realist.

"Well, would *you*?" He sounded hurt. She shouldn't have laughed.

"I doubt if I could love someone enough to say I'd marry them and really mean it. So I wouldn't say it."

"But if you did say it then, logically, you would

mean it."

"What?"

He watched her through those deep brown eyes. "You'd only say you loved someone if you meant it," he said.

"Right." She looked at her hands. Couldn't face that gaze. Why not? He made her uncomfortable. Not how Kyle made her uncomfortable. When George looked at her it was as if he saw right through her, saw how her brain worked, saw how stunted her emotions were and how she couldn't trust herself to love someone. Except Jessie. But he didn't seem to mind what he saw.

She must not give him false hope. Why were they having this conversation? Much too intimate for their level of friendship.

"What will the band do without Kyle? They're on a tour." That hadn't occurred to her before.

"I don't know. Lloyd would try to get a sub, I imagine. It'd be very short notice for last night unless they found someone local which is unlikely. They probably had to cancel."

"What a bummer. Kyle thought they were on the way up."

"They were, which makes this even weirder."

"Makes it weirder and makes it more likely that something has happened to him."

"Plenty of people will have taken photos at the gig," said George. "The cops will only need to ask around."

"Okay." She stood up. "I'd better go to the police station."

"Want to have lunch at the pub first?" he asked.

"Sure."

****

The bistro wasn't crowded, a far cry from the Wednesday night of the gig when it was heaving with bodies and noise. A poster announced that the act for Saturday night was a local country singer, a very popular young woman called Ellie who sat on a stool with her guitar and sang about lost love, missed opportunities, and broken hearts. Not Poppy's style. That part of her life was long gone.

"What will you have?" asked George.

Poppy scanned the blackboard menu on the wall near the bar. "A burger."

"Me too. Drink?"

"Water's fine."

He nodded. "You bag a table and I'll order."

Poppy chose a table a little away from the nearest group, two older, gray-haired couples. The man raised his hand to her and his wife, Dorothy, turned and smiled. She came to Poppy's Tuesday morning Creative Writing Class at the Community Center and rarely spoke and when she did it was barely audible. She'd probably lost the knack because he dominated every situation in volume and quantity.

"G'day, Poppy," he boomed. "How's it going?"

"Hello, how are you?" She groped desperately for his name, and failed. "Hello, Dorothy." Dorothy smiled and nodded.

"Can't complain," he said. "When are you going to come and visit us? We've got a good crop this year. Bring the little girl and pick some apples." He almost glared at her, daring her to refuse.

"Thanks very much. I'll call first," she said.

"No need for that. Come any time. Fairview Orchard. We're always there."

Except now, she almost said. Fortunately George joined her with a bottle of water and two glasses for the table.

"Will do, thanks."

George sat down. Poppy gave him the money for her order and he simply said "thanks" and put it in his wallet. Smart man.

"Did Kyle ever have a steady relationship with a woman?"

George shook his head. "He was married for a few years but that broke up and he always said after that he wanted to remain free of those shackles."

"Fair enough."

"Is it?" His eyes bored into hers.

"Just because *you* want a wife and ten kids doesn't mean everyone else should."

"There's nothing wrong with remaining single but 'shackles' is a bit harsh on the concept of wanting to live with and share your life with someone you love."

Kyle tried it and didn't like it, but she wasn't getting side-tracked into that subject with George. Whatever she said would come out sounding selfish and bitter because he was so understanding and only had experience of happy families. He hadn't even reacted to her crack about ten kids.

"Kyle wasn't big on tact though, was he?" she said.

The rest of lunch passed in amicable chitchat. George asked her opinion on his ideas for the school concert and she offered a few suggestions which he seemed to appreciate, although it was hard to tell whether he was simply being polite. That was the problem with him—she couldn't tell what he was thinking.

Chapter 4

Duncan and Lloyd arrived at the Currong Police Station just before midday. A chunky, brown-haired woman was behind the desk, and she took one look at Duncan and said, "You must be Duncan Barnett, Kyle's brother."

Not surprising. They were only eighteen months apart in age and people often assumed they were twins even though he was taller and more solidly built than Kyle, and women preferred Kyle.

Her manner was brusque, and her dark eyes flicked from him to Lloyd.

"That's right. This is Lloyd Johns from the band."

"Yes, thank you for coming. Mr. Johns, we have a few questions in regard to Kyle's movements on Wednesday night."

"Have you found my brother?" Duncan demanded. This chick didn't seem very fussed about the situation.

"Not yet, I'm sorry. Sergeant Davis will speak to you."

She came from behind the desk and knocked on a door at the end of the reception area. A gray-haired bloke opened the door, introduced himself as Sergeant Alastair Davis, shook hands, then ushered them into his office.

"So what happened to Kyle?" asked Lloyd.

"We don't know. We have a search beginning

shortly of the wider area around where the car was found and we're waiting for the forensic report."

"Why is there a forensic report being done?" asked Duncan.

"Because of the circumstances in which we found the car and the fact that Kyle is missing. To rule out certain scenarios. And to collect any evidence in case a crime was committed. Because we don't know anything for certain at this point, we have to cover all the angles."

Duncan shared a frown with Lloyd. Sounded more like covering their arses but this had gone from Kyle being a bloody nuisance to something else entirely.

"What scenarios are you trying to rule out?"

"Violence, and to help us determine if Kyle was removed from the car or left of his own free will, and if anyone else was in the car."

"Was anything in the car? His phone?"

"No, only a folder of music and his suitcase."

"Were there bloodstains?"

"Not immediately visible."

"How long will it take to get the results?" asked Duncan.

"We don't know if there's a crime yet, so it won't be a priority at the lab. We've listed Kyle as a missing person and he could turn up. Did anyone else drive his car regularly, or recently? Or was anyone else in it?"

"No idea," said Duncan.

Davis went on to ascertain when each of them had last seen Kyle. Duncan hadn't seen him for two years so wasn't any help at all although the cop did seem interested in the reason they'd become estranged. He didn't turn it into an interrogation, just nodded and made a few notes. Lloyd wasn't much more use even though he'd seen Kyle on Wednesday night. Both strongly denied Kyle was prone to depression, in trouble of some sort as far as they knew, or suicidal.

"Was your brother in a relationship?"

"Not that I know of. Lloyd?"

"No, he has plenty of women floating about but no one special."

"He was married for a while but that fell apart about five years ago. She remarried and lives in Brisbane."

"I'd like a recent photo of Kyle if you have one. We'll circulate it in case someone remembers seeing him."

Lloyd flicked through his phone. "This do?" He showed Davis and then Duncan a shot of Kyle laughing into the camera with a stage behind him. Duncan swallowed a rush of emotion at the sight of his little brother enjoying the music he loved so much.

Davis stood up. "Thank you."

"Could it have been joy riders? Kids?" asked Duncan as they left the office.

"That's one avenue we're looking at although they usually burn the vehicle to destroy evidence. And it doesn't explain where Kyle is."

"Unless they…"

He couldn't finish as the enormity of what he was thinking suddenly overwhelmed him, but the cop said, "Don't jump to any conclusions, Mr. Barnett. We just don't have enough information yet."

He nodded dumbly. Davis held out his hand and he shook it.

"We'll keep you informed."

Outside on the footpath, Lloyd said, "Come on, mate, let's get lunch at the pub. We need a beer."

Talking to the policeman had created far more questions than answers. What the hell had happened to his brother? The more time ticked by the more he was sure it was something bad, very bad. And the more he realized that he'd miss Kyle. Even though they hadn't spoken for years and harbored bitter feelings that had taken on a life of their own, festering away quietly at the back of his mind, Kyle was his little brother, his only sibling. No one knew him better than Kyle and no one knew Kyle better than him. They'd experienced things together as children no one else had and that was irreplaceable.

"I haven't told Dad yet," he said.

"You should, I reckon."

"Yeah, but I didn't want to worry him although he's too pissed most of the time to know what's going on."

"He's not that bad." Lloyd had met him a few times at gigs.

"He is. He hasn't worked since that accident and now he just sits around all day drinking and betting on the horses."

"Do you see him much?"

"I drop in every few weeks to see if he's still alive. I get abused and I leave. He was always a miserable, angry bastard. Kyle and I should have left when Mum did."

"That's tough when you're a kid."

"Yeah."

It was. Being seven and your mum runs off with another man, leaving you with a rage-filled father. He and Kyle grew up hating both of them. Dad for being useless and Mum for leaving them behind. Then they switched to hating each other. Stupid now, in hindsight.

They turned the corner and went into the bistro bar of The Royal. There were plenty of free tables, but Lloyd headed for the bar.

"Beer?"

"Yes, please."

Orders in and beers in hand Duncan and Lloyd glanced round the room deciding where to sit.

"Hey, look who's here," said Lloyd. "That's George, over there in the corner with that chick. She was at the gig. Kyle talked to her."

Duncan looked. "Yeah, that's George. He's lost a bit more hair."

The woman had her back to him, but her hair was collar length, smooth, glossy, and black.

Lloyd was halfway across the room already, heading for their table. Duncan followed reluctantly. He didn't want to sit with anyone and hash over what might have happened to Kyle, and he especially didn't want to have lunch with a stranger. He wanted to sit in silence and absorb the inevitability of the bad news coming his way. The way people prepared for a natural disaster like a flood, raging bushfire, or a cyclone.

George and Lloyd were already greeting each other, and the woman began moving things on the table to clear space.

"G'day, Duncan," said George. He stood up, smiling. "Join us. This is Poppy."

Duncan summoned a smile and glanced at her. She looked up and he registered green eyes before her expression froze, just like when a DVD stops mid frame. A split second later she blinked and life moved on. Did he know her? She was attractive with a wide mouth, smooth tanned skin, and a straight nose under the straight cut fringe. Good body under the figure-hugging white T-shirt.

He ran through the possibilities, but nothing sprang immediately to mind. He'd had his share of women. Nothing like Kyle's total and he'd slowed the pace and become more discerning in the last few years, but for a while partying had been the way to live and there were always eager chicks ready to please a guy in the band. She could easily have been one of them in some other place. Either that or it was love at first sight, but she'd looked more as if someone had punched her in the stomach.

George was waiting for a response.

"Thanks," he said. "If that's okay with you."

Poppy gave a tiny reluctant shrug. "Sure."

It sounded like the opposite and the set of her mouth confirmed her displeasure. What was her problem?

George hadn't noticed. He was too busy making introductions.

"Are we intruding on a date?" Duncan asked her.

"We're just friends," said Poppy in that tone women used when they were pissed off. Kyle regarded it as a challenge. Duncan regarded it as bloody rude, especially when they'd only just met. Was it because they'd crashed her cozy lunch with George and she wanted them to be more than friends? Too bad if he preferred their company to hers.

"Any news?" asked George.

"No. We were just at the police station talking to

the guy in charge. He's got no idea," said Duncan. He took a few swallows of the beer.

"He's good at his job." She sounded defiant.

"I didn't say he wasn't. I said he had no idea." Duncan flicked her a look then away. Her face was stony, and she wasn't looking at him.

"None of us do." George, ever the peacemaker.

"The cop's name is Alastair Davis. Reckon you can call him Al?" asked Lloyd.

Duncan and George laughed. Poppy didn't. Too young to get the reference.

"So you live here now, George?" He roused himself to a level of civility, ignoring her and her shitty attitude.

"Yes. I moved here at the beginning of the year."

"How's it working out?"

"I really love it. I was surprised actually. I hadn't expected to fit in so easily. People are very friendly."

"Apparently not all of them are." The one sharing the table being a perfect example. His comment landed like a shower of cold water.

"Whatever happened to your brother may not involve a local." Her again. "He didn't make himself very popular by what I've heard."

"And what might that be?" He glared at her, and she glared right back. The green eyes had flecks of brown, catching his attention, holding it.

"That he didn't have any compunction about picking up women at gigs and taking advantage of them."

"He never forced anyone to do anything they didn't want to."

"Consent is doubtful if she's too drunk to judge

what's going on properly."

He shrugged. "No one ever accused him of rape or assault."

"Kyle had his share of guys wanting to beat him up from what I gather."

"And where did you gather that?" So, another aggressive feminist.

"I met one in action." She'd modified her tone suddenly. Maybe she suddenly remembered he was the missing man's worried brother. Or she knew more than she was saying.

The food arrived. Lloyd immediately began sawing off chunks of his burger. Duncan had lost his appetite, but he pierced a chip with his fork and ate it. He wanted to question her, press her on that last comment but not here. Later.

She pushed her chair back. "I'd better get moving, George."

He made to join her, but she said firmly, "No, you stay and chat."

She stood and slung her bag over her shoulder. "Nice meeting you, gentlemen." She turned to Duncan. "I hope your brother turns up, I truly do. It must be horrible not knowing where someone you love is."

"Thanks," he muttered, taken aback by the genuine sentiment.

She hesitated a moment, studying his face as though deciding whether to say something or not, then turned and threaded her way between the tables on the way to the door.

Duncan stabbed another chip. "Someone you love," she'd said. Did he love Kyle? He supposed he did—he was the only person in the world who would qualify and vice versa. If Kyle was gone where did that leave him? Alone with a waste of space drunk for a father. Some family.

He looked up to find George's sympathetic eyes on his face and for some reason it made him angry.

"She's a real piece of work, your girlfriend," he said.

****

Poppy walked around the corner to the police station on automatic. It was him for certain. Not Kyle; his brother Duncan. It was definitely him. The Celtic tattoo on his wrist, his height, his body all snapped him into focus—he was the man she'd pushed into the dark shadows of her memory. But it was the eyes and the shape of his mouth that clinched it beyond any doubt. They were Jessie's eyes, albeit a brighter blue, looking at her with an arrogance and disdain she'd never see in her baby's soft eyes, and the mouth that framed those words and shaped that cold smile was a harsh model for the mouth of her loving child.

She'd never known his name. He'd never known hers. He didn't remember her, and she'd done her best to forget him, but it was harder for her with the constant living reminder. For him she was the briefest of encounters with a willing stranger at a party, in a cramped dark cupboard filled with brooms, a vacuum cleaner, boxes, and empty suitcases.

She'd met a lot of people after she'd left home. That was during the period she thought of as the black hole. The time when she left the safety of Aunty Evie's after leaving school and her home followed by the years when she headed to university in Melbourne, consumed by a passion to liberate herself from all constraints, exercise her newfound freedom without a care for her parents, her past, or anything that might catapult her back to that stultifying home life.

Two years later, Evie died shockingly and suddenly, having kept her illness secret to the end. The last link to security shattered.

God only knows who she met and what she did during that period. Lost was the only word for it. She lost herself but fortunately didn't lose her life. Good friends kept her afloat and somehow she kept her degree on track. And then came the pregnancy that shocked her back into existence. Jessie. She smiled. Her savior and the love of her life.

But this man. Duncan Barnett. Coming here for such a reason, smashing into her safe, happy world like a giant asteroid. Not only was he unwelcome, he brought with him gigantic problems. She'd have to keep right out of his way and under no circumstances allow him to meet Jessie. One look at her daughter's eyes and it wouldn't take much for him to comment. It wouldn't be too difficult—he was only in town for today. The realization calmed her breathing the more it solidified in her mind. He was highly unlikely to run into either her or Jessie again so her secret would remain a secret. If George happened to remark on any similarity she'd have to deny it, laugh it off. After all, lots of people have blue eyes.

But that wasn't the only problem he represented. What she'd seen in him that first time despite the thick haze of alcohol was still there, untarnished, glowing deep inside, a forbidden flame of desire. She had to keep out of his way not just to preserve her life with Jessie but to preserve herself. Duncan Barnett had the potential of a wrecking ball.

****

Steph called that evening, busting to discuss the news that had burst over the town like a skyrocket showering everyone with sparkling theories and speculation. It was the most exciting and interesting event since Greta Callow laid into her husband in the main street nine years ago, belting him with a leather strap and accusing him of cheating on her with the hairdresser's attractive young assistant, Janine. The police had arrived and shortly after that Greta and Kevin had left town, never to be heard from again. Janine had hotly denied the accusations, but rumors still floated about even after she quit the hairdresser's and moved to the Central Coast seven years ago, where it was said she was now causing similar trouble.

"You saw him just before he disappeared, didn't you? That's what everyone's saying. He had a punch-up at George's, and you intervened and stood between them before he got beaten to a pulp."

Poppy closed her eyes briefly. "Not exactly. George came home a minute after I went in. It wasn't that bad. He only had a split lip."

"But that guy, Ralph, he could be a killer. You might be in danger because you saw him threatening Kyle. You and George." Steph was loving this. Poppy had to be careful what she said.

"No, that's not…that won't happen. Ralph isn't dangerous and he's not like that. Take my word for it."

"I guess you can't blame him for getting angry," she said. "Fancy cheating on someone so publicly? How humiliating for him."

"He was really upset but he'd calmed down by the

time he left. And he was truly horrified when I said not to go home and beat her up instead. He said he'd never hurt a woman and I believed him."

Steph moved on to the next item for discussion. "The police asked for everyone at the gig to come forward if they had information."

"Did you?"

"Of course. I told them what I saw."

"What did you see?" Steph would have stayed much longer than Poppy.

"Kyle and that blonde. Sarah. She was all over him after you left. She's got a reputation according to Joey. Pretty wild. She sure won't be marrying Ralph now."

"How does Joey know that?"

"He works with a guy whose sister went to school with her or something. She's from Crookwell but she wants to be a model. Joey said she's gone to Sydney, left after the breakup with Ralph and she's not coming back."

"Poor guy, but it wouldn't have worked out, would it, if she does that sort of thing?"

"Yeah, he's better off. Did the cops talk to you?"

"Yes. Today. They wanted to confirm what happened on Thursday afternoon and exactly when I saw him leave George's place."

"Do you reckon she took off with Kyle?"

"I don't know. I don't know why he'd drop the band to be with her. More likely she'd follow along on the tour."

"A groupie." Steph laughed. "Like some stupid teenager? She's a bit old for that."

"You'd think so, but who knows? She went home with him."

"God, I wouldn't. He's so not my type," said Steph.

"Nor mine. I didn't like him at all."

"Someone liked him even less than you."

"Do you really think he's been murdered?"

Steph said more seriously than before, "I reckon given both their reputations and seeing them in action at the gig, that they've run off together, had a fight, and he'll turn up soon. He'll have been on a bender or something. He is a rock muso after all, don't forget. They do stuff like that."

Chapter 5

Duncan went back to Currong on Sunday. The rest of the band were heading to Sydney for a couple of days before the three Canberra gigs the following week, but he wanted to be close at hand if there was news of Kyle. None of the people he phoned in Sydney had heard from Kyle for nearly a week and none had expected to knowing he was on tour. No one thought he'd miss a gig deliberately; he was too much of a pro for that.

He sat on the bed in the Royal Hotel and wondered how to fill the next few days. A hick town, the guys in the band had said, what are you going to do there? But he couldn't pretend he didn't care about Kyle and something drew him back here, as if his proximity might help somehow. Guilt, probably, if he looked closely.

The town offered little in entertainment, but the pub lunch had been okay and the café in the main street did good food and coffee. He'd go back to the police and see if the search yesterday had turned up anything although someone would have told him if they'd found anything.

And he could call in on George, see what his thoughts were without Lloyd and that girlfriend listening in.

He decided to walk around town, check it out. The

fresh air would do him good and it was warm today. Walk, cops, George—but he'd call him first.

"G'day, mate, Duncan," he said.

George sounded surprised and not overly pleased by his call.

"Sorry, I'm heading out to play tennis soon," he said when Duncan asked him about calling in.

"Nice day for it."

"Yes. How long are you in town?"

"A few days. The next gig's in Canberra on Wednesday night. Maybe we could do dinner tonight?"

Was that a slight hesitation before George spoke?

"Okay. How about the Chinese restaurant?"

"Seven?"

"Sure. Sorry, I have to go."

Duncan slipped the phone into his pocket, irritated by the brush-off. Why didn't George just say no? It was obvious he didn't want to meet up. But of course George wouldn't refuse. He was too nice, too polite, and he'd feel sorry for the guy whose brother was missing. George was someone you could take advantage of.

He wouldn't, nothing to gain, but Kyle had, the bastard. How did he know George was living here now? No doubt he kept tabs on people in case they came in useful down the track.

Kyle used to be like that when he was young. He'd store up information about kids at school, even some of the teachers if a juicy bit of gossip was circulating. When he was thirteen he blackmailed Owen McDonald out of ten dollars a week for two terms because he caught him cheating on a test. Maybe he was still doing that stuff and it had finally got him into trouble.

As predicted the cops had nothing new to impart other than that Kyle's car had been gone over by the forensic team and was in the shed behind the police station.

"Can I leave it here until I decide what to do with it?"

"We're not releasing it yet." Constable Alice Bannerman her name was, the chunky one.

"Oh, right. Why not?"

"We might need to look at it again."

"Or Kyle might turn up."

"There is that." She smiled and her face changed completely, like the sun coming out and warming him briefly before it disappeared behind a cloud again. "We'll let you know as soon as anything comes to light. There's plenty of gossip around town. Don't listen to it."

"Thanks."

He strolled along the main street, passed the pub, and kept walking. For a hick town it was pretty busy on a Sunday. The café across the street was crowded and the takeaway and the bakery had a few tables outside. He paused at a real estate agency to look at the photos of property for sale or rent. A couple of houses but more farms or blocks of land. Cheap compared to Sydney. No wonder people were moving out of the cities.

Hopeless for a professional muso to live here, though. There'd probably be a gig a week in town if you were lucky. More if you were prepared to notch up hundreds of k's driving to towns in the area and then only if you were happy to play in the pub or the local RSL to a bunch of people who weren't listening. He'd lost count of the number of gigs he'd done where they set the band up in the same room as the pokies and had the races or footy going on the TV at the same time. And who knew if there were any decent musos out here? They would have headed to the big smoke long ago. That was the thing about music—you couldn't do it by yourself for long. You needed other musos for nourishment unless you were up for solo gigs. Which he wasn't.

He was approaching what looked like the end of the town center. He stopped at a cross street. A supermarket sign was visible in the next block after a few buildings that looked like houses that had become offices for an accountant, a massage therapist, and a lawyer. A sign pointed to the Currong Primary School, so he turned left and strolled past houses, a playing field, and then a couple of cream painted weatherboard school buildings. Nice place to go to school. His had been all concrete with a fence cordoning the playground off from a busy road. These kids had large trees and grass, fresh air and birds flitting about.

Duncan continued walking and cut back around the block, crossed the main street, and headed up a rising tree lined road. A community center hall was on the corner block with a few cars parked down the side. Sounded like choir practice was in full swing, warbling "The Banana Boat Song". Light on male voices as usual, heavy on sopranos with the ubiquitous loud one incapable of moderating her voice to blend in. More likely not even trying.

He was in need of a beer and food. He walked around the block and back to the main street. At the café he slowed and looked in at the crowded tables. A group of gray-haired old ladies had joined two tables together and were talking and laughing like crazy and several families sat with kids enjoying a Sunday afternoon ice cream treat. Old style wooden booths lined one wall. They probably had a juke box playing hits of the fifties and sixties as well.

An unexpected pang of envy shot through his body like an arrow. What did he have? A drunken abusive father, a mother who cleared out and was never seen again, and a brother with whom at the time of his disappearance he shared a mutual dislike and was now causing more trouble and grief by disappearing. A mediocre career as a musician. No wife, no girlfriend, no kids, no close friends. Added up to bugger all.

He turned and walked on. He wasn't sorry for himself, didn't wallow in that pointless "poor me" crap, never had. It was up to him to look out for himself, and it was up to him to care what happened to little brother Kyle because no one else would.

****

Duncan arrived at the restaurant a few minutes early and had a tall glass of beer in front of him, already a third down when George pulled out the chair opposite.

"Hi, George. Thanks for coming."

"No worries. Any news?"

"No. I don't know whether that's good or bad."

George filled a glass with water from the bottle on the table.

"I don't either."

"How was your tennis?"

"I didn't play very well but it was fun. It always is."

Duncan nodded. "I surf a bit when I get the chance."

"Really? I didn't know that."

"Yeah, started as a teenager."

"I was never into surfing."

"You should give it a go." He smiled. "Bit late now you're living here, I guess."

George smiled and picked up the menu.

"What's good?" asked Duncan.

"Everything. Depends what you like. I'm having the chilli prawns. Do you want to share?"

"Sure."

The smiling Chinese waiter took their order. "Good choice," he said.

"Jason always says that regardless of what you order," said George after he'd gone away.

Moments later he was back with George's glass of wine.

"Do you reckon Kyle could be hiding?" Duncan asked.

"Hiding from what?"

"Who, more likely." Duncan pulled a face. "Like your girlfriend said in the pub, Kyle made a few waves for himself."

"It'd have to be pretty serious to scare him so much that he'd hide out somewhere without telling anyone. Cranky boyfriends and dumped women are hardly likely to hunt him down mobster style."

"I don't know what else he was into, do you?" Duncan asked.

The look George gave him was surprisingly sharp. What did he know?

"Me? Why would I? I hadn't seen him for ages."

"But you hung out with him, didn't you? Back then."

"For a while. He was a bit out there for me."

"Yeah. But he could be very persuasive, couldn't he? And he had a long memory. Filed information away for future use."

George hesitated, then said, "Kyle had a way of making people do things they'd never think of themselves. He made it seem a bit of a lark, adult pleasure, nobody hurt, everybody willing. Up for it. Parties where anything went…" He stopped.

What was he hinting at? Had Kyle told him anything?

"He could be very persuasive. Maybe—" Duncan leaned forward, lowered his voice. "—Someone didn't like what he made them do."

"Like what?"

"You'd know. You were there at those after gig raves."

"Once or twice. So were you." George's voice hardened.

Duncan sat back. "Yeah, I was. Don't remember much about those times."

"But do you think Kyle did remember? What people did, I mean? Who did what and with who?"

"Sure, if he thought it would be useful down the track. I wouldn't put it past him to use something for a spot of blackmail, coercion or whatever. He was a nasty bastard when he wanted."

The waiter placed steaming dishes of food in front of them.

"More to drink?" he asked.

"Yes, please. Two refills," said Duncan.

George spooned rice and prawns into his bowl.

"Have you told the police?" he asked.

"Should I?"

"Why not? It might give them something to go on."

"Could be uncomfortable for you, though, couldn't it?"

"Why?"

"I don't know, you seem…concerned."

George frowned. "I'm not concerned."

"Okay."

The fresh drinks arrived.

George ate in silence which suited Duncan. He didn't want to put George completely offside, but his reaction had been interesting. George put his chopsticks down and drained the wine, made a show of checking his watch.

"I have to go, I'm sorry. I have some prep to do for tomorrow's class."

"Yeah, I'm up for an early night," said Duncan. "Those gigs are tiring."

"They go all right?"

"Not bad. Singing lead isn't my thing but it was okay."

Outside the night air had turned cool.

"Thanks, George." Duncan thrust out a hand and Georg shook it with no mention of another get together.

"Good luck."

Duncan nodded and turned away.

****

On Monday morning Poppy walked Jessie to school and continued on to the supermarket for a couple of items. On the way home with her laden backpack she had to wait to cross because a bloke was trundling down the road on his tractor towing a large piece of farm machinery and holding up traffic.

"Good morning," said a voice behind her.

Poppy's shoulders stiffened. What was he doing here? Hadn't he left yesterday? She turned her head, said, "Hello" and turned back to the street.

He moved beside her. "Listen, I'm sorry…Poppy, isn't it?" His tone had altered, lost the mocking, derisive edge.

She nodded acutely aware of his body beside her and the faint smell of aftershave combined with soap. Words got stuck somewhere between her brain and her mouth.

"I'm sorry about the other day. Put it down to stress. I'm worried about Kyle."

"Accepted. Thanks."

"The police don't seem to be getting far. Or at least they're not telling me much."

Her brain and tongue suddenly let loose an avalanche of words.

"I don't think they know much except that they don't think he left the car in that spot and walked away and got lost. It'd be hard to do there. It's close enough to town to walk even if you didn't know where you were. They think someone else was there."

"You know a lot about it."

"Word gets around," she said.

"I reckon they're right."

A gap opened up and Poppy stepped off the gutter and strode across the road. Duncan went with her. She swallowed her annoyance. How to get away from him without being rude again? Although maybe that was the best way of keeping him at bay. She stopped at the corner of the street leading up the slope toward her house.

"What are you doing here? I thought you'd left," she said.

She looked him in the eye, but he broke the contact and stared over her head at the trees. Wind rustled the leaves and a crow flapped overhead, its mournful call lingering in the air.

"I felt I should hang around until they know something."

There was something sad about him all of a sudden, an aura of loneliness quite different from being alone. She'd been alone and adrift at times but never lonely. Here, people assumed because she was a single mother she must be lonely for a man in her life but she wasn't. George knew and accepted it about her which was one of the reasons she enjoyed his company. Poppy was and always had been independent and liked it that way.

"It's very quiet here," he said. "I mean no traffic, hardly any people." He looked at her again and this time he frowned. "You look familiar. Have we met before? Before the other day?"

Poppy's lungs stalled for a moment. "I doubt it."

"Where did you live before here?"

"Melbourne."

"When were you in Melbourne?"

For God's sake! She glared at him. "Why?"

He raised his eyebrows and she looked away because there was a little uptilt at the corner of his mouth that made her pulse quicken, and that made her cross.

"Is it a secret?" he asked. Laughing at her now.

"I was at Melbourne Uni until about five years ago. Did you go to uni?" She doubted he had even though it was probably a student party he'd been at. Or maybe it wasn't. Whose party she had no idea.

He shook his head. "I wanted to be a musician. Didn't need to go to an institution to do that."

"I suppose not but people do."

"If they want a piece of paper, yeah. I'd rather play. I learn what I need to learn by myself. Can you understand that?"

She nodded. He was serious, not being sarcastic, wanting her to understand.

"I'm not saying I don't learn from people better than me, but I don't want to waste time doing stuff I'm not interested in."

Why was he so eager that she hear all this? She didn't say anything, should start walking and leave him standing there but he'd follow her, and she didn't want him to know where she lived. He was still talking.

"Kyle is a natural talent. He listens to the greats all the time. He learns that way, but he did have vocal lessons for breathing and proper voice production. Protect the instrument, you know? He's out of control about a lot of things but not his music."

She couldn't cut him short. He was stranded, alone in this strange situation. This was a different man to the one she'd met yesterday. This man was talking about his brother and something they both loved. This man was sensitive, and his words were heartfelt.

He was Jessie's father. She could learn something about him.

"And you wrote songs together."

"I'm better at that than he is. Lyrics, melody, and

harmony." He said it without boasting, as a fact. "He's a better singer and performer."

"Did that come from your family?" And through to Jessie?

"Mum played piano and sang but she left when we were kids, and we didn't see her again, so I don't know how good she was. Dad is a drunk. An abusive one." That was delivered in the same matter of fact tone.

"Did he hit you?" She couldn't keep the shock from her voice. Her father, for all his faults, wouldn't dream of hitting anyone. He withdrew into cold silence instead.

"No. He hit Mum. He yelled at us."

"That's horrible. Do you see him?"

"I check he's still alive every few weeks."

He looked at her with a slightly raised eyebrow and a half smile. The image powered through her memory like an electric shock. That smile had been the catalyst for what happened. The smile and the lean body and the intensity of those blue eyes staring into hers. "What?"

"Nothing. Goodbye." She shook her head and started walking on shaky legs because if she didn't move she might collapse. She couldn't possibly be so attracted to this guy. Not now. Not again.

When she reached the corner she swung left instead of continuing to her house. She sensed his eyes on her until she'd turned out of sight but when she glanced back at the next intersection he wasn't following. She turned right and walked around the block back to the road along from her house then peered around the corner. He'd gone so she scurried home.

Safely inside she shook her head in exasperation as

she unpacked the groceries. What a total idiot. She must not let this man overwhelm her. If he was wandering about in town she'd stay home as much as possible. She had plenty of work to do.

****

Poppy immersed herself so deeply in her projects she almost forgot to have lunch and later it came as a complete shock when she heard voices outside and George and Jessie appeared on the front path.

"Good grief!" She sprang to her feet and ran to open the front door. "I'm so sorry. Time ran away from me. I had no idea it was so late."

Jessie dumped her bag on the floor and submitted to a kiss. "I walked here with George because you weren't there."

"Thank you so much, George."

"No problem. I sent you a text, so you'd know where she was if you were running a bit late."

"Oh gosh. I didn't even hear it."

"I'm hungry and I'm very, very thirsty," said Jessie in her Miss Grumpy voice.

"Okay, we'll have afternoon tea right now. Go and put your bag in your room and have a wash."

"My legs need a rest. We did running at school." Jessie produced the familiar pout which preceded trouble and a loud voice.

"Come on, pick up your bag."

Instead Jessie regaled them with her opinion of running around the school oval.

"I don't like running," she finished.

"It keeps you fit and healthy," said George. "My class does it too, but they run around twice. Your class only goes halfway."

"No, no, no we don't. Mrs. Morton forces us to go all the way round." Forces was given special, wide-eyed emphasis.

"You must be very good runners," said Poppy, trying not to laugh. Maybe Tracey Morton cracked a stockwhip behind them and flicked stragglers on the bum with it.

"We are. She said we were the best runners in the school."

"Well done," said George. "I'll tell my class that to make them run faster. See you later."

He turned to go but stopped.

"We ran into Duncan."

Oh God!

"What did he say?" she asked.

"Nothing new to report."

"He said I have beautiful blue eyes," said Jessie. "He has blue eyes too. I like him."

George's gaze met hers. Did he realize? She held her breath.

"He's at a bit of a loss, poor guy," he said. "It's a tough situation to be in."

"Okay, Jessie, wash. Now."

Jessie dragged her bag behind her as she stomped to her room.

Poppy stepped onto the veranda and closed the screen door. "I saw him earlier and thought the same thing. He apologized for being rude the other day. He was different. Kind of worn down. He told me a bit about Kyle and their family. Not good."

George shook his head. "No, not that I know much more than you, probably. We had dinner together last night. He was worried about Kyle and tired from the gigs, too, of course."

"Thanks for walking Jessie home. I'll make sure it doesn't happen again."

"It's no problem unless I have an after-school meeting."

She didn't want Jessie getting used to having George as a close friend. Neighbors was fine but it might give him ideas about his relationship with Poppy. And there was always the chance he'd see the resemblance between Jessie and Duncan. Her father. He may already have. If he mentioned it she'd brush it off.

"Boundaries," she muttered.

"What?" asked George.

"Boundaries. Jessie needs to learn there are boundaries."

"Don't look so ferocious. You'll scare me," he said mildly. "What boundaries?"

"You're a staff member and she has to remember that."

"She knows that, and she also knows you and I are friends. We're neighbors so of course we chat and are friends. It'd be odder if we didn't. Unless that's not..." He stopped. "Unless you don't want her to be alone with me. If that's worrying you just say so."

"No! Of course not. I'd never think she wasn't safe with you. I just don't want her to make assumptions about...the relationship."

"She doesn't cross any boundaries at school. There, I'm a teacher. We both know our places. Anyway, I don't see her much at all. She's in the infants' area."

He looked at her steadily waiting for her to respond. Or explain properly what she was on about. She didn't know now what she meant. It was Duncan lurking in the back of her mind, upsetting her with Jessie's blue eyes and the way his mouth curved like hers when he smiled.

"She's fine," he said. "I'm fine, you're fine. We're all fine. Don't worry."

"Okay. Thanks." She opened the screen door. "I'd better feed the monster," she said.

"See you later." He strolled down the path, and she went inside. Had she just made a total idiot of herself for the second time today? Make that the third. First with Duncan, second forgetting to collect Jessie, and third just now. Her mind was going.

In between slurps of orange juice Jessie said, "I like George."

"So do I."

"I'd like him for my Daddy."

"He would be a good Daddy for someone but not you." Was this going to turn into another "where's my daddy?" discussion?

"Why not?"

"Because to be your father George and I would have to love each other a lot, live together or be married and we're not going to do any of those things."

"Why not?"

"Neither of us want to and we don't love each other."

"George would want to. He likes us."

"No. And that's enough of this topic. George is just a friend."

Jessie ate her apple slice in silence for a few minutes then said, "Can we have a kitten instead?"

Poppy was so relieved to switch topics she said, against all her better judgement, "Maybe we can."

The rest of afternoon tea was taken up with nonstop chatter about their possible pet, the likely color, sex, age, and name. No way could she back out of that ill-advised statement now—but she hadn't made a real commitment and a kitten was a better option than a husband.

And Jessie hadn't raised the father subject. With any luck Duncan would leave before they ran into him again and she could keep her secret locked away.

Chapter 6

Duncan had spent a few hours after lunch going over the songs for the upcoming gigs. The guys seemed pretty happy with how the first two had gone and assured him he'd be fine to finish the last few gigs of the tour. Then they'd given him a list of repertoire they wanted to add.

Most of them weren't difficult vocally but remembering the lyrics was tricky because having been written by Kyle, they had similar phrases and ideas. Unfortunately, because they were songs the fans would know, he couldn't fake the words.

He sat on the bed in his room and strummed chords, singing quietly. At about three he needed a break and walked to the café for a coffee and something to eat. Just as he was about to go in George crossed the road holding the hand of a small girl. She chattered nonstop while he smiled and said something which made her laugh.

"G'day, George," he said. "Who's this?"

The child looked up at him through big blue eyes. A cloud of dark curls framed her pretty face. Something tickled his memory. Something about her looked familiar…

"I'm Jessie," she said.

"Hello, I'm Duncan. You have beautiful blue eyes," he said before he thought about how weird that might sound—as if he had a pocketful of boiled lollies to offer unsuspecting kids. In actual fact he rarely encountered small children and wasn't sure how to deal with them.

"Thank you. You have blue eyes, too."

"Yes, I do."

"Any news?" George asked, cutting off further discussion or offering an explanation of who this child belonged to. Maybe he thought the eyes remark was out of line. He'd be hyperaware of predators in his job.

"Nothing. I think I might leave tomorrow. No point hanging around here. If anything happens they'll tell me. They've got alerts out for any sightings or information."

George nodded. "You can always come back if necessary." He held out his hand. "Sorry, mate. Good luck."

Duncan gripped it firmly. "Thanks. Goodbye, Jessie."

"Bye bye, Duncan."

He went into the café, picked up a copy of the free newspaper, and ordered coffee. Who did that little girl remind him of? What was it about her? Those eyes, clear and blue like his own and Kyle's. Inherited from their mother. Not that he remembered her very well. Was that it? The blue eyes reminding him of his mother and Kyle? Could be. There was that photo of his mother when she was young. One of the few reminders he had of her. But she had blonde plaits. This kid had dark curly hair.

He hadn't thought about his family so much for years as he had this last week. Not even a week. More like five days. Time slowed down in this town.

He opened the paper and read the first page. Local doings. More went on here than he'd thought. The waitress brought his coffee and Danish.

"Do you know George, the schoolteacher?" he asked.

"Yep, he's new in town." She seemed ready for a gossip because she didn't rush off to serve anyone and eyed him with interest. She'd know who he was and Kyle would be the topic du jour.

"Who does that little girl Jessie belong to? I ran into him outside just now walking her home."

"Oh, she's Poppy French's daughter. He walks home with her after school sometimes if Poppy is busy working. They're next door neighbors."

"Right. So they're good friends, are they?"

Interesting combination. What did a strong chick like her see in George?

She shrugged. "Friends yes, but people help each other out all the time like that here."

"And does Poppy have a husband?" Not that she gave that impression, too independent.

He wondered if he'd asked one question too many, but she said, "Not that anyone knows. She came here when Jessie was a baby, but she never talks about the father. He was probably a real bastard. Maybe he knocked her around or something. Guys like that should be castrated."

"Isn't she a local?"

"No. Her parents have a property over Dubbo way. Poppy used to stay with her aunt here when she was young. Eve left the house to her when she died. That was about seven years ago. Maybe eight. Very sad." She added as an afterthought, "It can't be easy on her own but Poppy's a great mother."

He nodded. "Jessie's a cute kid."

"Gorgeous," she said and went away.

He went back to the paper. Over the page the band's gig shared the space with a big pumpkin grown by some old bloke for a festival. He studied the photos. In one shot Kyle was in full flight with the band pumping away behind him. In another he was caught in close-up and the image of his pain-in-the-neck brother brought an unexpected lump to his throat. Where was the bastard?

His phone buzzed.

"G'day, Duncan. Lloyd here."

"Hi."

"Any news?"

"No. When are you guys arriving?"

"Yeah well, that's why I'm ringing. We only have Canberra on Friday. Bastards canceled the rest of the tour on us. Tickets weren't selling and the bloke said it was because Kyle wasn't singing. Word got round that he's missing."

"Geez, that's bad. Are they paying a cancellation fee?"

"Yeah, you'll get your share."

"Okay. I guess I'll head back to Sydney and see you Friday."

"Sorry, mate."

"Not your fault."

Duncan finished the call and took a bite from his Danish. The money from those gigs would have been handy but at least they'd get something. He couldn't afford to hang around here now.

He went back to studying the article and the

photos, searching in vain for a clue, something that might give away what had happened that following Thursday evening. It looked like every other gig the band had done and the punters looked the same: dancing, grinning at the camera, enjoying their night out.

His phone rang again. The cop. You Can Call Me Al. That name was going to stick regardless if the man used Al or not.

"We've had a call from someone who thinks they saw Kyle on Friday, late morning," Al Davis said.

"Friday? Where?" His heart thudded.

"The person he thinks was Kyle was a passenger in a car heading toward Sydney near Marulan."

"How reliable is it?"

"Pretty good, we think, or I wouldn't be telling you. The guy was at the Wednesday gig, and he was surprised to see Kyle because he knew they were playing in Goulburn that night."

"Can you find the car?"

"We're in the process. Look, I wanted to tell you that we're pretty sure he hasn't wandered off and got lost in the bush or fallen in the lake, but we still don't know who he was with or why."

"No, I realize that…but…how many people were in the car?"

"Our witness only saw Kyle but someone was driving, obviously."

"A woman?"

"He couldn't tell. Why do you think that?"

"It's more likely he'd be with a woman, I guess."

"Okay."

"Thanks for calling. I appreciate what you're

doing."

"No worries."

Duncan ordered another coffee to replace the one that had grown cold while he was on the phone.

So, Kyle had left his car by the lake and gone off with someone. Why would he leave his bag and the car keys? Because he thought he wasn't going anywhere? Someone arranged to meet him there and he got into their car to talk? Or something else, more likely, if it was a woman. A liaison. A bit of rain wouldn't stop him.

Would he run off with her though, to the detriment of the band and their gigs? No way. This piece of news threw his plan to leave into doubt. Maybe he'd stay another day. The room was booked till Wednesday. After his coffee he'd drop into the second-hand bookshop and stock up. He'd have plenty of spare time on his hands tonight and tomorrow. There was no rush. He continued reading the paper and did a couple of the puzzles until the chatty waitress hinted apologetically that they were closing soon.

On the way back into the hotel he stopped and read the chalkboard of events. Monday—tonight, was multicultural night. Greek food. Sounded good and offered three courses for a very reasonable cost. Moussaka and baklava washed down with ouzo? He went in and booked a table. George might join him again. He was good company. Undemanding. Kind. Maybe that's what that woman Poppy liked. Especially if the waitress was right and she'd lived with a guy who abused her. George would cut his arm off rather than hurt or offend someone.

He went up to his room and rang George.

"Duncan?" George's astonishment came through the phone. "Everything all right?"

"Yeah. Listen, are you up for dinner again? At the pub tonight? It's Greek night apparently." He gave a little laugh as a silence grew. What was George thinking? Impossible to tell. He sucked in a silent breath. Was he trying to work out how to say no to two nights in a row?

"Look, don't worry, mate. It was just a thought. Forget it. You'll have things to do." He spoke fast, embarrassed by the disappointment that caught him unawares and the overwhelming thought that he didn't want to eat alone again in this town. "Sorry."

But George had got over his surprise or shock or whatever and his inherent politeness took over.

"Sure, why not? I haven't even thought about dinner so Greek sounds good. What time?"

"I booked for seven but, mate, don't feel you have to."

"It's fine. Thanks for asking."

"No, thank *you*, George. I…I have to admit, this is getting to me a bit."

"I'm not surprised. Listen, I have a student but we're just finishing."

"Sorry, I didn't realize. See you tonight. Thanks."

"Okay. Seven it is. See you there."

Duncan sat on his bed. George was giving music lessons as well. He was a talented guy and would be pure musical gold in a small town like this.

****

"If someone saw Kyle on Friday," said George. "Where did he spend Thursday night?"

"Does it matter?" Duncan took a big mouthful of

77

the red wine that came with the set menu. A mix of tasty Greek appetizers, a mains choice of Greek style roast lamb with vegetables or a spinach and feta pie with Greek salad, and then a choice of chocolate baklava or spiced orange and honey sorbet. Sounded great.

The bistro was decorated in blue and white, with big posters of Greece on the walls and Greek music playing through the sound system. A couple of statues of Greek gods, probably liberated from someone's garden or local theatre props, stood in the corners silently eyeing the diners.

"There aren't that many places to stay in this area. Have the police tried to find out?" George asked.

"I guess so. They didn't actually say but they sound on the ball."

"At least we know he was alive on Friday."

Duncan looked at George sharply. "Alive then doesn't mean alive now."

"Sorry. I mean…at least we know…" He stopped. "Sorry."

Duncan saved him. "It's okay. I know what you mean."

"Was it morning or afternoon?"

"Late morning."

"And they found his car on Saturday. It must have been left on Friday morning, mustn't it?"

"Looks like it."

George sighed and toyed with his wine glass.

"I think he was abducted," said Duncan. He leaned forward but the waitress arrived and slid a platter of appetizers between them.

"Enjoy," she said.

George took a piece of flatbread, spooned hummus onto it, and took a bite.

"I wonder if he was drugged in that car when the guy saw him," Duncan said.

"Do you think that's the only reason he'd go off with someone?"

Duncan told George his theory of the car being left the way it was, that Kyle wasn't planning to leave it there.

"He might have spent the night with a woman and stayed at the motel using her room, so left his car out of sight for privacy reasons. Hers maybe. It's not far from the motel near the corner of the main road and the road to the lake. I took a look out there. About a five-minute walk."

"How did he know about that particular spot? It's only a small clearing that barely fits two cars."

"She told him and she picked him up. It wouldn't be spotted there."

"And then abducted him?"

"Had her wicked way with him first." Duncan raised a smile. "I don't know, I'm grasping at straws."

"It could be something like that. Or maybe her angry husband turned up."

"Are you thinking of that guy you met? That couple?"

"No idea." George shrugged and took a stuffed vine leaf. "Eat, Duncan. This is really good."

Duncan ate but his mind whirred. An angry husband could be the key. Maybe he took Kyle back to his car but something happened and the guy lost control. Kyle had the knack of mouthing off when he shouldn't. He'd be quite capable of having a go at a guy whose woman he'd just screwed.

He drank some of the wine.

George was chewing more flatbread and hummus across the table.

"Nana Mouskouri," he said suddenly.

"Who?"

"Singing," George said. A woman with a high-pitched folky voice was wading through "Plaisir d'Amour". "She was very big back in about the seventies. Straight black hair and glasses."

"Oh right. Not my thing." He vaguely remembered seeing an album or two.

"Mine either. She was incredibly popular though. Wonder if they've got Demis Roussos lined up."

"Big guy in a kaftan with a high voice and a nanny goat vibrato?"

"That's the one." George grinned. "Then we'll have "Zorba's Dance"."

Duncan laughed. "Nothing wrong with that."

"No. Will you stay with the band?"

"Doubt it. They've already had the tour canceled because of Kyle not being there. We're doing Friday in Canberra and that's it."

"That's bad."

"Sure is, and it's all the more reason for Kyle to stick around."

"Meaning he didn't disappear deliberately. Don't we already know that?"

"Yeah, I guess so." Duncan swigged some more wine and topped up both their glasses. "What if he's dead, George?" His voice rasped, surprising him with the strength of the emotion his words roused.

"Mate, that's only one possibility and if it comes to

that well…we deal with it then."

The "we" clogged his throat causing him to cough and drink more wine. He wasn't as alone as he'd assumed.

"Yeah," he said when he was able. "Thanks."

The waitress took away the demolished platter of antipasti and returned with their main courses of roast lamb.

"Thanks for asking me tonight," said George. "I don't eat out much and if I do it's Chinese."

"Don't you take your girlfriend out?"

"Poppy's not my girlfriend."

"Why not? She's not married, is she?"

"No."

"What's her story? She's an odd sort to live in a place like this."

"I don't know much about her, but she had an aunt here who left her the house when she died. Have you got a partner?"

Duncan shook his head. "Not at the moment. Poppy looks familiar."

George frowned and gave him a sharp look. Jealous? "Have you met her before? She didn't say anything to me."

Did George think she should run and tell him everything she did and thought? Maybe he did and was more interested in her than he let on. Or than she wanted.

"We might have met in Melbourne. We were both there at the same time, went to a lot of parties." Duncan eyed George. Tried a little probe. "If she's not your girlfriend I might ask her out."

George's jaw tightened but he didn't object. How

could he?

"There's something attractive about her…" Duncan ate some rosemary flavored potato. "This food is great."

"Don't mess her around." George put his knife and fork down.

"What?" Duncan smiled. "Asking her out for dinner isn't going to mess her about. She'll probably say no anyway. I don't think she likes me much."

George seemed mollified by that comment because he resumed eating. The unmistakable opening notes of "Zorba's Dance" filtered through the noise in the room. Duncan caught George's eye and laughed.

Chapter 7

Poppy rode her bike to the community center the next morning for her Creative Writing class. She had six students all of whom were keen and one of whom had real talent and was working on a fantasy adventure story with a great premise.

Fran, the volunteer manager of the center was clearing the main hall of chairs for her yoga session. Poppy helped her stack them then went to the smaller room she used, flung the window wide to let out the stale air, and began unpacking her briefcase with notes on the work her students had sent her for comments.

She looked up as footsteps sounded on the wooden floor. Duncan? What did he want? Why wouldn't he keep away from her? Perspiration prickled her neck and her fingers fumbled closing the catch on her briefcase.

"Good morning." There was the smile that twisted her heart.

"Hello," she said with as little as enthusiasm as she could given something deep inside her insisted it was pleased and excited by his appearance.

Before she could organize a question he said, "What are you doing for lunch?"

"No idea. I've only just had breakfast." A stretch, breakfast had been over two hours ago.

"Would you like to have lunch with me at the pub? Or somewhere else?"

The sane part of her screamed no, she was supposed to be avoiding him, protecting herself and Jessie, but the stupidly reckless part, the part that had got her pregnant to this man in the first place, insisted yes.

"My work time is limited." She kept her tone cool.

"Oh right. Can you spare an hour?" He gave her an icy stare in return. "Don't feel you have to if you're too busy."

"Why?" His attitude made it easier to hold out against that relentless force that drew her to him.

"Why do I want to have lunch with you?"

"Yes."

"I thought it might be nice to get to know you better and…" He sighed and glanced around the room as if embarrassed to give her the real reason. "I'd like some company."

"Oh."

"It's fine. Sorry to interrupt you."

He turned to go, and that aura of fragility and aloneness destroyed her resistance in a heartbeat.

"No, wait. Thank you. What time?"

"How about twelve thirty?"

"I'll be there."

"See you." He smiled again and this time she returned it.

As she cycled home after class the invitation expanded in her mind until it became unbearable. She should have said no and stuck to it. The more he saw her up close the more likely he was to remember her. She should cancel. Lie. Tell him something had come up unexpectedly. Out of his presence it was easy to be strong, in the same room, impossible.

But if he was lonely and just wanted a companion, turning him down would be rude and bordering on cruel. He was in a tough situation at the moment, a kind of limbo, waiting for news that as time elapsed was more and more likely to be bad.

She couldn't deny that same overwhelming attraction, the insidious tide that got her into trouble before and would definitely do so again if she indulged it. She wouldn't. Couldn't. He wasn't a man she wanted in her life and certainly not in Jessie's. She knew as much as she ever wanted to know about him especially about his brother and that miserable family they had. They weren't something Jessie needed to be aware of. She was better off without relatives.

She'd go to lunch this once. She would not let herself feel overly sorry for him. Sure, he was in a difficult and emotional situation, but she could not allow that to color her view of him. And she would not allow her personal feelings to intrude. This was purely an act of charity.

****

Tuesday lunch wasn't a busy time. Only two other tables were occupied and those were by people Poppy didn't recognize. Duncan was already seated by the window and would have seen her coming. He had a beer in front of him, a quarter empty. Hopefully it was his first. She summoned up a smile and sat opposite.

"I wasn't sure you'd show," he said.

"Why?" She slung her shoulder bag onto the spare chair.

"Call it instinct."

"Well, your instinct was wrong." She picked up the menu.

"Like a drink?"

"House red, thanks. One won't hurt. And I'll have a burger, please."

"Okay."

He went to the bar. Poppy watched him chatting to Julia. She laughed as she poured the wine. He was making himself at home in town by the looks but as a working musician he'd be used to making idle chat to waiters and bar staff, fitting in, being unobtrusively friendly in all sorts of situations.

He placed her wine in front of her and slid into his seat.

"Thanks."

"I was going to leave tomorrow but now I won't," he said.

"Because of the sighting? That's good news, isn't it?"

"Yeah, but it's not confirmed yet."

"Don't you have gigs to go to?"

"Canceled except for Friday in Canberra."

He must be getting used to the way word got around because he didn't ask how she knew Kyle had been spotted.

"Bummer." She grimaced. Freelance musos live a precarious existence if work can be canceled so fast. Who'd live like that unless they loved making music and couldn't conceive of doing anything else? George couldn't do it and opted for the steady pay and conditions.

"Sure is but…" He shrugged. "That's how it goes."

"You should ask if they'll put you on here for a few nights."

"Solo?" He shook his head. "I couldn't do that. I'm

not a singer, not really."

"You play guitar."

He laughed. "People wouldn't come to hear me play guitar."

"Just a thought." People might come along as a gesture of good will, knowing his situation but it would probably be insulting to suggest that. He was a talented man not a sideshow.

"Thanks, but I'm okay for a while."

"Oh, I didn't mean that…" What did she mean?

"Whatever." He leaned forward and pierced her with those blue eyes. "I can't get it out of my head I've met you before."

"I thought we sorted that out," she said tightly.

"Not really. Melbourne," he said slowly. "It was in Melbourne, but I can't pin it down."

"I met lots of people in Melbourne and you probably did too."

"I never knew your name. It's unusual. I would have remembered. Have you changed your hair or something?"

Heat flooded her neck. He picked up his beer, sat back still eyeing her with a slight frown. Her hair had been short and she'd changed the color randomly to orange, red, blue, or streaks so it could have been anything at the time.

"What do you think happened to Kyle?" she asked.

"I don't want to talk about Kyle."

"But surely you're pleased he was seen."

"Yes, but that doesn't mean anything. He's been missing for nearly five days."

To her surprise he leaned forward and outlined a theory whereby a couple of people colluded to lure him into a trap and abducted him.

"Isn't that a bit over the top?" she asked carefully when he'd finished.

"Is it? Why? There are all sorts of nutters out there doing unspeakable things to innocent people."

"But that would need planning and he was only here for a few days. It'd be more likely to be someone he knows. Why would a nutter pick out Kyle?"

"Haven't you seen that old Clint Eastwood movie called *Play Misty for Me*?"

She shook her head.

"It's about an obsessed fan. He's a late night talk back radio host and she calls in asking him to play a tune called "Misty". It's a ballad, a standard. They have a fling and she goes crazy when he's had enough of her. She keeps calling, saying play "Misty" for me."

"You think Kyle might have an obsessed fan?" She pulled a face. "Interesting. But who was the other person? You said a couple of people would have to be involved. And don't ask if I've heard of Bonnie and Clyde and those serial killers who work in pairs."

"Lots of them do." He relaxed back.

"Good grief, Duncan. Don't spread that serial killer theory around town."

Luckily the food arrived with another beer for him and he was distracted. He ate a few mouthfuls then emptied the first glass of beer.

"You can't tell me," he said. "That you aren't intrigued by my theory."

"In all honesty no I can't," she admitted.

"George thought it might be true, too," he said. "Although we were thinking more along the lines of that couple he met. You know, the guy who came around to beat up Kyle."

"I was there. I can't imagine him planning a murder."

"The police aren't coming up with much," he said.

"They can't just come up with wild theories and no proof." If he was trying to irritate her with that remark he succeeded.

"It's not a criticism. I'm sure they're being very thorough and they're keeping in touch with me. Apparently there were a few hardcore fans who followed the tour. I met a couple of them after the gig."

She managed a thin smile.

"What sort of people were they? Apart from the Kyle angle, I mean. Who does that for a band that's not very well known yet."

He shrugged. "They seemed normal. But those sorts of fans know him and maybe he pissed some of them off. Not here but earlier." He gazed at her intently.

"Duncan, I don't think speculating like this is a good idea."

"Yeah, well…I have to do something."

A pang of sympathy nearly derailed her. Did he do it deliberately? Was he manipulating her? Drinking wine during the day must have mellowed her, taken the edge off her defense. Allowed him into a place she didn't want him to go. Again.

She sighed and drained the glass.

"Like another one?"

"No way, but thanks."

"What are you working on?"

She glanced at him. Was he asking for real or did he think she'd lied about having work to do? But he was concentrating on the remains of his burger and looked innocent enough.

She started in on a summary of the types of projects she did, and to her surprise he listened and asked reasonable questions. She'd seriously misread this man. But then her original impression of him was colored at the time by her own out of control, messy life and total lack of judgement. Blaming him for what was at least half her responsibility.

Either that or she was drunk.

"I'd better make a move. Thanks for lunch." She meant it, could have stayed longer, but she wouldn't tell him that.

"No problem. I enjoyed it."

She smiled. "So did I."

He held the door for her when they left, and she stepped out into bright sunshine.

"Summer's hanging on," he said.

"Yes. You'll miss the autumn leaves—they're beautiful."

He strolled beside her chatting about nothing much until she realized she'd almost led him home without meaning to. She stopped.

"Have you told your father about Kyle?" she asked.

"No point. He'd use it as an excuse to drink more."

"I'm sorry."

"Don't be. It's not your fault my family is shit."

"My life was shit for a while," she said softly. "I can't blame my family though. It was me."

"But not now?"

She couldn't look at him. His eyes were too penetrating, too observant.

"No. Having my daughter...I had to get my act together. Maybe you should give your dad a try..."

He shook his head. "Too far gone, I reckon. As far as he's concerned Kyle may as well have been dead for the last twenty years or more. Not much incentive to have kids, is it? Your daughter's cute."

Poppy's lungs seized for a moment then she gulped in air. "She is. Would you like to have kids?"

"Not much chance of that. No point thinking about it."

That wasn't an answer, but it was good enough.

"Thanks for lunch," she said.

"Thanks for agreeing to come." He flicked a smile on and off and sauntered away.

Poppy continued along a few more houses to home. Inside she slumped into her office chair. His expression and tone when he said "not much chance of that" belied the words. The overwhelming impression she got was resignation. Add regret perhaps, with sorrow underpinning it all. Why? He wasn't too old to have kids. He certainly wasn't too old to find a wife able to have children. He couldn't be much more than mid-thirties. Was there another problem? A health one? What if Jessie would ever be his only child? Did she have the right to keep his daughter from him? And vice versa? He would always be Jessie's only father.

She put both hands over her face and leaned forward, the secret expanding within her, rising up malevolent and demanding attention. A potentially soul destroying and heartbreaking problem and one she'd ignored until now pretending she was the only person affected.

"Oh God," she moaned. "What will I do?"

Chapter 8

"Hello, sweet pea." Poppy dropped a kiss on the warm cheek.

"Hello." Jessie handed Poppy her backpack. "I'm hungry. I want to go home." She set off with a determined stride.

George came along the path from the main entrance to the school.

"Hi," she said.

"Hi. Everything okay?" He studied her face. What did he see? Signs of the emotions raging within? He was an uncomfortably astute observer where she was concerned. Too much so.

"Sure, are you going home now?"

"Yes. Are you all right?" he asked again.

Clearly she mustn't look all right but she said, "I'm fine."

Half a block passed in silence then George said, "Have you seen Duncan?"

"Yes. He's staying in town."

"When did you see him?"

He asked casually but there was an underlying tension in his voice, a note of interrogation that irritated her.

"Lunchtime," she said as they rounded the corner to the main street. "I need to pop into the bakery, Jessie," she called.

Jessie turned and came back. "Can I have a lamington?"

"I'm only getting bread. There are Anzacs at home."

"We can wait outside," said George.

Inside there was a queue and when she came out George and Jessie had moved along to look in the window of the news agent.

"Come on, let's go," Poppy said.

"There's that man with blue eyes." Jessie pointed across the road. "His name's Duncan."

Duncan was strolling along parallel to where they were. Poppy held Jessie's hand as they reached the pedestrian crossing. George stood on her other side. Duncan raised a hand in greeting as he too turned to cross but he waited for them to reach him on the footpath.

Poppy's heart pounded as Duncan looked at Jessie. How could he not see what she saw every day? How could that piece not fall into place? Had George seen it? Or was it so far out of left field that it didn't register to either of them as a possibility. A pair of blue eyes wasn't so rare. They could have come from a northern European ancestor of hers for all anyone knew. The worst thing she could do right now was act oddly and arouse anyone's curiosity, particularly George's.

"Hi," she said. "You've met Jessie, I think."

"Yes." He smiled at her, open and friendly. No suspicion there. Luckily Jessie's face was partially concealed by the obligatory wide-brimmed school sunhat. "Hello, Jessie. G'day, George."

"Hello. Come on, Mummy." Jessie tugged at her hand.

"Sorry, have to keep moving."

"Okay if I walk a bit with you?" Duncan glanced at George who nodded but wasn't his usual welcoming self. He started walking and Duncan followed with Poppy and Jessie.

"Do you have any news?" George asked tersely. What did he have against Duncan?

"The police found the owner of the car the witness saw, and it wasn't Kyle. It was the guy's brother."

"Sorry, mate," said George, slowing a little.

"How very disappointing," said Poppy. "I'm so sorry."

"I wasn't all that hopeful anyway." Duncan moved to walk beside her. "It always sounded unlikely."

"What will you do now?" asked George.

"Go home. I'm leaving today. Soon."

"Will you be back?" asked Poppy.

He looked at her, held her with his eyes. "If something happens."

Did he mean with Kyle or was he implying something else, to do with her? Stupid—why would she think that? Poppy broke the connection.

"Safe trip," said George and the relief in his voice was unmistakable.

The tone annoyed her. Did George think he had a monopoly on her friendship, or her attention? If so he could think again. She wasn't putting up with a clingy, possessive anyone, be they friend or lover. She'd seen that in action firsthand with a girlfriend at university. True love turned into a nightmare within months. Everyone had seen the signs before Rebecca admitted there was a problem. Now Poppy was hyper aware of unreasonable behavior. That query from George if she'd seen Duncan and the follow up question when had tinkled a warning bell but the bakery and Jessie had interrupted, and she might never know where that was going. Unless he tried to question her again.

Duncan stopped walking. "I guess I should head back and pack up. Get going."

George held out his hand, expansive and friendly now. "Good luck, mate."

"Thanks."

"Goodbye," said Poppy. Again, the blue eyes met hers, not icy, warm.

"Catch you later, Poppy French." The half smile appeared. He switched his focus to Jessie who'd stopped and turned indignantly, hands on hips. "See you later, alligator."

"Bye bye," Jessie said.

He said, "You can say, when your legs are straighter. See you, later alligator."

She giggled. "When your legs are straighter."

He didn't linger, simply gave Poppy one last fleeting look and walked back the way they'd come, leaving her with a tight throat and the ridiculous feeling she might cry.

"Good decision for him to leave," George said.

"Why?" The irritation returned with a vengeance. He sounded almost smug.

"He's wasting his time sticking around here."

"George, he's concerned about his brother. How would you feel if it was one of your siblings who was missing?" She frowned at him, conscious of the rise in her voice.

"Give me a break. He doesn't care about Kyle. Those two detest each other. Always have. Duncan's jealous of Kyle and vice versa."

"I didn't get that impression at all. Duncan's worried."

He made a scoffing noise. "Well, he's got you fooled just the way Kyle does."

"Kyle didn't fool me!" She rounded on him, the anger bubbling to the surface. "What's wrong with you?"

"I meant the way Kyle charms women. Duncan is the same. He turns it on when he needs to and he's just done it to you. The poor me act."

"Do you think I'm a gullible idiot or do you think I'm so sex starved that I'd jump into bed with Duncan if he crooked his little finger, because I feel sorry for him? That is the most insulting thing anyone's ever said to me."

Jessie ran back and flung her arms around Poppy. "Stop shouting," she cried.

"I'm sorry, sweet pea. I won't shout anymore. It's okay." Poppy ran her hands over the curls. "I'm sorry."

George, very wisely, said nothing.

"You have to say sorry to George," Jessie said with a frown.

"Sorry for shouting, George," Poppy said but couldn't summon a smile.

"That's okay." He smiled at Jessie. "All good now."

But it wasn't all good and he'd better understand that. He'd just overstepped a boundary big-time, and he hadn't apologized.

****

The rest of the week passed quietly with no further developments in Kyle's case. The little bevy of reporters who had arrived in the first days had moved on pretty quickly to cover more exciting events. Word was that a Missing Person's expert detective had arrived from Sydney to help out. No one had anything new to add to the gossip circulating round town, but the general consensus was that the bloke was dead. What else could have happened to him? The cops were stumped as far as anyone could tell, even the new detective. It was all very matter-of-fact. Sad thing, but he wasn't local, so the impact wasn't personal. The unspoken implication from some people seemed to Poppy that because he was a rock musician he lived in a less savory world where this sort of thing might be, if not expected, at least more likely. Probably involved drugs. Some deal gone wrong.

"They'll add the poor man to the missing person's list. Those cases are never closed," said Helen from next door when Poppy saw her weeding in the front garden and stopped for a chat. "But I think they'll find he's been murdered."

"Wouldn't an accident be more likely?" asked Poppy. Helen did have a tendency toward the dramatic. She was an avid crime novel reader and watcher of Nordic Noir thriller series on TV.

"Doesn't make much difference, does it? Someone knows where his body is hidden and isn't saying." She pulled a face. "Hard to believe that one of our community is a murderer. I've lived here for about a hundred years, and we've never had something like this happen." Her words belied the evident relish she was taking in churning over the different scenarios.

"But he might have slipped and fallen into the lake or something."

Helen fixed her with a beady gray eye. "They'd have found his body by now. You mark my words. If he's in the lake he'll have been weighted down in that deep part where the rocks are. Either that or he's been buried somewhere and they'll never find him."

"It's all horrible, isn't it?" said Poppy.

"Unfortunately a lot of people are, but the worst ones hide it well." She stabbed her weeder into the earth with enthusiasm. "It could be drugs, of course. If it is the police will figure it out. They know who those people are. Biker gangs and so on."

Poppy went back inside with Helen's words ringing in her mind. Biker gangs in Currong? The closest anyone came to that were a few of the agriculture students who rode motorbikes and newcomers, gray-haired Evan and his jovial husband Alfonso from the boutique winery who were a pair of left-over hippies with Easy Rider fantasies.

A murder seemed highly unlikely but if Helen was right was anyone safe? Was the culprit picking victims at random and Kyle was the first of many? She couldn't believe that.

Had Kyle died accidentally? Were they both wrong and this hypothetical killer followed him to Currong, or he was alive somewhere, abducted and held captive?

The abduction scenario hadn't been given more than a cursory once over and dismissed as pointless by the gossipers. Why would anyone do that? Kyle had no money for ransom and no power to wield on anyone's behalf as would a judge or a politician. It was a massive overreaction for an angry, jilted lover or boyfriend. Not something a man like Ralph, a local, would do even though he was in an extremely emotional state at the time. Sympathy lay with the cheated-on man rather than the pair of cheaters.

It was an extraordinary situation with any number of possible scenarios but whatever the truth of the disappearance it was nothing to do with Poppy and she could no more divine the outcome than anyone else. Her life could regain its steady routine. The disruption and heartache caused by Duncan had faded with his departure, making a decision about revealing his fatherhood academic. He hadn't shown the slightest interest in Jessie beyond the normal and the physical attraction between them would fade naturally without nourishment. She didn't know him well enough to pine for him. As long as he stayed away life would go on as before, apart from one aspect.

Her relationship with George had taken on a different complexion. He was wary of her now, polite, but kept his distance like someone who'd suddenly been scratched by a cat he'd thought was passive and friendly. Poppy made a point of collecting Jessie from school on time, not wanting to slip back into relying on George as backup. If something delayed her she'd ring one of the other mothers for help.

On Saturday morning the phone rang while she and Jessie were having a lazy breakfast and discussing where to go for a picnic on their bikes, with the lake the preferred destination. The weather would turn soon, and the warm days would dwindle and fade into the chill of autumn and winter. Today could be their last opportunity.

"Hello. Poppy French speaking." She didn't recognize the number but that wasn't unusual. Could be a query from a prospective client.

"Poppy, it's Duncan."

His voice in her ear sent a rush of hot blood to her cheeks and she stood up and went to the living room leaving Jessie to munch her cereal.

"Hi, where are you?"

"In Canberra. I'm about to leave and wondered if I could drop in on my way back to Sydney."

"Oh, I'm not sure…"

"If you have plans it's fine. It was just a thought." Disappointment had edged its way into his voice.

"Jessie and I are planning a picnic."

"I could be there by ten thirty at the latest. I'd like to see you…Would you still be around?" Brighter now she'd tossed him a crumb of hope.

What could she say? What should she say? Ask him why he wanted to visit her? It must be something important to him. He couldn't stay long. He knew they were going out.

"We weren't leaving till about eleven thirty."

"Thanks. Should I come to your place, or would you rather meet in town?"

"Umm. Probably here is best." The less public, the better. She gave him the address before she could think, and said goodbye. Now she knew why George had said yes to Kyle about staying at his house. Couldn't think of a fast enough excuse. But she knew she didn't try hard enough. Weakened by the unexpectedness of his voice. Unprepared to defend herself.

"Who was that?" asked Jessie.

"Duncan is coming to see us."

"But I want go on our picnic."

"We will go. He's coming earlier and only for a quick visit."

"Why?"

"I don't know but if you've finished eating you should get dressed then help me decide what we'll take for our lunch."

Jessie scampered away.

"Teeth," called Poppy. She poured herself more coffee. Duncan. Why was he coming? Had he remembered where they'd met and what they'd done? She reached for the phone to call him back. Her hand hovered then relaxed, didn't pick it up.

How had he got her number? From George when he was here before? But George wouldn't pass that on without asking her first, if ever, especially given his attitude toward Duncan. She shook her head at her slowness. All he needed to do was search for her webpage. She'd told him all about her work at lunch that day. Her contact details were there. Not her address, of course, but email and phone. Too easy. She'd even thought it could be a client.

If he had remembered her, she'd just have to face up to it, get it over with because her decision would be made for her, and she wasn't a coward. When confronted with a direct question she wouldn't lie. If, however, he was only coming because he was interested in her as a woman…well…that was different. She could fend off any advances if that was his intention. Getting to know each other on a platonic level, however, would make any future revelation about Jessie easier because she'd know whether the man was worthy of being part of her beautiful child's life.

If that was selfish and arrogant, tough. Her duty was to protect her child. Said child reappeared cute as a button in a pink denim skirt, white tights, and a long sleeved pink and white striped T-shirt, immediately putting a crack in her resolve.

Was it right to stop him sharing this treasure? Without him *she* wouldn't have Jessie either.

"What will we take?" Jessie asked.

"Sandwiches are easiest, and we'll need our water bottles."

The next half hour was spent discussing and preparing sandwich fillings and whether to take bananas or mandarins to eat after finishing the choc chip muffins Poppy had made yesterday.

"We should check our bikes," said Poppy.

With the tires pumped and puncture repair kit safely stowed in the backpack with the lunch and sunscreen, Jessie was eager to leave.

"When's Duncan coming? I want to go now," she said.

"It's too early. We want to get to the lake for our lunch."

"We could swim."

"I don't think it's swimming weather. The water will be too cold. He'll be here soon."

Fifteen minutes later a black sedan stopped in the street outside the house.

"He's here," said Jessie who'd been anxiously watching out the window. "Don't talk too much. You always talk and talk and talk."

"I promise I won't. but we mustn't be rude. He's a visitor."

"I won't be." She ran to the door, hovering while Poppy opened it.

He strode up the path, long legs encased in jeans, lean body in a navy shirt with the sleeves half-rolled.

He smiled when he saw Jessie peeping around the doorframe. Then his eyes fixed on Poppy, and she couldn't move, pinned in place by the sight of him as all her defenses and resolve melted like butter.

Chapter 9

Not for the first time since he'd spontaneously phoned Poppy that morning Duncan wondered what he was going to say to her. Why he should choose her to confide his emotional reaction to the latest news from the police and what she would make of it. Of him.

Several times during the drive he was tempted to pull over and call her, apologize and say he had to get back to Sydney, lie and say a gig had come in. He doubted she'd care and now he had no idea why he hadn't cried off, and still had no idea what he was doing there walking up the front path, smiling at the kid, but his attention focused on the green-eyed, dark-haired woman standing by the open door watching him approach. Not smiling but not radiating irritation or annoyance. He didn't know what it was about her but if they had met before he was a bloody idiot for letting her go.

"G'day, Jessie. How are you?"

"Okay." She backed away behind the safety of Poppy's legs.

"Hi, Poppy. Sorry to barge in on you. I won't stay long."

"That's all right. Come in."

Jessie stared up at him. "We're going on a picnic to the lake after you've gone."

Poppy glanced at him and gave a tiny apologetic

grimace.

"Sounds like fun," he said to Jessie.

"It is. We're riding our bikes."

He nodded. "Is it very far to ride?"

"Yes," said Jessie.

Poppy said, "About twenty minutes by road on bikes but it's walkable in less, cross country. There's a path that cuts over the ridge." She pointed vaguely across the road where a glint of reflected sunlight in the distance indicated water.

"Do you like picnics?" asked Jessie.

"I can't remember when I last went on one," he said. "I go surfing and sometimes I eat when I'm there but that's not really a picnic like yours."

"Would you like coffee?" asked Poppy. "Use the bathroom if you want. It's along the hallway."

"Thanks."

"Jessie, why don't you do a drawing of a picnic for Duncan?"

"Okay. I'll draw him at the beach."

She went away. Poppy led him through to a large, bright, old-fashioned family sized kitchen. Creamy white walls set off a high, sunshine yellow ceiling. Basil and thyme stood on the wide window ledge in pots. A wooden table sat against one wall, and an antique dresser with glass fronted doors displayed crockery and glassware against another. The fridge and stove were modern, the fridge door covered in reminders, childish drawings and a calendar covered in writing. The whole room radiated coziness and happy families.

"This is really nice," he said.

She indicated he should sit, and he pulled out an

old, solid, wooden chair. She already had the coffee making underway, no doubt for a speedy dispensing of hospitality to the uninvited guest.

"I inherited the house from an aunt," she said.

"Lucky." He didn't dare tell her that thanks to the waitress in the café he already knew about Eve the aunt and how Poppy used to visit.

"I guess so. But I loved her very much and she died way too young. I'd much rather she was still here. She would have loved Jessie."

"I'm sorry."

"I think my luck was more that I had her to myself when I was a child. She was…like a mother."

He looked around. "It certainly has an aura about it, this place. A real homeliness to it."

Poppy stared at him for a moment then said softly, "I always felt it too, when I came to stay. And I still feel as though Evie is here with Jessie and me. As if she's just gone into another room or the garden and will come back in a minute." She gave a little laugh. "Crazy."

He shook his head. "No, it's not. I've never had that feeling of home in my life, but I can understand why you feel it in this house, and I've never been here before."

She turned abruptly and finished making the coffee.

"Why did you come here today?" she asked with her back still turned.

"I don't know. I asked myself that on the way here and I nearly called you and said I wouldn't come."

He didn't dare move. Her back was rigid, shoulders tight. Thinking what?

"But you didn't," she said after a moment. She turned and placed a mug of coffee before him along with a little jug of milk and matching sugar bowl. Aunt Eve's?

"No." He added milk.

She sat opposite, hands wrapped around her own mug.

He sipped the coffee but barely registered the flavor.

"It's not true," he said. "I do know why I came." He met her gaze suddenly. "The police are shifting the focus to finding a body. Which means they're sure Kyle's dead."

She didn't reply straight away. Wouldn't know how.

He wanted to talk it out with someone and there wasn't anyone else he could confide in, reveal his inner feelings. He wouldn't approach George again. Something about his attitude last time they met made him wary. The guy was interested in Poppy, that was obvious, and he also resented the fact that she was friendly toward Duncan. He was probably next door right now wondering what was going on.

Somehow he knew Poppy was the right, the only, person. She'd met Kyle, had been one of the last people to see him alive and she was sympathetic.

"They're going back to the car and how it got there. Someone might have seen or heard something that night, so the cop was talking about going house to house near the lake and asking again. Maybe do a re-enactment of the route the car took."

"Do they think he was…"

"Murdered?" The word crashed into the room.

"Or died accidentally," she said. "Or there could have been a fight and the other person panicked."

"They're not saying. God knows I've wanted to kill him often enough over…" Broken and rough, the words came in little bursts of sound. He stopped as an intense rush of emotion jammed his throat. He rubbed a hand over his eyes embarrassed to feel the moisture against his fingers. "Sorry," he murmured.

Her chair scraped lightly on the floor then she rested her hand on his shoulder. Somehow it seemed natural and easy to relax against her body and feel her hold him as he struggled for control, feel her warmth and the reassurance that he wasn't alone.

Time ceased and then he drew away, unsure how long he'd leaned against her like a child, trying not to cry. Poppy resumed her chair and sipped her coffee as if nothing had happened. He picked up his own mug surprised his hand wasn't shaking. Couldn't look at her, couldn't utter a word.

Jessie burst back into the kitchen waving a piece of paper and put it in front of him. A stick figure with an outsized blue shirt and black shorts stood on a strip of bright yellow sand with more blue in the background. A big yellow ball with radiating lines hovered in the top left corner and odd looking lines represented things he couldn't identify. Her name was printed in crooked letters at the bottom.

"That's very good," he said. "Me at the beach in my blue shirt. What's this?" He pointed at a red blob with a smaller green one next to it.

"That's your beach umbrella and that's your towel. And those are birds." A little finger pointed at a couple of black squiggles in the sky.

"Seagulls."

"Yes. They want to eat your sandwiches."

He smiled at the intent little girl by his side. Cartoons were his forte at school and his depictions of teachers had got him into trouble more than once, but he hadn't picked up a pencil for years.

"They're cheeky pests," he said. "One nearly took my chip out of my hand once."

She laughed.

"Can I keep this drawing?"

"Yes, I drew it for you."

"Thank you very much."

"I can draw another one."

"I have to leave soon," he said. "And you're going on your picnic."

"You can come too, can't he, Mummy?"

Before Poppy could respond with a negative, he said, "I don't have a bike."

"Do you have to be home for something today?" Poppy asked.

"I have a gig tonight, so I'd have to leave here by about two at the latest. I could stay but I don't want to intrude." He couldn't judge by her expression what she wanted him to say.

"Come on our picnic," said Jessie, gazing at him with big blue eyes. Darker than his he saw now but striking coupled with the smooth pale skin, dark lashes, and bouncy curls. A heartbreaker in the making.

"You could drive and meet us there or walk over the ridge. It's a nice walk, takes about fifteen minutes if you dawdle," said Poppy.

It was a matter-of-fact statement with no indication of trying to influence his decision either way. The truth was he wanted to stay, draw on the effortless happiness this little family created purely by loving and respecting each other, having fun together. How much he and Kyle had missed out on! If their mother, or father, had been as loving and caring as Poppy their lives would have been completely different. But it was never that simple. Poppy had her problems, and she was as alone with them as he was with his.

He looked from Poppy to Jessie and saw only the desire to share a simple picnic with a friend. For them a natural and uncomplicated invitation.

"I'll need to go via the shop for some food," he said.

"I'll make a few more sandwiches and we have muffins and fruit, but you'll need a drink," she said.

"Choc chip muffins," said Jessie.

"I can never resist a choc chip muffin," he told her. "I have a water bottle in the car. Are you sure?" He looked from one to the other.

"Why not?" Poppy asked and Jessie said sternly, "And you need your hat and sunscreen."

"Yes, boss," he said and saluted. "I have both those in my car as well."

Jessie giggled again and the sound lightened his heart. He could pretend he belonged, for a couple of hours at least.

The cyclists took him along the street and around a couple of corners to the beginning of the path with instructions on where to wait for them at the other end because he was sure to arrive at the lake first. The first hundred meters of dirt track went through open grassland with a few gumtrees and wattle growing in clumps along the way, then the land rose slightly and the bush crowded in. A small group of elderly hikers came striding toward him, calling cheerful hellos and lovely days as they passed by.

The shade of the tall trees was welcome. Despite obeying Jessie's admonition to wear a hat the sun beat down on his head with surprising strength for late March, and it wasn't long before a trickle of perspiration ran down his back. The path was narrow but well-trodden, one of those paths made by people's feet rather than planned and as Poppy said, not a difficult walk. The ridge she'd mentioned was more a gentle slope up from where he'd started, and it wasn't until he reached the highest point that he realized the land dropped away more steeply on the far side. The view was expansive. The lake wasn't very big, but it stretched away and around a slight bend with a rocky promontory making a picturesque feature in the bright sunshine sparkling off the water. A small sailboat moved slowly across to the right and the faint sounds of children's voices and laughing floated up from below where the water's edge was still obscured by trees.

Off to the left the road from town appeared and disappeared but he couldn't see any bike riders. He smiled and drew a deep lungful of fresh eucalyptus scented air. He needed this break more than he'd realized. At home he'd go surfing but hadn't managed to get to the beach for several weeks what with Kyle's disappearance and unpleasant weather over the last couple of days in Sydney.

He sat on a large sun warmed rock, swigged some water, and gazed out past the lake to the distant hills and rolling pastureland.

A family group came from the direction of the

town and smiled and nodded as they went by. Friendly people here. Did they know who he was? Some might, but his photo hadn't made it into newspaper or TV reports. He waited until the family were out of sight and strolled on, downward now. Suddenly the gently winding path ended, and he stepped out into a parking area with two cars in it. The family were disappearing along a path between trees on the left, by the lake's edge.

Poppy had said walk to the right to the picnic area and wait there. A woman read a book at the only occupied table while two young boys tossed a Frisbee nearby with lots of laughing and shouting at each other to throw properly.

She looked up and said, "Hello. Lovely day for a walk."

"Yes."

"You're not local, are you? Are you in town for long?"

"Just visiting a friend."

She waited for him to give her more information, but she'd find out soon enough when Poppy arrived.

He chose a table close to the water under a tree and sat down to wait and watch the ducks waddling about.

The rocky promontory wasn't far from where he sat. How deep was the water in the lake? Kyle's car had been found a bit farther along the shoreline, but in a small cleared area set back from the water where the usual picnickers didn't go. Al had told him people didn't come out here during the week and there'd been a cracking great storm the night Kyle had disappeared, so the ground was very soggy the next day and not conducive to hiking or picnics.

Duncan had driven out to have a look the previous week but wasn't sure where the spot was and by the time he did that, there was nothing to see anyway. Certainly nothing the police searchers would have missed. One thing had become clear however during his very pleasant walk. Whoever had dumped the car here could easily have gone back to town on foot after leaving the car and disposing of the body. The storm was the perfect cover for returning unseen in the dim light. How long would that take? Not long. Despite the rain and slippery conditions someone who knew the way and needed to hurry could do it easily in ten minutes. Someone desperate and frightened.

No one else would be out here in that weather, no one to spot a person coming along the lake path. Not the elderly hikers, the families or dog walkers, and probably not the residents who lived nearby.

Chapter 10

Jessie pedaled steadily along with Poppy close behind making sure she stayed well to the left when the few and far between cars came along. All the drivers knew them and took extra care, waved and called out hello as they slowed to pass.

When they reached the motel, turned the corner, and were safely able to pedal side by side on the quiet lake access road, she asked Jessie why she wanted Duncan to come along. To her surprise Jessie said, "He's sad and I wanted him to be happy."

"How do you know he's sad?"

"His brother's lost," she said. "Everyone knows that."

"That's very kind, Jessie." Her heart swelled with pride. Somehow this little girl had inherited the kindness and generosity of spirit Poppy had so loved about Aunty Evie. Maybe it was growing up in the house imbued with her presence.

"I know. He's nice and he liked my picture."

"It was very good. He won't be here for much longer."

"I know. He's going home after our picnic," she said in the tone of voice that implied her mother didn't know a thing.

The road sloped gently down to the water and ran along to the main parking area.

"Duncan should be waiting for us at the picnic ground," said Poppy.

"There he is." Jessie accelerated over the parking area, little legs pumping fast.

"Be careful," called Poppy.

Furzia and her boys were the only other people at the picnic ground. Furzia deep in her book at a table and Adam and Ryan throwing a Frisbee at the far end on an open stretch of grass. Furzia was a driving force on the school committee, organizing cake stalls and trivia nights with practiced ease. She also liked to know everything she possibly could about everything.

Duncan turned and stood up as Jessie pedaled toward him making Poppy's heart beat just that bit faster than was justified by cycling.

Furzia waved. Poppy waved back but didn't stop to chat. The last thing she wanted was a friendly but invasively thorough interrogation about the man who was obviously waiting for them. No doubt she'd already asked him some questions and no doubt he'd deflected them with ease. She'd met her match with Duncan.

Was it good that Jessie liked Duncan? How could she tell whether her kind, sweet little girl was going to be badly hurt by this whole situation? Deep in her heart she believed allowing them to know each other was the right thing to do, but the right thing wasn't always the wise or best thing. Evie would have given her good counsel. As it was, she was on her own.

"Hi there. You're a good bike rider." Duncan steadied Jessie's bike for her and she got off.

"I beat Mummy," she said.

"I saw."

Jessie handed him her helmet and he hung it on the handlebars. Poppy propped her bike against the tree next to the picnic table. Duncan did the same with Jessie's.

"Nice walk?"

She took off her helmet then shook her head, running a hand through her hair to loosen it.

"It was," he said after a moment, during which she realized he'd been studying her breasts in the tank top, an awareness that gave her a little unfamiliar thrill of pride. How long had it been since a man looked at her body that way? A good-looking man. Even if it was this one.

She slid the backpack off and dumped it on the bench seat. "Here's your drink, Jessie."

Jessie dutifully swallowed a few mouthfuls of water then went to look at the ducks.

"Shall we have lunch first or walk around the lake for a bit?" It was cooler in the shade. She took her white linen long-sleeved shirt out of the backpack and put it on but left it unbuttoned.

"I wouldn't mind walking to the rocks over there." He pointed to the promontory.

"Sure."

"Are you leaving the backpack here?"

"Why not? Furzia's over there."

She called, "Hi, Furzia. We're just going for a walk to the rocks and back. Keep an eye on our stuff for me?"

Furzia looked up. "No worries, Poppy. Lovely day for it."

"Sure is. Thanks."

With Jessie running about like a puppy, Poppy and

Duncan strolled along the water's edge.

"She's wondering who I am," he said. "She was busting to give me the third degree before you arrived. Now she'll be even more frustrated."

"Furzia really likes to know what's going on." Poppy laughed. "People think I need a man."

"I've never met a woman less in need of a man," he said casually.

Coming from Duncan that stung in a way that surprised her. Was she some sort of ultra-feminist in his eyes? "Really? Why do you think that?"

"You're managing very well, you have your own business, you're raising a happy healthy kid in a secure home." He shrugged. "Strikes me you don't need anyone else, man or woman. Wanting is a different thing."

"Thank you." It sounded more defensive than she meant but the whole conversation was striking too close to her secret dilemma for comfort. "But no one can function properly completely alone. I don't think humans are designed like that. We like company."

"You don't think a woman needs a man to function properly though, do you?" he asked.

"Plenty of men and women get along fine without a partner by choice or circumstance," she said tartly. "I don't think it's a matter of need. It's more from desire or lack of opportunity. It's not like the old days when women were married off to any bloke who'd take them. And men needed a legitimate heir. No one has to get married these days." The irritation had crept into her voice and wouldn't go away. "Do people tell you, you need a wife?"

"No. Don't get bent out of shape. What you do

with your life is your business."

"Exactly." She walked in silence for a few meters while he wisely did the same. "Just for the record, I haven't sworn off men for life. I'm not scarred by a previous lover who dumped me or cheated on me. Most of us have experienced that and forged on, wounded pride, broken heart, and all."

"I'm sure George is pleased about that."

If that was some sort of joke she wasn't laughing. She glanced at him sharply, but he was looking out over the water.

"I'm not interested in George. He's a bit...he's not my type."

"I guess options are limited in a place like this. How deep is the lake?" he asked. Her non-existent love life had lost his attention. Good or bad? Probably good in the grand scheme. And was he talking about her options or George's?

"Not sure," she said. "But the deepest bit is in the middle." She pointed. "What are you thinking?"

"I'm thinking it's not far to walk—or run—back to town from here."

"After dumping a body and the car?"

"Yep."

"Surely the police have thought of that."

"I would hope so. They're doorknocking the area closest to the start of the path again."

"That storm was pretty intense."

"Exactly. No one would be out in it by choice."

"But I saw Kyle leave just before the rain started." Or had she? "It have might have been raining a bit, a few drops, but the storm hadn't hit. That came about five or ten minutes later. Jessie and I were going to do

118

some gardening when I finished working but we couldn't."

"Hmmm." That seemed to stump him.

"And," she said. "He would have had to go straight there for his murderer to be caught in the storm on the way back to town."

"We don't know where he went or who he met after he left. The police haven't got any definitive sightings of the car except for one person in the main street."

"There's not enough time for it all to fit, is there?" Poppy sighed. "There's nothing we can do that the experts can't."

"No and it makes me feel so…useless."

Jessie was waiting at the start of the footworn track that led up and over the rocky section. Parts of it were almost vertical with natural steps up from rock to rock that were too big for her short legs.

"Are we going up?" she asked.

"Yes, and then we'll go back for our lunch."

"You go first, and I'll lift her up the high bits," said Duncan.

Poppy did as he suggested and held out her hand to steady Jessie as she came up the makeshift path, puffing and panting with the effort of the climb but extremely proud of herself.

The top was flat rock for a few paces with a couple of trees and shrubs clinging to the inhospitable surface. From this point and with macabre thoughts of body disposal in mind, the water appeared sinister and almost threatening in its mirror-like calm.

Duncan walked across to the edge and peered over at the three-meter drop.

"Careful you don't fall," called Jessie. "It's very high and you'd drown in the water."

Duncan turned, smiling. "I won't."

"Can I go and look too?" she asked Poppy.

"Hold my hand."

When she reached Duncan's side Jessie took hold of his hand, too. He looked down with a surprised expression but didn't brush her fingers away, and he caught Poppy's eye over the head of their daughter.

"Now I won't fall," he said, his eyes fixed on hers as he spoke.

"It's deepest off this spot," Poppy said, breaking the contact abruptly. But it would be impossible to lug a body up to where they stood, and even if that was managed, rolling it off the cliff edge wouldn't clear the rocks below.

"You'd need a boat," he murmured. "Far too complicated."

"No one leaves their boat out here. And it'd be a ridiculously tough climb to where we are even on a perfect day like today."

"Couldn't do it."

Jessie tugged at their hands. "Can we have our lunch now? I'm hungry."

Back at the picnic ground, Furzia and her boys were sitting at their table eating. She waved. Poppy waved back. Duncan, his back turned to Furzia, grinned and raised his eyebrows at Poppy and she laughed.

"Is she a single mother, too?"

"No, maybe Bruce is away. He's a lecturer at the Agricultural College and she's the director's PA."

"Adam and Ryan go to my school," said Jessie. "But they're not in my class."

Lunch passed in companionable chit chat, with Duncan making Jessie laugh at silly jokes he must have dredged up from somewhere in his childhood. By his face, Jessie's innocent delight and non-judgmental friendliness had taken him albeit briefly away from the pain associated with Kyle, and for that Poppy was glad because he needed some relief. The problem was the more that pair bonded the harder it would be to keep the truth from him.

Could she count on this being a short, never to be repeated interlude? If he came back to Currong, as he inevitably must given the situation, would she be able to avoid him after today's visit had altered their relationship? An independent, insular man like Duncan would rarely show the emotion he had displayed in her kitchen which made his reappearance more likely. They could now be classed as friends when before they'd been mere acquaintances, and she'd have to strive to keep it that way. The weird thing was she kept telling herself to keep him at arm's length, and somehow he kept avoiding her defenses without even trying. After today he wouldn't realize there had been any defenses, if he ever had.

After lunch Jessie wanted to look at the ducks again so Duncan offered to pack up the remains of the picnic while Poppy walked to the water's edge with her. He came to stand by her side and watched Jessie following a couple of waddling ducks.

"I should get going, Poppy."

"Of course. We'll be a little while yet." She kept her tone light, but it wasn't as easy as she'd thought. The picnic had been relaxed and fun and Jessie had kept the conversation away from the topic which was eating away at him. He'd fitted comfortably into their little family, more so than George because he made no demands and expected nothing from her.

"Thanks for the invite and lunch. I'm not around kids much but she's a real sweetie."

Poppy smiled. "She is. Jessie," she called. "Duncan has to go now."

Jessie ran across. "See you later, alligator."

"In a while, crocodile," he said.

"When your legs are straighter," she said with a beaming smile.

"That's right." He touched her hair briefly. "Ride safely."

"I will."

He turned to Poppy. "See you."

She nodded. "Safe trip."

He studied her for a moment then turned and strode away.

She watched him go. Duncan had unknowingly filled a space she hadn't fully acknowledged or more accurately, had denied, was there. The space filled by a father.

****

Duncan timed the walk back, moving swiftly. The beginning of the path was steeper going this way but easily managed by anyone reasonably mobile and he reached the first houses in nine and a half minutes, panting a little and sweating in the afternoon heat but he hadn't jogged, figuring the rainy and slippery conditions would have slowed down the suspect. He paused on the tarred surface, looking around the quiet dead end street. The nearest house was across a stretch of rough grass and the next closest faced it. The blocks

122

were bigger than suburban city ones and most had old, established gardens crammed with shrubs and trees.

He started walking toward Poppy's house, more slowly now because who knew where the phantom assailant went after reaching the town? It was all conjecture anyway, built on nothing but vague assumptions. Trying to make sense of the senseless.

He reached the car and leaned against it while he drank the rest of the water. He looked at Poppy's front garden and spied the tap. If he filled the water bottle here, he needn't make a rest stop until Marulan. Mission accomplished, he went back to the car just as George came out of the house next door and strode toward him, face set in an unfamiliar expression. Was he angry?

"What are you doing here?"

"I'm on my way to Sydney," Duncan said mildly.

"This is hardly on your way." Angry and jealous. Very jealous. He was bristling like a guard dog.

"You seem to forget the police here are running the case and I check in with them as much as I can."

"Poppy's house isn't the police station."

"Yeah, so?"

"So what are you doing at Poppy's house? Your car's been there for hours."

"Saying hello and good bye. Not that it's your business, George."

Was that steam coming out of his ears? Duncan forced back the laughter bubbling in his throat. "Are you spying on her? Do you spy on her?"

"I keep a neighborly eye on her. She's all alone." He'd retreated into indignation.

"So are you. So am I."

Duncan opened the car door.

"Where is she? Where did you go?" asked George. A note of desperation had crept into his voice.

"See you later, George."

Duncan got into the car, gave him a little wave, and drove off. When he checked the rearview mirror George was standing in the street staring after him. The lightning bolts of hate spearing from his eyes at the car were almost visible. Like those red hot blasts the wizards let fly in the Lord of the Rings movies.

What the hell was all that? The man was insanely jealous. Duncan could have attempted to diffuse him by insisting that he and Poppy were just friends but doubted it would have made any difference. Anyway, he didn't want to. Why should he pander to that man's jealousy? Poppy wasn't interested in him. She'd told him herself quite plainly. He wasn't her type, she said.

And he wouldn't tell George anything because he didn't want Poppy to be just a friend. But he didn't want her to know that.

A short way out of town he pulled over and called her.

"Duncan? Is everything okay?" The concern in her voice warmed his heart at the same moment as he belatedly realized she might be alarmed by a call coming so soon after they'd parted.

"With me? Yes, yes, I'm fine. Are you home yet?"

"We're just about to leave the lake."

"Listen, I ran into George when I was back at the car. He was acting a bit oddly and he worried me a bit."

"Why?"

"He appeared from nowhere and wanted to know why I was visiting you and where you were and so on.

He was pretty angry, but he tried to hide it. He sounded jealous. I just wanted to warn you."

"What did you say to him?"

"Nothing. It's none of his business what either of us do, but he seems to think it is. He said he keeps an eye on you because you're all alone."

"Oh my God." It was a groan of annoyance rather than an expression of alarm.

"Can you handle him?"

"Yes, don't worry. Now that you've gone, he'll calm down. He thinks you're out to seduce me and that I'm too silly to resist."

"Did he say that?" He snorted with laughter, couldn't help it. Did the guy know the woman he was talking about? Poppy? No one could seduce her unless she wanted it to happen.

"More or less. He said I shouldn't trust you because you're the same as Kyle."

"Do you think I am?"

"No, you're not."

"But he thinks I'm irresistible to you…" His fingers tightened on the phone, waiting for her response.

A little voice said something in the background.

"I'd better go. Sorry. Jessie's complaining that I talk too much."

He exhaled. "Do you?"

"Always. Thanks for calling, Duncan, but don't worry. I'll be fine."

"Let me know."

"Okay. Bye."

He drove on, smiling. She hadn't said no need to call with an update. She'd said okay.

Chapter 11

George was nowhere to be seen when Poppy and Jessie arrived home, hot and puffing from the final stretch up the gently rising slope.

"Boy, I'm pooped," said Poppy as they reached the shed and got off their bikes.

"Me too. I need ice cream." Jessie wheeled her bike in and carefully propped it against the wall. She loved her hot pink Christmas present and took great care of it.

"I think we can manage ice cream. We've earned it, and you did really well. It was a long ride." Poppy closed and locked the shed. Jessie had insisted she find a padlock to ensure the beloved bike was safe from thieves.

"I want chocolate sprinkles on mine."

Jessie wanted to eat her ice cream on the front veranda so Poppy sat with her and chatted about the picnic and the ducks as they spooned up the deliciously cold treat.

"When is Duncan coming to visit us again?"

"I'm not sure. He didn't say."

"I want to draw him another picture. He'll like that."

"He will. What will you draw this time?"

"Him and his brother to make him happy."

"Have you seen his brother?" Poppy glanced at her.

When could she have seen him? When the band arrived in town they went straight to set up at the Royal, changed, and ate there, George said. Kyle only came to the house late that night after the gig.

"No, but that doesn't matter. Have you?"

"Yes, he has blue eyes, too but he's shorter."

Jessie absorbed that piece of information as she licked her spoon. "I'd like to have a brother."

"What about a sister?"

"No, a brother."

"I don't have a brother or a sister," said Poppy.

"That's because you're an only child like me. I don't want to be an only child anymore."

"That's just how it is at the moment."

"Maybe one day," Jessie said in a world-weary voice.

Poppy smiled. "Maybe one day."

"Maybe Duncan would like to be my Daddy," she said after some studious ice cream eating.

"We've talked about this before."

"That was about George, but you said you didn't want him to be, and he didn't either. Duncan is nice and you like him, don't you?"

Jessie's version of Duncan's eyes gazed at her with a similar intensity to the look he'd given her when he said goodbye. Poppy couldn't speak for a moment as her secret and its accompanying dilemma crashed back into the spotlight.

"You do like him, don't you?"

"Yes, but not enough," Poppy said weakly. "Have you finished?"

Jessie handed her the spoon and empty bowl and Poppy escaped to the kitchen where she leaned against the bench and drew deep breaths to steady her thumping heart.

Get a grip. This wasn't a new conversation and Duncan wouldn't have any reason to come back for a while. She straightened and rinsed the bowls for the dishwasher. Jessie came in and sat at the table.

"Duncan left his drawing behind," she said.

"I'm sure he didn't mean to."

"No, he liked it. He just forgot when we went on our picnic. We can post it to him. And we can send my new drawing, too."

"We don't know where he lives," said Poppy, knowing it was the feeblest of excuses.

"Mummy," Jessie said in that exasperated tone she used when something was blindingly obvious. "We can ring him up and ask him."

There was no answer to that piece of logic.

****

Duncan had plenty of time for thinking on the drive back to Sydney. If the police were working on the premise Kyle was dead, he really should tell his father. Al had asked if he would break the news or if he preferred the Sydney police to do it. The police had already been in contact with his father to ask when he'd last seen Kyle, but as Duncan could have told them, he was no use whatsoever and basically told them to piss off and leave him alone.

Like it or not, putting off the visit wouldn't benefit anyone so when he reached the highway exit which would send him home he made the turn but detoured to go via Randwick. Twenty minutes later he pulled up outside the house he'd grown up in. The sloping block was narrow and the front yard minimal, a slab of stained concrete raised five steps above street level stretching from one side of the house to the other. The only greenery softening the disaster was a flowering bush hanging over from next door and the street tree arching across the footpath. The neglected old house was badly in need of repair and painting. In the row of better maintained properties, it stood out like a rotten tooth in a healthy mouth.

There was no point getting involved in any sort of discussion about it, he'd learned many years ago, so he ignored the eyesores and strode to the front door and thumped loudly.

He knew his father would be there. Light was showing through the fanlight over the front door even though it was nowhere near sunset. After an interminable wait during which he banged twice more, shuffling footsteps sounded, and the door creaked open.

"Oh, it's you." The usual welcome.

He left the door ajar and retreated so when Duncan stepped inside and closed the door his father was disappearing into the living room at the end of the corridor, a shambling figure in baggy gray track pants, thongs, and a crumpled shirt.

"Hello, Dad."

"What do you want?" he growled when Duncan came through after him. The room was a mess. Plates and mugs along with dirty glasses, full ashtrays, and empty beer bottles littered the flat surfaces. Crumpled newspapers and form guides lay on the floor and the couch. An all-pervading smell of unwashed body, garbage, stale food, cigarette smoke, and something unidentifiable but resembling mold or decay hung in the air. His father sat in the old dark-red armchair that had always been his favorite. Now the fabric had scorch marks from a multitude of forgotten cigarettes left to smolder and stains from God only knows what. The TV blared in the corner on a sports channel.

Duncan glanced around, made up his mind. No use offering assistance or cleaning up. Get straight to the point and get out.

"It's about Kyle," he said loudly.

"Bloody useless bastard."

"You know he's been missing for almost all of the last week?"

A grudging grunt which he took to be assent. His father muted the TV, lit a cigarette, and sucked in smoke like a man drowning.

"The police think now that he must be dead. They're looking for his body instead."

Awareness flashed in the watery, bloodshot eyes. "Dead?"

"They think so."

Duncan tossed some papers on the floor and sat down on the other chair, careful not to touch the fabric with his hands.

"He was always in trouble, that one," his father said.

"Yes."

"You too."

"Yeah, well...not anymore."

Silence sank over the room like a shroud. Duncan stood up.

"What happened?" his father rasped, then coughed,

"They don't know," he said.

"Don't care more like it."

"Maybe, but I don't think so."

He moved toward the door. "See you later, Dad."

"Someone came looking for him." The words brought him up short.

"Who was it?"

"Dunno."

"When?"

Another pull on the cigarette. "A week ago, two?" He shrugged.

"Did you tell the police?"

"Nah, why would I?"

"Did he give a name?"

"It was a woman. Some blonde-haired piece. Cheap looking, you know?"

"Why did she come here?"

"Dunno, didn't ask."

"Did she leave a phone number or anything?"

"Don't remember. I wouldn't have kept it."

"Call me if you find it or think of anything." Duncan looked at the piles of paper and rubbish lying about. Hopeless asking him to look.

Something about his tone must have penetrated the fug in his father's brain because he nodded. "Yeah, yeah. Get us a beer on your way out, will ya?"

Duncan closed the front door firmly behind him and sniffed, wrinkling his nose. One cigarette in close confinement and he stank of it. Luckily he'd be at home in Bronte in fifteen or twenty minutes and could shower and change.

Should he call Al Davis and tell him about the visitor? He didn't have much information to pass on, and what little he had raised more questions. Unanswerable questions starting with her name and why she would look for Kyle at a house he hadn't lived in or been anywhere near for at least ten years. Who would give her that address? Kyle himself? He wouldn't put it past him in order to throw someone off. It would certainly *put* someone off. He should have asked his father if there had been others asking for Kyle.

Cheap looking. He snorted. Who was his father to judge anyone's appearance?

Traffic was becoming heavy now. Going via his father had delayed him enough to enter deeper into weekend peak hour. Everyone going home from their Saturday activities and visits to the beach. Traffic lights turned red on principle at those times of day and now he crawled from block to block. He should have left before lunch as he'd planned, but then he wouldn't have spent the time with Poppy and been invited to join them on their outing.

What were Poppy and Jessie doing right now? The question popped into his head from nowhere. The lazy, relaxing picnic seemed as remote as another country now. In another world altogether.

The lights turned green up ahead, but nothing happened. A removalist's truck finally lumbered across the intersection, and he moved forward to wait again. He turned the radio on for some news but got football, the last thing he was interested in. He flipped through channels and came to the classical station, paused to listen to a guitar quartet playing something Spanish. Nice rhythms with interesting harmonies.

He stayed on the station enjoying the quietly soothing vibe of the music and the skill of the guitarists who turned out to be Australians, Guitar Trek, based in Canberra. Impressive. The announcer said the title of the CD and he made a mental note to look for it.

Back in his apartment at last, he stripped off, tossed his stinking clothes in the washing machine, and walked straight into the shower. Couldn't turn up at the gig smelling like his father's pigsty of a house. Something must be rotting in there. Did he ever empty his garbage?

The gig tonight would be fun. Charlie, a bass player he worked with now and again had rung yesterday wanting him to sub for the guitarist at their regular restaurant gig.

"If you're up to it and in town," Charlie said. "It's very late notice for a Saturday and everyone's working already. I know what's been happening about Kyle and wouldn't have called…but on the off chance…"

"Sure," Duncan had said from the coffee shop in Canberra where he'd been filling in time before the gig. "I'll be back home tomorrow."

He'd played with the trio before. Guitar, bass, and a girl singer. An eclectic mix of blues, funk, soul, and anything that took their fancy. Background music at a busy Italian pizza and pasta restaurant, a good gig with dinner thrown in.

Next week starting on Tuesday he had three days in a recording studio working on a singer friend's third CD. He'd done lots of gigs with Leon and they were recording tunes he'd help write and arrange. He was looking forward to that and the pay was good.

The work would be a good distraction. Sitting around in Currong was pointless and the only upside was Poppy. She'd tire of him soon enough though, hanging about and looking for sympathy. The last thing he wanted was to annoy her and get in her way. She'd been kindness itself today when he'd put on that humiliating and embarrassing display in her kitchen. He scrubbed at his hair in an effort to blot out the memory. She was probably as embarrassed as he was. She didn't mention it, for which he was grateful.

Oddly, at the time, there in her cozy kitchen, it had felt natural to accept the comfort she offered. It was now, later, that he regretted the weakness he'd displayed. That wasn't his style. He'd always managed on his own, didn't need anyone else. Like Poppy. They understood each other in that sense. Independent and happy with it. His usual routine would remove any traces of the emotional floundering he'd experienced in the out-of-the-way little town.

George would be pleased not to see him there again. He frowned as he closed his eyes and let the water sluice the shampoo from his hair. Would he bug Poppy about his visit? The display of barely concealed anger was surprising coming from a man everyone assumed was Mr. Nice. Just goes to show—never assume you know what's going on in someone's head. Especially if emotions are aroused. And he didn't know George well at all. Did Poppy?

She seemed to think she could handle him, but could she?

He turned off the tap with an annoyed flick of the wrist. Of course she could, and she'd be pissed off to think he thought she couldn't. Anyway what could he do from here and what business was it of his? Exactly the words he'd tossed at George.

They'd go back to whatever their relationship was, and their lives would jog along as before. Like his.

He dressed in clean jeans and a dark-red shirt and

went to sit on the balcony with a cup of tea and a couple of pieces of toast with tomato and cheese. The gig was from seven till ten, so dinner was a long way off. He gazed out at the ocean. His apartment was on the third floor of an old building surrounded by million-dollar houses, back from the beach but close enough to walk and he'd been living there for fifteen years. The weather was much milder here on the coast than inland Canberra or Currong. He'd get in a surf tomorrow with any luck. Have his own picnic on the beach. He smiled, remembering the earnest little girl explaining the red and green blobs she'd drawn.

Where did he put the drawing? Had he left it on the table? He didn't remember taking it to the car when he collected his hat and water bottle. She'd find it and think he'd deliberately left it behind, not caring. He didn't.

Without thinking he pulled out his phone and rang Poppy's number.

"Duncan?" The tone was mild surprise. Fair enough.

"Hi, sorry to bother you but I left my drawing at your place."

"We found it."

"I didn't mean to. Is Jessie upset?"

"No, of course not. She wants me to post it. What's your address?"

He gave it to her. "Tell her I'm sorry I forgot it."

"Don't worry. She's a forgiving type."

"That's a rare thing."

"Yes…she's a rarity."

"Yes."

The line hissed faintly. She didn't say goodbye. He

135

should hang up.

"I'd better go. I have a gig…"

"Okay," she said quickly. "Thanks for calling."

"I saw my father," he said. "Gave him the latest news."

"How did that go?"

"The usual, but he said a woman came to the house a few weeks ago looking for Kyle." He couldn't bring himself to tell her that his father more or less said it was to be expected that Kyle would meet a violent end. And lumped Duncan into the same category. A pair of troublemakers who deserved what they got. He didn't want her sympathy.

"Why?"

"He didn't ask, she didn't say. Kyle hasn't been there for ten years, at least."

"That's odd. You would be a more logical person to contact."

"You'd think so, or someone in the band." He glanced at his watch. "I have to go soon. Sorry."

"Bye."

The line went dead. Duncan finished his tea and snack. Poppy thought it was odd and so did he. He had a few minutes without cutting it too fine. He phoned the Currong police.

Chapter 12

Life went on. Poppy posted three drawings to Duncan at Jessie's insistence but refused to send weekly offerings. He sent her a card with thank you written on it in pink glitter and a picture of a rainbow. Jessie stood it on her bedside table. Poppy groaned when it came but he didn't follow up with anything else and she had to admit it was an unexpectedly kind thing to do. For a man with no experience with small children he sure had a knack of doing the right thing.

By the end of the following week, a month after Kyle's disappearance, the mystery had slipped down the list of hot topics in town with only occasional desultory comments when someone would wonder if anything new had happened in that disappearance case. A mystery was the general consensus, and poor bugger was the prevailing opinion. It had to be someone from out of town who was responsible. Who else could it be? Certainly none of the locals would bother killing the bloke, not even poor old Ralph who had the most reason of anyone. He was better off without that Sarah and was sure to find another, better girl. He'd get over it. Everyone had their heart broken at some stage.

No one assumed there was a serial killer roaming the streets of Currong. If there was, he would have struck again or done it before, and anyway didn't those loonies go for young women? A serial killer who targeted rock musos would run out of victims pretty quickly in this area, and it was a narrow field of choice anyway.

Poppy's strained relationship with George slowly righted itself. It was difficult to avoid him completely. Difficult and unnecessary because she saw him most days coming or going from school and apart from an obviously broken friendship catching attention and becoming a new subject of gossip, it was awkward to wait until he'd gone or rush to be ahead of him on the school route.

On the days when they happened to be leaving school at the same time Jessie made it impossible to walk separately because if Poppy tried, she knew her daughter would demand to know why they were going so fast in a loud and insistent voice and order her to wait for George.

George talked about the fifth grade trip to Canberra coming up in the second week of the school holidays, to visit Parliament House and the War Memorial, amongst other school related things. Poppy listened and made appropriate comments. Sensitive topics were carefully avoided, and she never mentioned the call Duncan had made on the day of the picnic and George never mentioned Duncan or Kyle.

Something had fundamentally changed in the friendship, however. Where before she'd enjoyed his company, now she realized he was, as Steph and Lindy had said, a bit dull. Previously he'd chatted about school a lot, but it hadn't bothered her because he was new in town and still a mostly unknown quantity. She was also a new school mum and interested in anything to do with the inner workings of the primary school.

Had he changed, or had she? Maybe they both had, but that jealous streak and the antagonism toward Duncan he'd displayed while superficially treating him as a friend was unnerving and left a bad taste.

He didn't seem to notice any difference in her reactions but she couldn't help comparing him to the other man, the one who'd reappeared in her life so abruptly, catching her unawares and shocking her into the realization that underneath the independent, focused, single, working mother she was still a young, passionate woman capable of desiring a sexy, extremely attractive man when she saw one—that one, that man. The only difference now was that she had a measure of restraint and the foresight gained by harsh experience. And so, fortunately, did he.

He hadn't acted on any of the attraction he'd displayed while he was in her presence which was a relief but also made her wonder if perhaps those two brothers were a tiny bit similar in that respect. Out of sight, out of mind.

Easter came and went closely followed by the school holidays. Poppy hadn't planned on going anywhere because there was plenty to do around the house. She'd decided to take the first week off, with her study door firmly closed and a sign saying On Holiday stuck to it, and the second week with limited hours which she could do mostly at night. The community classes were taking the school break, so Jessie was her priority.

Steph had triggered a long-postponed decision by saying casually that she was getting a cat to keep her company. She'd dropped in for a visit the preceding weekend to deliver an Easter egg to Jessie and return a book she'd borrowed from Poppy, and stayed for lunch. Jessie's eyes lit up at the news and Poppy's vague promise to maybe get a kitten was resurrected with full force.

"Pleeeeeeaaaase," she said. "You promised."

"Can't break your promise," said Steph innocently.

"It wasn't exactly a promise, it was an 'I'll see.' "

Jessie and Steph looked at each other. "Close enough," said Steph, the traitor, and Jessie nodded. "Close enough," she said.

"Where are you getting your cat from?" asked Poppy.

"The shelter in Goulburn."

"Can we go, too?" Jessie gazed at her like a puppy.

"We could go next week in the holidays."

"I want an older cat that's housetrained," said Steph. "Kittens are too much trouble."

"That sounds good, if they have any."

"They have an online page with photos so you can make an appointment to visit one you like. Mine's a tabby and white one called Peach. I'm collecting her tomorrow after work."

"Can we see the photos, Mummy?"

"No harm in looking," said Steph. "I'll show you Peach."

Poppy knew she was doomed to become a cat owner. Not that she didn't like cats, she did, it was just that it added another layer of responsibility, not to mention expense on a budget that was finely balanced. But looking at Jessie's glowing face as she and Steph discussed the merits of the cats on show, she knew caring for and loving a pet would add immeasurably to Jessie's childhood. And it might also take her mind off the desire for a brother. Or a father.

Steph and Jessie had focused on a serious looking nine month old black cat called Maurice.

"I like him," said Jessie. "Can we tell them we want him?"

Poppy met Steph's gaze over Jessie's head.

"Go on," said Steph. "You can borrow my cat carry box to bring him home in."

"Thanks a lot."

Steph laughed. "He's a gorgeous boy. Look at him. How can you resist that face?"

At the end of the week on the first Saturday of the holidays, Maurice, pronounced the French way they discovered, took up residence in their house and within two days had established exactly who was in control, and it wasn't Poppy.

"Can we tell Duncan?" Jessie asked a couple of days later.

"Why do you want to tell him?" For heaven's sake. What was it about the man that so attracted Jessie? She'd been hoping the cat would upstage him for her attention and she'd forget about him.

"I'll draw him a picture of Maurice and it'll make him happy. No one knows where his brother is yet. He's still lost."

Poppy looked at the earnest little face and couldn't refuse. "All right. If you do it now while I finish weeding, we can walk to the post office after lunch."

****

Duncan was immersed in writing a song when the Currong policeman phoned. He cursed when the ring tone sounded because once his concentration was broken it was hard to get back into the same head space.

"We've managed to track down that woman you said visited your father," Al said. "Her name is Fiona Howard. Do you know her?"

Duncan frowned. "It doesn't sound familiar. Did you speak to her?"

"Not personally, the Sydney detective did. She said Kyle gave her your father's address as his own as well as a dud phone number."

"Knowing she wouldn't get anywhere with Dad." What a miserable thing to do. But typical.

"I'd say so. He may have done it quite often with insistent women."

"What did she want?"

"She's pregnant and she wanted him to help her. Take responsibility."

"Does she want to keep the baby?"

"Yes."

"Do you have her number?"

"I can't give you that," said Al.

"Why not?" The penny dropped with a clang. "Is she a suspect?"

"Not exactly, but we're still investigating."

"But she didn't know where he was."

"She did. She asked around and contacted Lloyd Johns after she'd tried the house."

"Was she a fan of the band?"

"No, she met Kyle at an event he was playing at with a different group, and never went to any of the rock gigs. She didn't know much about him and hadn't seen him for over a month. She didn't know he was on tour until she spoke to Lloyd."

"Did she speak to Lloyd before or after Kyle disappeared?"

"Three days before. We're reinterviewing everyone at the gig but the only women matching her description in any of the photos are locals."

"She might have been at the gig in Goulburn," said Duncan.

"She says not but as I said, we're checking."

The phone call brought the whole thing smashing back into focus. Being at home, with work continuing as usual, writing songs and practicing, Duncan had been able to put Kyle away in a corner of his mind and not go there. He was able to pretend, on a superficial level, that Kyle was out there somewhere carrying on as he had been for the years they'd been estranged. Duncan had barely given him a thought during that time, so it was easy to slip back into the same mode.

There'd been no updates from the police for several weeks which had made his charade easier, but now Kyle was center stage again and the rawness of his loss was still painful. The news wasn't particularly surprising that the woman was pregnant. Kyle's modus operandi was well-known. The unsettling thing was her appearance so close to his disappearance. Was it a coincidence?

Who was Fiona Howard and how many other Fiona Howard's were there? Women in other states who Kyle had screwed and left pregnant with no way of contacting him or if they did, had paid off or avoided? How many children did he have out there wondering who their father was?

Duncan went back to his guitar and note pad and strummed the chord sequence he'd written down, but it was hard to concentrate and the words he'd been tossing around were rubbish now he read them back.

Other thoughts crowded in demanding space.

He was a prospective uncle to at least one child. Should he approach this woman at some future time and offer assistance in Kyle's place or would that open a can of worms on something that wasn't his responsibility? She could be crazy or an addict.

The prospect of being involved with a child was appealing. The contact with little Jessie had opened his eyes to how enriching one could be in his life. Yesterday another drawing had arrived when he thought she wouldn't send more. He looked at the paper stuck to his fridge door and smiled. A black four-legged animal of some sort with a tail, surrounded by flowers and hearts. On the back she'd printed, MAURICE OUR NEW CAT, the wobbly letters taking up most of the page.

The fact that she'd wanted to tell him touched his heart. Poppy must approve or she wouldn't post the letters and that was in itself very pleasing. Poppy, he had to admit, was a major part of his appreciation of Jessie. Her wide smile flashed into his mind's eye as did the smooth tanned skin on display when she wore the tank top for cycling. The way she tossed her hair loose when she removed the helmet, oblivious to the effect she was having. The urge to phone her became overwhelming. Did she know of the latest development? He had a good excuse to call.

She answered just before he thought he'd have to leave a message.

"Hi, Duncan." Friendly and cheerful. Panting slightly.

"Hi, am I interrupting something?"

"No, I've been gardening. Digging in compost for

planting veggies. I left my phone on the veranda."

"How's the cat?"

"So you got the picture." She laughed. "He's fine. Jessie spends all her time rolling around on the floor playing with him."

"I just had a call from Al Davis."

"What's happened?" Her tone changed immediately to one of apprehension.

"No news of Kyle. They tracked down that woman who turned up at my father's."

He outlined the situation and for a long moment she didn't say anything.

"Poppy? Are you still there?"

"Yes." Now she sounded very subdued, as though she'd had a shock.

"Do you know her?"

"No, of course not. Why?"

"You sound…I don't know. Upset."

"I feel sorry for her."

He closed his eyes, grimaced, and stifled a groan as the obvious dawned on him. She was a single mother. Jessie's father could well have done the same thing to her. Cleared off and left her to deal with the pregnancy and baby on her own. Ignored her pleas for assistance. Fobbed her off. A married man? Or just a complete bastard.

"So do I, but I'm not sure if I should offer to help. That baby is my nephew or niece." Would she have wanted help from her baby's family? Her parents weren't very involved but whose choice was that?

More silence.

"I can't say," she said eventually. "Depends on how involved you want to be and if she wants a reminder of Kyle. And if you can afford to. It's a lifetime commitment or at least connection to both of them. Are you prepared for that?"

"I can't do anything right now anyway. Al Davis won't give me her contact details."

"So you're off the hook."

That had an edge of bitterness, but he couldn't blame her given her situation.

"He's checking whether she went to Currong or Goulburn when she found out he was there. She wasn't at the Currong gig as far as he can tell."

"Outsiders stand out here."

"Maybe Goulburn. It's bigger."

"Does he think she abducted him? Killing him wouldn't do her much good if she wanted child support."

"He doesn't think anything yet."

This call had been a mistake. He should have thought through how it would affect Poppy. And so stupid blurting out that stuff about helping the Howard woman.

"I'm sorry," he said.

"For what?"

"Bothering you with this."

"It's okay." Curt but not so bitter now.

"Thanks, Poppy. Tell Jessie thanks for the drawing. I really like it. Bye."

He disconnected before she could respond.

****

Poppy shoved the phone into her pocket and put her gardening gloves back on. She hadn't heard that piece of news but no doubt it would hit the streets pretty fast. How many children did Kyle have spread across the country? More than this one, she'd bet. And Duncan? Those brothers were the same, just as George had said.

She resumed her digging, wielding the spade with savage fury until the plot for the winter greens was turned over several times and her back was aching. She took the spade to the shed. Clouds had gathered and the wind had picked up. Brown and yellow leaves fluttered down and danced across the grass. Still plenty more clinging on so no point raking them up yet. Fortunately because she'd had enough yard work for today.

Jessie was sitting on the couch with Maurice on her lap purring. He'd settled in like a champion, but who wouldn't given the gold class attention he got?

"Duncan just rang and said thank you for the drawing. He really liked it."

"I knew he would."

"Like a snack?"

"Can Maurice have one?"

"He has to wait until dinnertime or he'll get too fat."

Someone knocked on the front door. When Poppy opened it, George was standing there. For a crazy moment she wondered if he'd come to berate her for talking to Duncan but dismissed that as the idiocy it was. She stepped out onto the veranda. She hadn't seen him at all in the preceding week even though she'd been in the garden quite a bit.

"Hello."

"Hello. I'm off on the school trip tomorrow so I wondered would you mind collecting the mail for me?" He gave her an uncomfortably penetrating look. "If you'll be here, that is."

"Of course. We're not going anywhere."

"I thought perhaps you might be heading off somewhere. Sydney maybe. The beach." Smiling now but there was an unmistakable edge to it.

"No. We've just got a cat, so Jessie's completely absorbed in playing with him. I'd forgotten you were going so soon."

"Time flies," he said.

"Have fun." Taking an excited bunch of ten-year-olds on a five day excursion wasn't her idea of fun but George was looking forward to it. She'd gathered that from his comments on those walks home from school.

"We will."

"What time are you leaving?"

"Eight in the morning. We'll be there by ten, go up Mt. Ainslie for a look at the city, then have lunch in Commonwealth Park, visit the Regatta Point tourist information bureau and walk around the central basin of the lake. We'll see the National Library, High Court, the Carillon, and National Gallery but we'll visit the gallery again later in the week and go inside."

Poppy nodded throughout the travelogue, maintaining a polite smile and hoping he wasn't planning to give her the daily schedule. "Have fun and we'll see you when you get back."

He delivered another one of the intense looks. Was he trying to memorize her face, or was he trying to figure out if she was holding something back about her holiday plans? Either way it was an unsettling experience, and she was glad he'd be away for most of the week.

"Right, thanks, Poppy. See you later."

She closed the door with a sigh. Dull was right but

there was something else going on, too. Could be anything—maybe he had family or work problems.

"Who was that?"

"George wants us to collect his mail while he's away with the fifth graders on their excursion. Let's have afternoon tea."

It was only later while she was cooking dinner that it occurred to Poppy that George might have been obliquely trying to find out if she was seeing Duncan in the break. Had he heard her on the phone outside? She wasn't working close to their shared fence. But that was ridiculous and anyway Duncan could as easily be coming to Currong. Except he wasn't.

Was she being harsh in assuming Duncan was the same as Kyle where women were concerned? He'd asked if she thought it was a good idea to contact the pregnant woman which indicated he had some sort of conscience, something she doubted Kyle had.

Should she tell him? No time was going to be the right time so it may as well be now.

****

To say Duncan was surprised when Poppy rang saying she had something to tell him, was an understatement. She didn't want to do it over the phone, she said. Could he come to Currong? He wouldn't need to stay long. It was hard for her to get to Sydney, and she didn't want to involve Jessie and make a big thing out of it.

He had no idea what she was on about and didn't really care because the thought of seeing her was very tempting. He'd missed her with a dull ache he knew wouldn't go away but tried to ignore. The time spent with her and Jessie was a memory he treasured. A glimpse of what could be, if he lived in a different world where that type of family life was taken for granted. He didn't but he recognized the joy of it when he saw it.

He couldn't get away until the following week. Monday or Tuesday were clear, then he had five gigs in a row from Wednesday to Sunday afternoon.

"Monday is fine. Jessie will be back at school then. Come for lunch," she said. "Thanks."

"Can you give me a clue what this is about?" he asked.

"I'd rather not."

So he headed for Currong on Monday morning with an overnight bag stowed in the back of the car just in case. The weather grew fouler the farther from Sydney he went. The forecasts he heard on the radio as he drove predicted gale force winds and torrential rain for the Southern Highlands. He was passing through that area, but Currong was farther west so with any luck he'd miss the worst of it by traveling this morning. Coming home later might be another story, but if it looked bad he could stay the night or take another route.

The weather bureau was right. A heavy band of clouds that had hung threateningly on the horizon when he started out consumed more and more blue sky until by Mittagong he was in the midst of it with wind buffeting the car and rain spattering onto the windscreen.

Currong wasn't spared as he'd hoped. The rain pounded down as he turned into Poppy's street just after eleven. Wary of the big old trees along the verge whose almost bare branches were thrashing wildly, he parked in her driveway as close as he could to the house. The last thing he wanted was a massive lump of wood landing on his car.

His umbrella was still in the boot after he'd dumped it there wet, after a gig. Useless now. Better to go straight to the house. He grabbed his jacket and held it over his head as he ran across the sodden grass to the veranda where he shook it out, soaked already, slipped the car keys into a jacket pocket, and ran a hand through his damp hair.

The door opened almost immediately revealing Poppy in a dark-red sweater and jeans with a small black cat winding about her ankles. Her jaw was tight and there was no smile. Not a good sign but his heart still lifted when he saw her. No matter how she looked, what she said, or how she acted, she was always beautiful and tugged at his heart in a way he couldn't explain.

He couldn't begin to guess what she wanted to say but it could only be about Kyle. Why? Wouldn't the police have called him with any update?

"Hi, Duncan. Come in."

She stooped quickly and picked up the cat. He opened the screen door and stepped inside, catching it before it slammed in the wind. She closed the front door, still clutching the cat like a life saver.

"Give me your jacket. I'll hang it up." She took it from him one handed and went away.

"I'll take these boots off. They're soaked." He left them on the floor by the door and waited for her to come back, standing uneasily on the mat in his socks listening to the rain pouring down outside, wondering why he'd come. He might get stuck here if the roads were closed due to flooding or downed trees. He should have said no, tell me over the phone. Why didn't he?

"Would you like tea or coffee?" She was back, without the cat.

"Coffee would be good, thanks. Could I use the bathroom, please?"

"Down the hall on the right."

The cat was sitting in the hallway, and it followed him with a few bounding, lolloping strides then sat near the kitchen door and watched. When he returned it was in the kitchen under a chair and she'd set the mugs and coffee pot on the table along with a cake. He inhaled warm smells of cooking. Something simmered in a pot on the stove.

"Been baking?"

She nodded. "It's banana cake, and that's soup for lunch."

He sat down. The cat rubbed against his leg, and he bent to scratch its head. "Hello, Maurice. Settling in, I see."

She sat opposite, back straight, fingers interlaced on the table in front of her. Gone was the confident woman. She was nervous, almost scared. Of him?

"You look as though you've been sent to the headmaster's office," he said lightly, trying for a joke. "What have you done?"

"Sorry." She looked away then poured the coffee with a hand shaking so much she nearly poured it over the table. "I haven't done anything."

He had to strain to hear her over the wind and the scrape of branches against the wall outside. What was he doing here? Attracted to her or not, this was crazy. As soon as she'd said whatever it was, he'd leave. He had no place in her life and hanging around only prolonged the uselessness of wanting it.

"Poppy, you asked me to come here, and I came. God knows why. I've driven for over two hours, the last hour in this shitty weather, and driving home isn't going to be much fun, so tell me what's going on."

She looked directly at him then.

"Jessie is your daughter."

Chapter 13

"My daughter?"

He shook his head with a strained laugh. Of all the things she might have said that was the wildest. Had she gone crazy?

"Yes."

"That's impossible. I met you for the first time here in Currong." The astonishment turned swiftly to anger. "Where has this come from? Did you get an idea from that Howard woman? Did you think you could tap me for a bit of cash? Is that what this is?"

He shoved the chair back roughly and stood.

"Jesus, Poppy!"

The disappointment and humiliation cut deep. He'd thought she was better than that. Couldn't believe how he'd been taken in by her. Liked her. Was attracted to her. Wanted to be with her. Why else would he have come here today for such a flimsy reason?

"No, of course I didn't."

He glared at her. "Why announce this now? You've had plenty of time to tell me your little item of news."

"It's not like that!"

Her eyes were wide, pale face stricken. She was good at doing the helpless, misunderstood thing. But she'd been good at the strongly independent thing, too.

"How is it then? Or shall I guess?" He turned away

a pace then spun back. "I know. You wanted to find out what sort of man I was first and then hey presto up pops the pregnant woman. That was a stroke of luck for you, wasn't it? Here I was asking you what I thought about offering to support her. What an opportunity that was. Didn't take you long to come up with the idea, did it? Duncan's a nice gullible guy. If he's willing to help out a total stranger, I'll give it a shot. He likes me and he likes my daughter."

She was on her feet now, her eyes flashing fire. "Just what do you take me for? I would never do that. Never."

"Wouldn't you? Seems to me you just did."

"I did not!"

"I won't stay for lunch. Say hello to *my daughter* for me. I seriously misjudged you, Poppy, but can you at least find the decency to make sure that poor kid stays innocent in all this?"

He strode to the front door. What the hell was he thinking, driving all this way to be treated like that? Such easy pickings for a conniving woman. And to think he'd been annoyed with George for his jealousy. The guy was welcome to her because he wanted nothing to do with her.

He shoved his feet into his damp boots. Dammit! Where was his jacket? His keys were in the pocket.

He turned to her, standing farther down the hallway, her face stony. "Where did you put my coat?"

"I'm not telling you until you listen to me."

"Don't be so bloody childish. Give me my jacket. Please."

"Not until you listen."

The laundry was the obvious place because it

155

wasn't in the bathroom when he'd been in there earlier. He took a few steps toward her, but she stood her ground. Where was the laundry? Running through her house looking for it would be the ultimate humiliation. Quicker to let her speak.

"Talk," he said.

"Can we be civilized about this? Finish your coffee." She stepped back into the kitchen. Who was the one acting like a child now? Throwing a tantrum. She'd made it look like him.

He hesitated a few moments then followed, resuming his seat opposite her.

"You thought you'd met me before," she said. "You had. We met in Melbourne. At a party."

He shook his head. "I don't remember," he said tersely.

"My hair was short and probably a different color. I used to change it a lot."

"When was this?"

"Jessie's five. Her birthday is on January 9th so nine months before that."

He did a quick calculation. "April, six years ago."

He'd been in Melbourne for about a month doing the music for a stage show. He'd been to a few parties, some of which had been pretty wild, most of which he'd forgotten. Who had he met? Who had he had sex with and forgotten? There'd been that girl in the play. Erica something. They'd had a week or two of fun, a lot of it in bed, until she'd had enough of him and moved on to someone more useful to her career. After her…a few of those parties had been good pick-up grounds. No strings one-nighters with willing strangers.

He picked up the coffee and took an absentminded

sip as he sorted through the blurred memories.

"It was at someone's house. We did it in a store cupboard," she said harshly. "I can't forget. I've never done anything like that before or since."

A store cupboard. An image clicked into place. He stared at her, shocked. She'd been passionate and unrestrained, that woman, couldn't get enough and neither could he. He wanted to see her again, later, when he discovered she'd lodged in his brain despite the alcoholic haze, but they hadn't bothered with irrelevancies like names. No one knew who she was, no one cared and a week later, when he went back to Sydney, she'd faded from his mind along with all the other excesses of that Melbourne trip. A low point in his life for all sorts of reasons.

After that he'd straightened up and flown right as the song goes.

"That was you?" Now his hand was shaking as he picked up the coffee cup again. The truth?

"Yes."

"And Jessie…" He couldn't say it out loud. A child? He was a father? It was a concept both exhilarating and terrifying. He wanted to run to the car and drive, escape from what was now becoming clear. An inescapable truth. How could he deal with a child? It was impossible. He had no experience to draw on, not from his parents or his own childhood. He'd be a disaster. He'd ruin her life, that sweet trusting innocent little thing. His daughter.

She nodded. "Can't you tell by her eyes and her mouth?"

"I…she reminded me of my mother. I have one photo of her as a child, but her hair was blonde."

157

"I kept expecting you to see it."

"Why would I?"

"To me it's so blindingly obvious. When I first met Kyle, I saw the similarity straight away. But I knew he wasn't right…that he wasn't you. I knew I never would have…you know…with him."

Her sudden prudishness almost made him smile. Almost. If he hadn't been so stunned. He had to admit her admission also soothed a tiny part of the anger and floundering humiliation of the preceding half hour. She didn't succumb to his brother, she preferred him. Still did, it seemed, while he…he had no idea how he felt about her. Not now.

"I guess there's no point asking why you never told me or tried to find me."

She shook her head. "You know why. It was a kind of madness, what happened. I knew nothing about you…not even a name."

He knew exactly. Madness was right.

"By the time I found out I was pregnant it was way too late."

"I was doing a stage show in Melbourne. I went back to Sydney the following week," he said.

She shrugged. "Right. Jessie keeps asking who her father is and I keep fobbing her off. When you turned up out of the blue, I didn't know you at all. I had to protect her." The eyes she trained on him were momentarily those of a lioness. Then she relaxed. "But…it's not fair on either of you."

"Does she know?"

"No." The word cracked the air like a gunshot.

"Fair enough."

"I needed to know more about you first. Make sure

you were the sort of person who would appreciate her, care about her."

Was he that sort of person? He hoped so.

"And now?"

"Are there others?" She was on the attack now. The interrogation had begun.

"Children?"

"Yes."

"Not that I know of, but I didn't know about Jessie, did I?"

Her mouth tightened. "But it's possible."

"Not really." Who was she to start judging his behavior? "And I don't think that's anything to do with you, is it?"

"You're my daughter's father. If you're to become part of her life I need to know what sort of man you are. If you have other children, it means she has half siblings."

"*Become* part of her life? I *am* part of her life. You've just seen to that. And no, there are no other children. Until you I was careful."

"I can prevent you seeing her."

Anger bubbled inside. "Why tell me then? What sort of game are you playing here? What do you want from me?"

She dropped her gaze to her hands, backed off. "It wasn't an easy decision to make, Duncan. Sharing her."

"So you want me to go away and never see her, is that it? Is that what you wanted, so you could pretend this never happened?" He drew in air, struggled to control the rise in his voice. "You regret telling me, don't you? A minute ago you were saying it wasn't fair on either of us. Well, you were right about that."

"I know," she said softly.

"I'm not going to walk away from my daughter, Poppy. I'm going to stay right here and we're going to tell her this afternoon. After that we can work out how we're going to deal with this."

The moment he'd said it he knew it was a mistake, that anger made him blurt out something he had no hope of doing. How could he possibly deal with a daughter? Saying and doing were entirely different. He wasn't ready to put forward any type of proposal, but he was still riding the tide of anger at her sudden change of heart. The implication he was somehow unworthy as a human being.

She didn't say anything. While he'd been speaking, she'd covered her face with her hands. Was she crying? He didn't know and right at this moment he didn't care. Women could be brilliant manipulators, with tears one of their best weapons, he knew that firsthand, the long gone and best forgotten Nancy having been a champion tear producer. He had no patience with any of that crap anymore.

"Don't take her away from me," she said through her fingers, in a voice filled with such anguish his anger was extinguished in an instant.

"Don't be stupid," he said, but quietly. "How on earth would I cope with a five-year-old?"

She lowered her hands and said in a flat voice, "You'd probably cope pretty well. It's amazing what a person can do when they have to."

An uneasy silence settled over the kitchen. Outside, the wild weather reflected the emotional turmoil inside, ranting and raving, rampaging about the house, hurling rain against the windows, relentlessly tearing at the trees with powerful gusts of wind.

"It's getting worse." Poppy went to the window. She turned round and opened and closed the fridge. "Power's off."

"That's not surprising."

"No."

"I hope the roads don't get blocked. I need to be back in Sydney."

She sat down but almost immediately stood up. "I'd better check that the windows are closed."

"Anything I can do?"

She hesitated. "Could you bring the cushions in from the chairs on the veranda, please?"

"Sure."

The force of the wind on the front door was ferocious when he released the catch, but he struggled outside and picked up the big blue cushions on the old chairs, tossing them inside two at a time. A few spots of rain had blown in, but the overhang sheltered the wide veranda from the worst of the deluge. A quick glance through the steely gray curtain reassured him his car was clear of trees and the danger of falling branches. He should get his guitar.

He dumped the last cushions in the hallway and shut the door, fighting the wind desperate to claw its way inside.

"Where do you want these?" he called.

Poppy appeared from the living room. "In the laundry, please. Past the kitchen on the left."

His jacket was there, hung neatly on a coat hanger from a hook behind the door. He wiped his hands dry on a towel draped over the sink, took the keys from the jacket pocket, and rejoined Poppy.

"Only a little bit damp," he said.

"Thanks."

"Do you have a raincoat I could borrow? I want to get my guitar from the car."

She looked at him steadily. "Are you planning a sing-along?"

"If you want to but no, I like to have it handy. Don't need power to play it."

"Nothing I have would fit you. I'll get an umbrella."

"Okay."

He took his damp jacket from the laundry. He'd misjudged her. She was far from tears. She'd pulled the shutters down and locked the gate to her heart, but she was determined to go through with the decision she'd made, regrets or not. It wouldn't be easy for him. Poppy was tough.

****

Poppy stood in her office and watched Duncan run to the car. His lower half would be drenched but too bad. He opened the back and slung a bag over his shoulder as well taking out his guitar case then, head down, ran for the veranda. He must be serious about staying. She'd have to provide lunch. Fortunately, the gas cooktop was still working so the soup she'd made would still be hot to have with the rolls she'd picked up from the bakery on the way home from dropping Jessie at school. She could boil water for tea in a saucepan.

The front door opened and slammed closed. She roused herself and went to the linen cupboard for a towel. She'd have to let him use the spare room. Her movements felt weirdly disconnected from her body as if she was in a dream, acting on automatic with no conscious control of what she was doing.

His guitar, the folded umbrella, and the bag were on the floor, leaving small puddles. She stared at them, watching the drips plop one by one. He straightened from removing his boots, holding them in one hand.

"I'll put these in the laundry."

She nodded and handed him the towel.

He looked at her with a slight frown. "Are you all right?"

"Use the spare room opposite the bathroom." She had to concentrate to form the words and force them out.

"Thanks."

She turned and on increasingly shaky legs went to the kitchen where she slumped onto a chair. What had she done? Panic churned in her stomach and rose through her body with crippling speed. Her breathing came fast and shallow and she leaned forward trying to control it.

He was moving in already. Hadn't even asked her permission. Was he intending to take over her life completely? Hers and her daughter's. She really knew nothing about him. He was a stranger, and he was in her house.

A sob burst from her throat, hoarse and uncontrolled, shocking her with its force. Another followed making her gasp for breath. Her whole body shuddered, and she wrapped her arms across her chest and gripped tightly, struggling for air as yet another sob broke forth.

"Poppy?"

She barely heard the voice over the crashing of the storm outside and the deafening panic within.

Then she was enclosed by arms drawing her up and holding her firmly against a solid chest.

"Shh, shh, shh," the voice murmured over and over. Gradually the tide of panic receded, and she was able to draw breaths again as the calmness radiating from the voice seeped into her mind and body. A familiar voice.

"Duncan?" she whispered.

"It's okay," he murmured. "It's okay. You're safe."

"Safe." She turned the word over in her mind. Was she safe being held in his arms? She didn't want to move. Couldn't move. Her cheek rested against his sweater. He smelled good.

"Jessie," she said. Tears trickled down her cheeks.

"She's safe too. She's not going anywhere."

He relaxed his hold on her and she eased away, groping for a tissue to wipe her eyes.

"Sorry," she muttered. "I don't know what that was." She sat down and blew her nose.

"I think it was a panic attack," he said.

He went to the bench and peered into the soup pot then gave it a stir. "Can we boil some water? You need a cup of tea."

"There's a saucepan in the cupboard."

He set about making tea while she watched, slowly regaining her strength, her brain clearing, body settling. He wasn't the monster her panic-stricken mind had conjured up. He was just a man. A man she liked.

"Is it okay if I stay, Poppy?"

She looked up to find him leaning against the bench gazing at her with a concerned expression. "I don't want to upset you."

"You can't leave in this," she said. The wind was

fierce out there and the rain was still pouring down.

"I will if you want me to."

"No. I invited you for lunch." She managed a weak smile.

He smiled. "Minestrone soup?"

"Yes."

"Perfect."

The water began boiling and he carefully poured two mugs of tea and gave her one. She wrapped her fingers around the warmth and sipped.

"What will Jessie think of me?" he asked after a period.

He sounded like a worried child asking if someone would like them.

"She already knows you. I think she'll be pleased to finally have a father."

"Any father?"

"She's five. It's a word to her rather than a reality. She wanted a cat, too."

"That's reassuring, thank you."

"I mean, she doesn't fully understand what it means. She asked me if George could be her father because she liked him."

"What did you say?"

"That George and I would have to love each other, live together or be married, and we didn't want to be any of those things."

"What will you say now? We don't want to be married or live together. And we don't love one another."

"But you really are her father so it's different."

"What did you tell her about me?"

"That you went to live in another city when she

was small."

"Does she accept that?"

"Less and less as she gets older. And one of her school friends teased her about not having a father. She told Jessie her father didn't want her."

"Nasty little…"

"Yes." She caught his gaze and held it. "I couldn't do anything about that. She wouldn't understand why I didn't know who you were."

"No. It'll be awkward at any age. So what do we say?"

We. It was we now, for the first time. How long would it last? It was nice for the moment, but he wouldn't be here for long, and the novelty would probably wear off given the long distance situation, and end up reduced to birthday and Christmas presents. Like her parents.

"That you were living in another city? That was always true."

"But why didn't we tell her immediately?" he asked.

"She might not ask but I'll say we had to work some things out first because we hadn't seen each other for a long time."

"Sounds okay. What things have we worked out?"

"What we say to her is good enough for a start."

"Good." He drained his tea. "Will this soup be ready yet?"

Chapter 14

After lunch Duncan took his guitar to the couch and worked on the song he'd been struggling with at home. Poppy went to her study with her laptop to do some work. Outside the worst of the storm had moved on leaving behind steady rain but strong wind rather than the gale force blast of earlier. With any luck he'd be able to go home later although the way Poppy had acted after her initial meltdown indicated she would let him stay overnight if necessary.

He'd decide what to do later. Going home was preferable. He'd checked for weather news on his phone but hadn't found anything useful for the area and the power wasn't back on yet. Could be days before anyone got around to fixing it out here in the sticks.

He strummed a chord sequence, tried a different resolution. Nice. He jotted it down. Played the verse again humming the melody. Worked well. He already had the chorus down. That had come more easily. The words still eluded him, playing hide and seek in his head.

Poppy surprised him when she appeared in the doorway. He put the guitar down.

"That's a really nice tune," she said.

"Thanks. I'm pretty happy with it now. Having trouble with the words though."

"I have to collect Jessie from school, so you'll need

to move your car, please. I can't walk today."

He'd blocked her in by parking in the driveway. "Of course. Sorry. I'll drive you."

"All right, thanks."

Five minutes later he turned into the main street. Nerves jittered in his stomach similar to how he'd felt before subbing for Kyle with the band. Jessie might be only five but her opinion was way more important than he could ever have imagined. How would she react when she saw him? She might be disappointed or annoyed that he was back in town and on top of that, in her house. He concentrated on the road to take his mind off what was about to happen.

The gutters ran like mini rivers. A few small branches had come down in Poppy's street but nothing major. No one was at the shops and all the lights were off. Only a few cars swished by in the main street but at the school a lot of parents had come to collect their kids. He joined the queue of cars crawling along the side of the road to the entrance.

"I'll go and find her," said Poppy. She disappeared through the school gate, her red umbrella bobbing along in the gloomy gray afternoon.

The line of cars stopped. The writhing in Duncan's stomach grew worse. He swallowed and tapped his fingers on the steering wheel. A mother and two small children hurried past all carrying umbrellas. Older children trudged by heading for home in bedraggled groups or by themselves. No one had ever come to collect him from school. He and Kyle walked regardless of the weather. He had dim memories of his mother walking him to school when Kyle was too little to go but his main memory was the two of them dawdling along arguing, shoving each other and laughing. Often with Sausage Boone and Fat Franco who lived in the next street.

The line of cars moved along again. He was almost at the entrance gate now. Parents jumped out and shoved their children into the car. Cars pulled out and drove off slowly.

A red umbrella appeared. Not Poppy. He craned his neck straining to see around the car in front and the groups on the footpath. Suddenly the car door opened and there she was, with little Jessie in a pink coat, smiling as she scrambled into the back seat.

"Hello, Duncan," she said.

"Hi, Jessie."

Poppy strapped her in then hurried around into the passenger seat. He carefully maneuvered the car with its precious cargo onto the road and joined the other parents leaving the school zone.

"All the lights went off," announced Jessie. "It was a blackout."

"The lights and the power are off at home, too," said Poppy.

"It rained really, really hard and a tree fell over. Some children were frightened in my class, but I wasn't. They thought the roof might blow off. It didn't but the third grade class had a leak and water went on Miss Brady's desk. Was Maurice frightened in the storm?"

Duncan listened to the chatter from the back seat and his heart swelled with pride that he'd been part of this extraordinary creation. He glanced at Poppy and smiled. She smiled back.

"Did you meet Maurice, Duncan?"

"Yes, I did. He's very handsome. You drew him very well."

"Mummy's friend Steph helped me pick him out. She has a cat too. It's called Peach but it's a girl and it's got white fur on it. Do you want a cat, Duncan?"

"I go away too much to have a cat," he said. "He'd be lonely."

"You can visit Maurice instead."

"Thank you."

Back at the house he parked in the same spot. The rain had reduced itself to a drizzle now, but the ground squelched as they walked across to the steps. A car went by slowly and turned in next door. George. He must have seen them. What would he make of Duncan's reappearance?

Poppy disappeared with Jessie to change her wet shoes and tights. Duncan took his boots to the laundry again and hung his damp jacket up. When was Poppy planning to break the news? He'd have to leave it to her. If he didn't, who knew what she'd do? The nerves had come back with a vengeance. Jessie's natural friendliness was one thing but discovering her new friend Duncan was her father might be another thing altogether. It could be as shocking to her as it had been to him.

Maybe he should tell Poppy not to tell her, to wait until he'd gone home. So she could judge a good moment and Jessie could absorb the information without him standing there. In case she was upset. Or even cried. Much better not to be here. Easier on all of them.

He went to the kitchen. Maurice was sitting on the floor waiting for attention with a sphinx-like look on his face. He had a sleek black coat, a narrow tapering jaw line, a penetrating, judgmental gaze, and was obviously a specific breed of some sort like Burmese. He was no street moggy—he was aristocratic and haughty but surprisingly friendly. Duncan ran his hand along the cat's back which earned him a demanding meow.

"Don't ask me," he said. "I'm not your boss."

"No one's his boss," said Poppy behind him. "He gives the orders in this house."

"Poppy, don't tell Jessie. Not yet," he said urgently.

"Why?"

"After I've gone might be better."

Her eyes narrowed as she studied him. "You're the one who insisted—" she said, but Jessie came bursting in and threw herself onto Maurice, hugging him and rubbing her face on his fur.

"Who wants banana cake?" asked Poppy.

"We do," said Jessie.

"Not Maurice."

"But he wants some, don't you?" Jessie peered into Maurice's face.

"Wash your hands, sweet pea."

She obediently put the cat down and ran to the bathroom. Minutes later she was back, sitting across from Duncan eating her cake, chattering nonstop to Poppy, himself, and the cat. She didn't wait for answers most of the time.

Duncan sat at the table and watched his daughter. She was perfect, a miracle and he was so far removed from either of those things it terrified him to think how badly he could screw up her life. Poppy had no idea what his father was like and how their relationship was toxic from the start. How that must have rubbed off on him no matter how hard he tried to avoid it.

He couldn't expose Jessie to her grandfather, but she'd be sure to ask about his, and now her, relatives. How much of his father did he have in him? He wasn't a drunk or a gambler, that much he knew for a fact, and his working life was on a totally different trajectory. It wasn't those things that worried him so badly. It was his personality and any unknowns that lurked inside him ready to explode and obliterate those around him. How far did the apple really fall from the tree?

"Duncan? Cake and tea?"

"Yummy yummy banana cake," said Jessie

He blinked and looked at Poppy. "Yes, please."

A mug of tea and slice of cake on a white plate with violets painted round the edge appeared in front of him. He a took a bite on automatic and washed it down with a mouthful of tea. The sweetness and the hot tea brought his mind into focus.

"Can I watch TV now?" Jessie asked.

"The TV isn't working because the power is off," said Poppy.

"When will it be on?"

"I don't know. The electricity men have to fix it. You could draw Duncan a picture."

"Okay." She beamed at him. "I'll draw rain and a rainbow."

"Maybe after that Duncan could show you his guitar," said Poppy with a meaningful look his way.

"It's…a…deal!" Jessie said as though she was a closing a multimillion dollar agreement. She slid off her chair and with the cat at her heels skipped out the door.

Poppy snickered. "God knows where she got that from."

"Playschool?" he suggested.

She laughed and sat down. "Don't worry," she said quietly. "You'll be fine. Why don't you stay tonight? See a bit more of each other."

"But you won't tell her?"

"Not until you're ready."

He nodded and the tension in his gut eased. "Thanks."

"It's not for your benefit," she said with a steely edge. "I don't want to give her a father and then have you back out and leave her upset and thinking it was her fault."

That hit home with a vengeance. How long had the guilt nagged at him? The soul destroying, stultifying knowledge that not even his mother loved him enough to want to stay. Had it ever really left?

Get over it the voice in his head said. You're a man, not a crying child. He wouldn't do that to his daughter. Never. If he decided he deserved to be in her life at all.

"I know what that's like," he said with as much nonchalance as he could muster. "When our mother left, at first Kyle and I wondered what we'd done wrong, why she'd leave us, not want us anymore. Kyle was Jessie's age, and I was seven. Later we realized it wasn't us, it was our father but even then…"

"Why didn't she take you with her?" The empathy in her voice nearly broke his fragile bravado. "She must have had a very good reason, Duncan. Don't be too hard on her."

That was doubtful. What sort of mother abandons

her children to an abusive drunk?

"I don't want Jessie ever to think I didn't want her. After I knew she existed…"

****

When Jessie appeared with his picture, he admired it and took it to the spare room where he placed it on the bed and collected his guitar.

Jessie, with the cat on her lap, waited in the living room. He sat next to her on the couch and adjusted the tuning under her watchful eyes—those eyes as clear and blue as his own but with far more innocence and confidence, more self-worth, than he'd ever had.

"George plays his guitar sometimes when we do singing at school."

"He's a good musician."

"George does that, what you're doing."

"We have to make sure the strings are in tune with each other." He strummed a chord. Not bad.

"How do you know when they are?"

"Listen and tell me what you think." He strummed the chord again. "Sound okay?"

She nodded.

"Right, now what about this?" He loosened a string so it was flat and played the chord again.

"That sounds bad." Thank goodness she heard it.

"Because it's out of tune," he said. "But when I turn this tuning peg the string tightens up and sounds better. I listen and adjust it until it's right, or I can use an electronic gadget to check."

He fixed the tuning. "What do you want to sing?"

"Old MacDonald Had a Farm."

"Off we go," he said and played an introduction. He nodded to show her when she should start. "Now."

She had a pure voice, sang in tune, and had an innate sense of rhythm which was a big relief. A tone-deaf daughter would have been extremely disappointing. He joined in with the animal noises which made her laugh so hard she couldn't sing. He hadn't had as much innocent fun in a long time. Who'd have thought it?

When they ran out of animals, she collapsed on the couch panting in exaggerated breaths, but her eyes were sparkling with joy. "Can we sing another one?"

Poppy startled them both by clapping from the kitchen doorway. She came in and sat down. Duncan met her eyes and smiled. "Like to join in?"

"Sing my song, Mummy."

"You Are My Sunshine," she said to him.

"Mummy sings that to me."

"It's an oldie but goodie," he said. "Still very popular. I've played it at a few wedding anniversaries."

"I only know one verse," Poppy said.

"I know more." He began playing and this time the three of them sang. A family sing-along. How corny could you get? But how close it brought them.

Poppy's phone rang as they came to the end and she looked at the caller ID. "George."

A frown came and went and she glanced at him with an unspoken question, but he nodded and said, "Answer it."

"Hi, George."

She listened for a few moments.

"No, all fine apart from no power. How about you?" Silence again. "Any damage?"

George went on at some length before Poppy said, "No problems, in fact quite the opposite." She smiled at

Duncan.

"Tell him we're singing with Duncan," Jessie said loudly.

"Did you hear that?"

"He'd hear that without the phone," said Duncan and Poppy snorted with laughter.

"Sorry. What?"

More silence.

"Not long. No, no need. Thanks for calling. See you. Bye."

She disconnected and put the phone on the table. "He was checking that everything was okay."

"It is." Was that a bit weird? Possessive even? "What does he think will happen?"

"Nothing. He thought maybe the roof leaked or something. A branch came down in his backyard. You heard what I said. He asked if you were staying long and if he should come round." She stood up. "I'll put your bath on, Jessie, but only a little one because we don't want to run out of hot water."

"Can I have bubbles?"

"All right but I'm putting the bubble stuff in. Last time you did it they nearly came out the door and I couldn't find you in there.

"Play another song, Duncan." Jessie leaned on his knee and peered into his face.

"Magic word," said Poppy as she went out.

"Please."

"Last one." It was all he could do not to bend down and drop a kiss on that sweet little cheek.

Was that an idle query of George's or was he checking up on Poppy and her visitor? He'd recognize Duncan's car from when he accosted him last time he was here. He'd be over there seething and that thought brought a certain amount of pleasure.

"Do you know this?" He strummed the opening to "Yellow Submarine".

****

After a dinner of sausages and mash in a candlelit kitchen, Duncan was coerced by a persistent five-year-old into reading bedtime stories by candlelight while Poppy started clearing away the dishes.

"Don't wash up," he said. "I'll do that."

"No, you peeled the spuds. Go and read. Maximum three stories."

Poppy hummed to herself as she rinsed and scraped and stacked the dirty plates. Candlelight was soft and gave everything a mellow glow. Thank goodness the gas was working, and she had matches on hand or they'd have been eating sandwiches in the dark. The hot water was running low with no sun today for the solar tank Aunty Evie had installed fifteen years ago and no electric booster.

Was Duncan always as helpful as this in the house? She'd bet he wasn't, but he was trying hard. She had to give him that. His sudden reluctance to tell Jessie was surprising but also a relief. It showed he was as decent as she originally thought. He wasn't one of those ego driven grasping men who wanted what was theirs regardless of the damage and the consequences. He was the exact opposite. Too insular, in fact, afraid of making intimate connections. Not surprising given his family. If anyone could break down those barriers Jessie could. But not yet. He was obviously smitten with her. How could he not be?

Would he suddenly blurt out the news?

Poppy froze. He mustn't. She wanted to prepare Jessie herself, reveal the truth carefully because there'd be questions he couldn't answer and Jessie would need comfort from her mother.

She put away the salt and pepper shakers, the place mats, and wiped down the table then crept along the hallway like a thief. He was reading. Okay. His voice stopped and she darted back into the kitchen, shoved the plug into the sink, and turned on the hot tap.

Moments later he came in. "I was going to do this," he said.

"You wash and I'll dry," she said tersely. "Is she asleep?"

"Just about. Anything wrong?" He swirled the dish mop in the water and began washing the glasses.

"I don't want you to tell her you're her father."

He gave her an astonished look. "I wasn't going to. You were. We agreed to that. And I backed off if you remember. I didn't want to tell her at all, and I'm still not sure. Have you changed your mind about it?"

She couldn't tell if he was relieved or disappointed.

"No. But you might tell her without meaning to because you've discovered how much you like her. The idea of her."

"The idea of her? What the hell does that mean?" He stopped washing cutlery to glare at her.

"The idea of having a daughter, of being her father."

"It's not an idea. It's a fact." He resumed washing.

"I know but I want to tell her when I think the time is right."

"When I've proved myself, you mean."

"If you want to put it like that, but no, not really."

"But you're putting it like that whether you mean to or not. You can't alter the fact I'm her father, Poppy. You know what I think?" He put a couple of dripping plates on the rack and turned to her.

"Tell me, why don't you?" She slammed the dried knives into the cutlery drawer.

"I don't think you want to share her with anyone. You regard her as yours and you like the fact that it's just the two of you. There's no room for anyone else, not even poor bloody George who's totally in love with you and jealous as hell but you don't even see it."

Poppy gritted her teeth and dried the forks and spoons.

"You missed a bit," she said and tossed a serving spoon back into the sink with a satisfying splash of sudsy water on to his front. What did he know? George wasn't in love with her, and she wasn't in love with him. She didn't need or want anyone else in her life and George knew that. They were friends, neighbors. Why would he be jealous? And of what?

"Like I said before, I think you're regretting telling me now that you see how much she enjoys being with me and now that I'm saying I won't turn my back on her. You didn't expect that. You counted on me to say I wanted nothing to do with her and leave you alone having done the morally right thing. And when she next asks about her father you can honestly say he isn't around. You could even tell her my name and feel good about yourself. Shift the blame to me."

"Keep your voice down," she hissed. "That's total bullshit. You know nothing about me. I did do the right thing telling you and I needn't have. I wanted you to meet her. I invited you here, for God's sake." Poppy stacked the plates in the cupboard.

"You did and now you regret it."

"I do not. All I'm saying is let me tell her."

"Okay. You tell her."

"You keep flip-flopping about changing your mind every five minutes, that's your problem. I've no idea what you're going to say next."

"Give me a break. You sprang this on me this morning with no warning whatsoever. What do you expect? A full plan of how I'm going to provide for her and how I'm going to deal with this…this…bombshell? I can't…I'm still trying to get my head around it."

"That much is obvious."

He began scrubbing the sausage frying pan.

"Why are you washing that before the saucepan?"

He grabbed the saucepan and gave it a quick swirl around with the scrubber. "Satisfied?"

"Yes."

A click and a whirring sound from the fridge startled her.

"The power's back on," he said.

Poppy strode across, switched the light on, and blew out the candles. Harsh light flooded the room. Did he really understand what she was asking and why? She paused, organizing her thoughts.

"Duncan the nice man she sang songs with is different to Duncan her father. She'll forget the first one but she won't forget the second. Ever."

"When will it be the right time?"

She frowned. "Are you saying you want to be her father now? With all that entails?"

"What does it entail?"

"Staying in contact. Regular contact rather than

just birthdays and Christmas. Visiting. Maybe financial contributions. It's more than just playing with her and being Mr. Fun whenever you feel like turning up."

"Aah." He nodded. "Financial contributions."

"I said maybe. When she's older. We've managed fine without you." She drew in air. "I could hit you for child support you know. But I won't," she said harshly.

"Thank you. I didn't think you wanted that level of involvement from me." His voice was cold.

"I don't. I'm just saying…" What was she saying? She'd lost track and she couldn't think straight with him standing there focusing so intently on her.

"You don't want that level of commitment, do you?" she asked but it sounded desperate.

"I said I won't take her away from you, Poppy," he said gently. "You're right. I can't take care of her. I wouldn't know where to start. But I had no idea the effect she would have on me. She's amazing. Extraordinary—and I had no idea she even existed. It's pretty overwhelming."

"I'm sorry." Tears sprang to her eyes.

Suddenly he was holding her hands in his large warm ones. "It's not your fault. We were both…" He stopped. "But I don't regret it one little bit," he said softly. "I'm glad we met again. And that we like each other apart from…"

Poppy looked at their interlocked fingers then made the mistake of looking up into his face, so close to hers. What was it that drew her to him so inexorably? It was impossible, would lead nowhere, but the attraction was real and he felt it too. She knew that fact as clearly as she knew her own name. If she let it happen he'd kiss her.

She didn't move as his lips brushed hers. It had been so long since she'd felt anything like this she'd forgotten how sweet it could be, how wonderful and exciting and how she'd missed the touch of a man's hands on her body, a man's mouth on hers. How her own body responded with a life all its own, leaving her brain behind, reveling in the rising passion, wanting more of what he gave.

He was as willing as she was. More than willing. Just like last time. And like last time passion overcame sense. Almost. Jessie was in the next room…shouldn't go further…

Before she could articulate the hazy idea that this was a bad move, should never have started it, he stopped, breathing hard.

"Not a good idea," he murmured. "Sorry."

"No, it's not." She didn't even convince herself.

"I agree. Not good but nice." He smiled and dropped a quick kiss on her mouth.

She nodded. "Look what happened last time."

Right on cue what happened appeared in the doorway. "I'm thirsty."

"This happened," he said.

Chapter 15

Duncan went to the spare room with his guitar and Poppy watched a movie on TV without taking any of it in, then peeked at Jessie before going to bed. The argument was upsetting. They'd been getting along well until then, but she had to tell him how she felt. She'd never been good at hiding her feelings and didn't think it ever did any good to stifle her opinion. In this case it was an extremely important point she wanted to make crystal clear.

But then the kiss.

They'd both wanted it, which was hardly surprising but rather, alarming. Despite the passion they'd shared six years ago and the lingering, intense physical attraction, she'd gone way past being naïve since then. Sex and desire needn't have anything to do with intimacy, empathy, or caring for or about another person. Nothing to do with love.

They both knew that and if he didn't it's about time he did.

She didn't think she'd been asleep, but she must have been dozing because a noise outside popped her eyes open. She lay still, listening. Something was moving about out there. Bigger than a possum or a cat, and dogs were locked up at night nowadays. It was moving too slowly and carefully for that anyway.

The bush by her window rustled and a branch

scraped against the glass.

A dark shape appeared in the doorway. She always left her door open in case Jessie woke up but because of Duncan, half closed it tonight.

"It's okay, it's me," Duncan whispered. "Did you hear that?"

"Yes." She sat up.

He came closer and sidled up to the window, edging the curtain aside with one finger before letting it go slowly.

He crouched by her bed. "Someone's out there. They were outside my window just now."

"What will we do?" she whispered.

"We could call the police but they'll be gone by then."

"Mummy," Jessie wailed.

"Damn." She switched the bedside light on and got out of bed.

Duncan was already in the hallway. "I'll have a look outside."

"No! What if you get hurt?"

"I won't but I might get a look at whoever it is."

"Mummy."

"Be careful."

He threw her a smile.

The night light in Jessie's room showed her sitting up in bed with tears streaming down her face.

"Someone looked in my window," she sobbed.

Poppy cuddled her close and stroked the hair from her damp face. "I think you were having a dream, sweetheart."

"I wasn't. I was awake. Someone banged on my window."

"I don't think so. It was just the lilac tree blowing in the wind. Tomorrow I'll trim the branches back. How about that?"

"Okay. Can I sleep in your bed?"

"All right. Come on."

Jessie scrambled out of bed and down the hallway. Poppy tucked her in.

"Are you getting in, too?"

"In a minute. I'll turn your nightlight off and go to the bathroom."

Poppy went to the back door and peered out. Duncan had turned the outside light on, and he came around the side of the house as she was stepping back inside.

"Nothing that I can see. I'll have another look in the morning." He shivered. "Jessie okay?"

"She said someone looked in her window."

"Could she see if they did?"

"I doubt it. Her curtains are closed, but something disturbed her. She rarely wakes up like that."

"I'm going back to bed. It's freezing out there." He locked the back door, switched off the light, and followed her to the hallway.

"You should have put a coat on." He only wore a long-sleeved T-shirt and jeans.

"Yeah, too late now. Good night."

"Good night. And thanks."

He didn't smile. "Why would anyone snoop around your house at two in the morning?"

"Robbery?"

"Is there much of that in this town?"

"Not really. Mainly kids being stupid. Opportunistic stuff, nothing serious."

"Okay. Tell the police tomorrow."

She nodded, suddenly overwhelmed by the realization that she didn't want him to leave and not because there could be a prowler in town.

Poppy woke early and discovered Jessie fast asleep next to her. What or who had been out there last night, and if no one had woken up what would have happened? Would they have broken in? She had nothing worth stealing. It was weird and for that reason, frightening. Not for herself so much but for Jessie.

Did the prowler know a little girl was asleep in the house? If they didn't at first, they should now because they must have heard her cry out.

Poppy slid carefully out of bed. Jessie could sleep for another hour and a half at least but for her, sleep was long gone. Too many questions, too many thoughts jumbling about in her head like clothes in a tumble dryer.

Duncan's door was closed when she emerged from the bathroom, dressed, and went to the kitchen to make coffee. It was still dark outside, but the approaching dawn was being welcomed by a few sleepy sounding birds. The wind and rain had packed up and moved on.

She leaned against the bench, arms folded, waiting for the coffee to brew and wondering how much she wanted toast and marmalade versus porridge. Coffee first.

The shower started. He was up early, too. She opened the fridge for milk.

Duncan came in as she was drinking her first cup. She'd put out a mug and plate for him.

"Morning." He looked as alert as she was. In other words, still half asleep.

"Morning." She held up the coffee pot.

"Yes, please." He yawned. "I couldn't get back to sleep and then when I did I kept waking up."

"Me too. What would you like to eat? I have bread, cereal, porridge, eggs, baked beans. No bacon."

"I'll make an omelet. Like one?"

"No, thanks. I'm having toast."

"Is Jessie all right?" He took a frying pan from the cupboard and began preparing to cook. Didn't need to ask where things were. He'd had time yesterday to take stock of her meagre supply of kitchen equipment.

"Yes, fast asleep. She didn't wake again."

"When it gets light I'll have a look around outside."

"I can't imagine why anyone would try to break in to steal things. Most locals know I've got nothing, and I live here with Jessie. They wouldn't try to scare me, if that was the intention."

"Promise me you'll phone the police." He stopped whisking the eggs and turned to fix her with a stern eye.

"Of course I will."

"Will you be okay here tonight?"

"Of course."

"You could stay with someone."

"I won't. I'm not frightened. No cowardly bastard is going to drive me out of my home."

He pursed his lips. "It could be a murdering bastard, Poppy."

"Oh! You're right. I'm sorry…" She hadn't given Kyle much of a thought since Duncan came to stay.

"Promise you'll take Jessie at least, to stay with your friend. The one with the cat."

Chastened, she nodded. "Steph. I'll think about it.

187

She could come here. I'd never put Jessie in danger."

"I know." He continued with his omelet. "Got any parsley out there with the prowler and that massive rosemary bush?"

She pulled a face at him. "A bit."

She went out the back door to the plot near the rosemary and picked a few sprigs of parsley. The morning light was stronger but not enough to show up any traces of the intruder. She shivered and went back inside.

"Chilly out there." She gave him the handful of parsley. "Sorry, it's slowed down in the cold."

"That's plenty, thanks. Home grown is much better."

"Do you have a garden?"

"Pots on the balcony. I'm good at herbs and lettuce. I've tried tomatoes a few times but wasn't home enough to keep them watered. I like gardening, though."

"That's surprising."

"Why?"

She shrugged. "I don't know. No proper reason."

Two pieces of toast popped up in the toaster. She put in two more slices.

"You have a very skewed idea of who I am based on that one night five years ago," he said.

"I could say the same."

"True but I haven't been full of resentment for the intervening years, so I have a less biased opinion of you."

"Ha! You weren't too impressed when we met in the pub."

"You were pretty rude."

"I might have been. A bit."

"You assumed I was the same as Kyle, didn't you?"

"Yes. But I was wrong." She put the two new pieces of toast on the plate and took them to the table.

He slid his omelet onto a plate and sat down.

Poppy slathered marmalade all over her toast—homemade and bought at the last school fete. Her store cupboard was full of jars of local honey, homemade chutneys, jams, and marmalades from the various fetes she'd been to over the years. So far every jar had been delicious. As had all the cakes, biscuits, and slices she'd bought. Currong had some super cooks.

"I was wrong about you, too." His eyes were on her again.

"I'm glad we've got that sorted," she said.

He laughed softly. "Me too. It's a pity I have to leave."

She couldn't indulge herself in that fantasy. The one where he stayed in Currong and they continued on from where that kiss had ended so abruptly. Eyes open, clear-headed, and in a more comfortable place than a cupboard… Stop.

"Unless you move here that's going to keep happening. What time are you leaving?"

"I don't want to get to Sydney too early and hit the morning rush—I'll go about nine."

Poppy finished her toast. "How old are you?"

"Thirty-six. Kyle's thirty-four."

"I'm nearly twenty-eight," she said before he could ask.

"A young mum."

"For these days, yes, but it's good. Kids require a

lot of energy which I have, and I'll be still young when she's independent. Mum and I are the same. She was young when I was born." And was so put off by her first effort she never had another baby.

"Unless you have a few more," he said casually.

"As you said, that's not likely."

"She might like a sibling."

What was he suggesting? "I'm not having babies just for Jessie's benefit. She has the cat."

"Fair enough." He grinned. "But still…"

"Are you saying you're offering? You want more kids now?"

"No. But if you wanted more, I'd give it some thought…our first effort turned out pretty well. You'd know what you were getting."

"You mean you'd provide the sperm and I'd look after your brats?" Poppy stared at him. "I hope you're joking."

He stared right back then burst out laughing.

"You rotten…" Poppy shook her head. She got up and took her plate to the sink, then picked up the tea towel, wadded it, and threw it at him as hard as she could.

He caught it and tossed it back, still laughing. "Truce," he said.

"Not funny."

"But it could be fun, you must admit."

The kiss danced between them. It could so easily have turned into more.

"Not interested. Men are more trouble than they're worth."

"Is George?" His tone changed.

"George is a friend."

"If you say so."

"Are you jealous?" she asked lightly. What was his problem with George? They barely knew each other.

"Not me. Him."

"Jealous of you?" Is that what he'd meant yesterday when he came out with that crazy remark?

"I'm serious. He as good as warned me off after we first met."

"He was worried Kyle had annoyed me and embarrassed that he'd introduced us. He's just looking out for me. He didn't want it to happen again."

"Do you need looking after? I wouldn't have thought so."

"No, I don't but it's nice that he cares. That's what he's like."

When he didn't say anything she said, "Don't worry about me, Duncan. I've been getting along fine without you so don't suddenly start being protective."

"Sorry." He began singing softly.

"What's that? It's lovely." She liked the way singing came so naturally to him, in the way he expressed himself.

"It's called "I Get Along Without You Very Well". Hoagy Carmichael wrote the melody. I wish I could write tunes like that."

"Don't you write in a different style?"

"Yeah, but a good song is a good song. I listen to those old songwriters a lot. They were brilliant." His smiled pierced her. "If a melody or words pop into my head I follow where they go."

Would she get along without him very well? She needed to know more about him. They'd done everything back to front. Questions swirled.

"Can I ask you something? Something personal?"

He shrugged. "Why not?"

"Are you able to have more children?"

His expression changed. Gone was the lightness replaced by...what? Was he offended? "Why on earth would you ask me that? What have we just been talking about even if it was a joke?"

"It's something you said when we were talking about families. You said there wasn't much chance of that and there was no point thinking about it when I asked if you wanted kids."

"Is that why you told me about Jessie? Because you felt sorry for me?" He gave a little snort of laughter. "I don't know whether to be angry or touched by your concern."

"Not entirely, no, but it was a factor. If she was the only child you were ever going to have it would be beyond cruel to keep her from you. And vice versa."

"You haven't answered my question."

"As far I know I can have children," he said. "When I said that, I meant I didn't want kids and had no partner so there wasn't much chance of it happening."

"Mistakes happen," she said mildly.

"You...you were a lightning strike, a thunderclap, a bolt from the blue. You totally scrambled my brains." He smiled. "Just like in "Orange Colored Sky." "

"Another song?"

He nodded.

"I don't think that was me did that," she said, but he did exactly the same to her.

"I wasn't so far gone that I wasn't choosy."

"That's good to know."

"What about you? You can't talk." The indignation was undermined by the hint of a smile.

"No, I know. But I wasn't that far gone either. You didn't even remember me."

"You looked different. You said so yourself."

"I remembered you the instant I saw you."

He shrugged. "You had a constant reminder. I didn't."

She dropped back to earth with a thud. "I don't blame you, Duncan."

"I know." The little smile lurked again, deadly coupled with the intense blue gaze of those eyes. "I don't think it was a mistake."

"I'd better wake Jessie up," she said. Why did he say things like that just when she was in control of herself?

Chapter 16

After breakfast Duncan went to his room and packed his bag. Jessie was grumbling about something while Poppy brushed her hair. He listened, smiling at the defiant tone in her voice as she said loudly, "I don't want a ponytail. I want a French plait."

"It'll take too long. We're late."

His phone rang. The police. He drew a quick breath.

"Duncan, it's Alastair Davis. I have some news. It's not good, I'm sorry."

"Yes?" He knew what was coming. Dreaded it because it made Kyle's death real.

Poppy and Jessie went by the open bedroom door. Poppy glanced in and Jessie said, "Hello, Duncan. I'm going to school now."

Poppy shushed her and sent him a worried frown.

"School," she mouthed and pointed to Jessie. "Back soon."

He nodded and they disappeared.

Al was talking. Duncan caught the word Kyle.

"Sorry, sorry. I…could you say that again?"

"A body was discovered this morning and we're pretty sure it's your brother. I'm very sorry, Duncan."

"Where? How?"

"Electricity workers discovered the remains earlier this morning when they were checking power lines.

Last night's storm must have dislodged earth and branches used as concealment and washed the remains into the open. The site is about thirty minutes from town on a side road that goes through some thick bush. We found his wallet there and the clothing matches the description we were given by George Caramani."

Duncan swallowed. When he didn't speak Al went on.

"There's a forensics team from Goulburn already at the scene and they'll be determining a cause of death but preliminary evidence suggests a head injury."

"Someone hit him?"

"Yes but not a punch before you jump to any conclusions. It was to the back of the skull." He paused for a moment. "Would you be able to identify the possessions found at the scene?"

"Yes. I can do that whenever you like. I'm in town at the moment."

"In Currong?"

"Yes, I'm at Poppy French's place. I was going home this morning but now…"

"It might be a good idea to bring her with you if you can. Have someone with you." He spoke kindly, didn't pry.

"I'll ask her." He knew she'd say yes and that was a small comfort.

"I'll let you know. It may not be till tomorrow. We'll try to do fingerprint ID first to confirm what we think but decomposition might make that difficult. If you'd rather not, I understand."

"No, no, I will. Thank you, thanks for letting me know and…" He didn't know how to finish that sentence.

"We can notify your father if you'd like us to."

The enormity of the situation overwhelmed him. Decision making seemed impossible. "I…I don't know. I can't…"

"Is Poppy there now?"

"She's taken her daughter to school."

"Okay. A team of homicide detectives will be coming in from Sydney, and rest assured everything will be done to catch the bastard who did this. I'm so sorry, Duncan. Take care and reach out if you need help in any way or have questions."

"Thank you."

After the call he sat on the bed, his mind empty of coherent thought and when Poppy returned he was still there with the cat curled up next to him.

She paused in the doorway. "Duncan, are you okay? Who rang?"

"They found a body." Her eyes locked with his. "Kyle's wallet was…" The next moment she was beside him with her arms around him and he leaned into her comfort the way he had that other time.

"That bloody idiot," he said in a strangled voice. "Getting himself killed."

Her grip tightened and she rested her ahead against his shoulder. "He didn't mean to," she said softly.

"He didn't deserve to die, even though he was a real bastard."

"No one does, not like that. Tell me what the police said."

He repeated what Al Davis had told him, the words coming in jerky little spurts punctuated by indrawn breaths.

"I know that road," she said. "It's dirt and winds up

196

a fairly steep hill through big trees. It's not used much."

"Good hiding place."

"Until a storm comes."

He straightened and she relaxed her arms. "You can stay here as long as you need to," she said.

"Thanks." He flicked her a tiny smile. "Would you come with me to confirm his belongings?"

"Of course."

"I thought…hoped you would." She hadn't even asked when, just said yes.

His brain was beginning to function again. "I'll have to cancel some gigs," he said. "I should do that now."

"All right. I'll make coffee. I have a class at ten at the Community Center. Will you be okay if I go to that?"

"Sure. You don't have to babysit me. It was a shock that's all, even though I knew…"

"Until he was found there was always hope," she said.

He nodded. "I need to tell my father."

Half an hour later Poppy went away to teach her class. He'd canceled the Wednesday and Thursday gigs, and the guys he spoke to were full of sympathy. Friday and Saturday were with a group he played with regularly and he figured he'd be back in Sydney by then.

Typical Kyle, stuffing everyone around even after he was dead. The thought brought a sudden rush of tears to his eyes which he wiped away angrily. He had one more call to make. His father.

He sat on the couch in the living room and dialed the number. Maurice appeared to have taken a fancy to

197

him because he jumped up next to him, walked across his lap with heavy little steps, licked his paw a few times, curled up against his hip, and went to sleep. His father took a long time to answer, probably still in bed, unconscious.

Finally, he answered.

"Whadda ya want?"

"Dad, it's Duncan."

"Yeah." Surly as ever.

He wasn't sugar coating this. "The police found a body and they think it's Kyle."

Silence.

"Dad?"

"Whadda ya mean think? Don't the bastards know?"

"They're sure but they'll try to do a fingerprint ID today. They found his wallet with the remains."

"What happened to him?"

"The cop I spoke to said he had a bad head injury. His body got washed out into the open from the storm last night."

"What storm?"

"Here in Currong where Kyle went missing."

"Never heard of it. No storm here. Somebody whacked him, did they?"

"Someone murdered him, yes."

"Poor bugger."

And that was as much sympathy as Kyle was going to get from his father.

"I'll let you know when I know more."

"Yeah, whatever."

Duncan was left with a dead phone in his hand and a familiar dull ache born of disappointed expectations.

He should know better than to keep hoping there was a glimmer of paternal affection left in there.

He drew a deep breath. So much for that. He'd done his duty and he was damned if he was wasting his time on that miserable bugger anymore. The way he was going his father would be the next of the Barnett men to die but he'd effectively do away with himself through drink. His body would pack it in—liver and kidneys shot to pieces. It's a wonder he was still upright. How come people like him survived and talented people like Kyle didn't?

For all his many faults Kyle had a gift that he honored and treasured. With his voice and musicianship he brought pleasure to countless thousands of people and contributed to society in a way only a few could. That alone made his life worth more than his father's, but his father was alive and Kyle wasn't.

"Rest in peace, little brother," he murmured.

****

Word of the discovery had flown around town and already news teams from Canberra and Goulburn had arrived with their cameras and their questions. No doubt they'd be on George's doorstep and possibly her own soon enough.

Poppy's class of creative writing students could talk of nothing else.

"That poor man," said Chi, her big dark eyes filled with sympathy. "It's very sad."

"Yes, but people like him lead different lives, don't they?" said Gordon who viewed the world through a prism of conservatism founded in the 1950's. "Pop musicians and those rock stars and so-called celebrities—whatever that means. Getting your face on

TV and social media is enough as far as I can see. They have looser morals. Lower standards of behavior."

"Musicians aren't more likely to be murdered than anyone else. What are you talking about?" asked Ursula.

"I meant a particular type of musician. The ones that are out late at night playing in bars and strip clubs and unsavory places like that. Not classical musicians—they're in another class altogether."

Ursula and Kerry burst out laughing. Poppy clamped her mouth shut. She'd shared a house once with a professional viola player whose tales of orchestral musicians on tour would make Gordon's remaining hair curl.

"You'd better not tell Aaron you think The Royal is an unsavory place," Kerry said with a cheerful grin. "He'll ban you for life."

A stay at home mum raising four boisterous boys, Kerry could hold her own in any conversation and wasn't afraid to let her opinion be known. Because it was always accompanied by her wide grin and a laugh she got away with an amazing amount that coming from anyone else would be plain rude. She tempered her comments in Poppy's class but poking at Gordon entertained her immensely.

"Julian and I were at the gig he did here," said Ursula. "And we didn't murder him. Neither did you or George, Poppy, did you? You were there."

"Not that I remember, and I think I would something like that. Can we move on, please?"

"Maybe it was one of those Ag students," said Kerry. "They learn all about pesticides and poisons and who knows what else. And talk about loose morals!

What about the breeding programs they study? Pimps for cows that's what they are."

"Don't be ridiculous." Gordon snorted and folded his arms. "That's livestock not people."

"Did you get much storm damage in the orchard, Dorothy?" asked Peter. Retired from the city and a career in investment banking, he and his wife Anna now lived as progressive and ecofriendly a life as they could. He wrote short stories and made thoughtful and tactful comments on the prose work of his classmates. Disagreements made him supremely uncomfortable, and he always tried hard to defuse any tension. As did Chi.

"We lost most of the unpicked crop," Dorothy said in her whisper-like voice. "A lot of branches came down and a couple of the older trees fell over."

Commiserations and other examples of damage filled the following ten minutes although, as country people, everyone knew how viciously indiscriminate the weather could be.

"Why don't we use the storm as our warm-up exercise," Poppy said. "A descriptive passage using all the senses. Don't think too much. Let your impressions and thoughts about it flow. Go."

"How long do we have?" asked Gordon.

"Until I say stop."

"How long will that be?"

"Not long for you if you keep asking silly questions," said Kerry.

When everyone was packing up after class, the topic du jour reappeared.

"How's Kyle's brother taking the news, Poppy?" asked Ursula.

"His brother?"

Ursula asked the question as if Poppy's relationship with Duncan was common knowledge, taken for granted. Coming from her, Poppy knew it wasn't information gathering for malicious gossip. Ursula wasn't judgmental.

"Yes, he's staying with you, isn't he? Duncan?" All eyes turned to her, some surprised, all interested in her response.

"Yes, he is."

Ursula must have seen them at the school pickup yesterday. Her kids were a few years older than Jessie and she was there with umbrellas for the walk home.

"Duncan's very upset as you can imagine, but Kyle's been missing so long it wasn't totally unexpected."

"Is he staying long?"

"I'm not sure. A few more days I suppose."

"I didn't realize he was a friend of yours," said Gordon.

"Didn't you?" Poppy said smoothly.

"I don't think Poppy or anyone else has to give you a list of their friends for approval," said Ursula with sudden fierceness.

"Oh no, no, that's not what I meant at all," he said. "I just didn't…"

An awkward silence fell as the class donned coats, picked up bags. They said their goodbyes and trooped out.

"Give Duncan my sympathy, please. It's a terrible thing to happen in our town," said Chi in her gentle way.

"Mine too," said Dorothy softly.

"I will, thanks."

Poppy pedaled home. The news had hit Duncan harder than he, or she, had expected. For all his casual dismissal of his family and the bravado with which he faced the world as a man alone, deep down he'd loved his brother and now wanted to do right by him. It was this same vein of caring and ability to love that drew her to him and gave strength to her growing belief that he was a worthy father for Jessie. He just didn't, or couldn't, recognize it in himself.

Duncan was sitting on the couch with Maurice and his guitar when she arrived home. They both looked up. One smiled, the other gave her a yellow-eyed appraisal then went back to sleep.

"Everything all right?" he asked.

"They all wanted to talk about Kyle and the storm. Chi sends her sympathy. So does Dorothy."

"That's nice of whoever they are."

"Chi is nice, very gentle. Her family were refugees from Laos in the seventies, but she was born here. She married a farmer, and they have goats and sell the milk. Dorothy and her husband have been here forever and run an orchard. Any more news?"

"The Sydney detective rang, and they want to talk to us both. Separately. They'll be here at twelve thirty but if that doesn't suit you, you can rearrange when they arrive."

She glanced at the clock on the bookcase. In about ten minutes. "That's fine. I'll make coffee. There are a couple of news teams in town, so they'll be after you for sure."

"Damn."

Promptly at twelve thirty the bell rang. Poppy

203

opened the door to a man and a woman. They gave their ranks but all she took in was their names. Rudy Dietrich was the senior of the two with steely gray hair, tired eyes, and a face etched with lines reflecting the stress and heartache of his job. Portia Mason was younger. Her short, ginger hair was stylishly cut, and she wore black slacks and jacket over a chocolate brown sweater. She smiled warmly as she accepted the offer of coffee, but her eyes were shrewd and assessing.

Poppy showed them to the living room where Duncan was putting his guitar in its case. He turned and shook hands as Dietrich introduced himself and his partner.

"Ms. French, would it be all right if we talk to you after we speak to Mr. Barnett?" asked Dietrich.

"It's Poppy. Yes, of course. I'll be in my office." She pointed across the hallway.

While Poppy worked, the murmur of voices filtered through the two closed doors. What could Duncan tell them? He'd know who Kyle's long-term friends were and which musicians he'd played with and the stories from their childhood that had given her a brief glimpse of a bleak existence. He'd help them build a picture of his brother, but he wouldn't know much about his recent activities except by hearsay in the music world.

Her own contribution would be brief but limited to her impressions of him when they met and the fight she'd interrupted. They'd be speaking to George if they hadn't already done so. Apart from one other obvious person he'd probably be the last to see Kyle alive.

She shivered. She'd only encountered death twice before this. The first was a schoolfriend tragically killed in a level crossing accident a week after he got his driver's license. Trying to race the train, was the general conclusion.

The second was Evie, her death a shock that rocked Poppy's paradigm in a way the earlier one hadn't. Both died far too young and now Kyle. Also too young.

The whole thing was horrible.

****

When the detectives eventually left wearing their non-committal but sympathetic faces and promising to stay in touch, Duncan faced Poppy over the kitchen table. He'd made sandwiches while they interviewed her, too hungry to wait and ask what she'd like to eat.

"Thanks, these look great," she said. "I couldn't tell them anything they didn't already know."

"They asked me a lot about our family. Growing up and all that, who his best friends were. I don't think he kept in touch with many school friends, but I know one lives in Thailand and another is in and out of prison and rehab. Not much use. Neither is in a position, or likely, to want to murder him. And of course his ex is a non-starter as a suspect. They ruled her out immediately."

"They'll talk to the band of course." She took a sandwich with lettuce and tomato hanging out of it. He wasn't the neatest sandwich maker, but she didn't seem to care.

"Yeah, someone in Sydney is doing that. I can't see any of them being involved. It would have to be all or none because they were together all the time from when they left. Self-defeating too considering they had to call me at the last minute because they couldn't find a sub."

"Have those two got any suspects?"

He shook his head. "Not that they're saying. They asked if I knew the road he was found on but I don't. Where does it start and where does it go?"

"If you go past the motel and the lake turnoff it's about ten k's on the left. It doesn't go anywhere really. It's unsealed and a bit rough. There are a couple of properties on it, and it eventually connects with another minor road that goes north. Anyone could have driven along there pretty much any time and not be seen."

"And it's nowhere near where his car was?"

"No." She looked at him with a frown. "Did they say how long he'd been where they found him?"

"They'll know more precisely when the pathologist has done a better examination, but they think at least seven or eight weeks."

"Close to the time he disappeared."

"Yes."

"So the murderer deliberately ditched the car straight away and then dumped the body either the same night or in the few days before anyone realized he was missing."

"Looks that way," he said. "If he waited a while, where did he keep the body? At home?"

"In that case it has to be a local and you'd think there'd be evidence."

"I think that's the main thrust of their investigation," he said. "But they don't know where to look."

He met her shocked gaze.

"It could be someone I know," she said. "But I can't understand why anyone would do that."

Chapter 17

The same question went round and round in Duncan's head as he ate. Murdering a person is an extreme action and would need a very good motive. Unless it was accidental but even then there'd have to be a fight over something monumental to arouse such violence as to pick something up and hit the person hard enough to kill them. That bloke Ralph was justifiably angry with Kyle, but he only punched him and probably not as hard as he was capable of. Self-defense? Kyle wasn't a physical fighter. He used words to inflict pain and damage. They must have been vicious to cause his murderer to use a rock to crack his skull.

He hadn't told Poppy but that's what Dietrich had said. "Hit with something heavy and quite large. Like a brick or a rock."

A rock? Who had a rock handy in the house? If it happened in a house—they didn't have a murder site because the body was definitely dumped in the bush, not killed there. Nor in the car. After so long and all the rain, it would be hard to find evidence at the lake.

Someone knocked at the door. Loudly.

"Reporters?" he asked.

"Will I go?"

"No. I will. Get it over with." He put his half-eaten sandwich on his plate and stood.

The woman on the doorstep was young and determined and had a TV cameraman hovering. He stepped outside and answered her questions politely and briefly then terminated what she was trying to turn into a wide-ranging interrogation. She thanked him and he went inside. He had nothing of great interest to say except for the fact of being the deceased's brother.

He resumed his lunch.

"That didn't take long," Poppy said.

"I didn't have much to say. Did you report the prowler?" he asked as the thought popped unexpectedly into his mind.

Poppy shook her head. "I totally forgot."

"You should."

"You don't think there's a connection, do you?" Alarmed eyes fastened on his.

"I don't know, but it's odd. You said so yourself. Do it now."

She got up and went out. Moments later she was on the phone, talking.

"Someone's coming," she said when she returned.

"Good."

A constable arrived an hour later, not someone Duncan, or Poppy, had seen before. Come from Goulburn, he told them, to help with the investigation. He moved carefully around the house taking photographs of the ground under the windows and where the intruder could have walked. One half footprint stood out clearly under Jessie's window in a muddy patch where the grass had thinned near the lilac bush.

"We'll talk to the neighbors and be in touch," he said. "But no one else has reported anything. Could you put something over the print please, like a bucket? We may take a cast of it."

After he'd gone, Poppy said, "They think it's connected, don't they?"

"They're certainly taking the whole thing seriously. They won't dismiss anything, I guess, and they've brought in extra people."

Poppy went to get a bucket. Duncan studied the print. It was a pretty standard man's foot as far as he could judge. Maybe a bit smaller than his own. Too big for a woman but not a massive man's boot. Half the men in town would take a similar size. The police would easily identify the tread and tie it to a brand and style. Then what? His only knowledge of crime investigation came from TV, and he didn't watch much of that being a night worker.

Poppy returned and carefully placed the upturned bucket over the print with a garden gnome lying on top to stop it blowing away or the cat knocking it over.

"Who's that? Sleepy?" he asked with a smile.

"More like Creepy at the moment," she said and pulled a face. "I'll have to collect Jessie soon. I'm walking. Do you want to come?"

"A walk would be good."

The reason was even better. Picking up his daughter from school. A new and exciting experience. Almost like a proper family but he had to tread as though he was walking through a minefield.

In these strange circumstances Poppy's natural kindness had kicked in, her concern for him in the face of the reality of Kyle's death overwhelming her concern over his relationship with Jessie. He thought he'd assuaged her initial fears and had established an easy connection with Jessie without trying too hard. Poppy was happy with that, he was sure, and his own doubts about being a reasonable father had subsided marginally from the first total panic.

Whether that truce would continue after Kyle's murder was resolved, if that ever happened, remained to be seen but he wasn't going to make demands or do anything Poppy might regard as undermining her control. He didn't want to lose his chance at knowing the beautiful treasure that was Jessie as she grew up.

****

The news teams were waiting at the school interviewing parents. Duncan hung back and let Poppy go on alone saying he'd catch up with them later. The reporters pounced on George when he came out surrounded by hurrying children when the floodgates opened at the school. Jessie was chatting and laughing with her friend Farah. She waved goodbye to Farah and ran across the schoolyard. Poppy gave her a kiss, took her backpack, and turned to go.

"I thought Duncan would come to get me." Jessie looked about hopefully. "Is he staying at our house again?"

"Yes. How was school?"

"Okay."

"Come on, let's go."

George was still caught up with the news people. Poppy hurried Jessie away before any of them recognized her. They must know her address and that Duncan was staying because that reporter had turned up, but perhaps they didn't know her face well enough. She didn't want to be highjacked in the street with Jessie in tow.

Duncan wasn't anywhere to be seen near the school or around the corner.

"Can we go to the bakery?" asked Jessie as they neared the main street.

Before Poppy could answer, George caught up, his expression one of concern.

"What a nuisance they are. I should have driven today but I didn't think."

"They'll know where you live, and they'll already have pictures of your house. One turned up to talk to Duncan earlier."

"Not surprising. It's impossible to keep it quiet. I didn't have much to tell them. Is Duncan still there?"

"Did you tell them he was?"

"No, but it's not a secret, is it?"

Duncan stepped out from a tree covered lane that led behind the shops and ended in the park.

"Hello, Duncan," Jessie said. "Did you come to meet us?"

"Hi there. Yes, I did."

George held out his hand to Duncan.

"I'm so sorry, mate," he said. "The detectives came to the school this morning to talk to me. It's hard to believe even though he's been missing so long."

"Thanks, George."

Was the smile he gave a tiny bit forced or was she hypersensitive after Duncan's assessment of his extreme feelings for her? If Duncan was right, for George, seeing the two of them here together with Jessie would be a blow. Not much she could do about it except maintain the friendship and make it clear that's where she stopped.

"George just got waylaid by reporters," said Poppy.

Duncan grimaced. "To be expected, I guess."

"Are you walking home with us, George?" asked Jessie.

"If you don't mind," he said.

"We don't," she said.

The footpath wasn't wide enough for four so George and Duncan walked ahead but the conversation was loud enough for Poppy to hear and take part in. She hoped they'd discuss only what was appropriate for the sharp five-year-old ears.

"I was going to come over this afternoon to give my condolences," said George. "Have they given you any information at all? Any suspects?"

"No, but they're thinking local."

"That sounds unlikely to me."

"Me too," said Poppy.

"I would have thought it was someone he knew. He's rubbed plenty of people up the wrong way over the years and I said that to the detectives. He didn't know anyone here."

George slowed so Poppy came level with him. She glanced at Duncan and indicated Jessie with a tilt of her head.

"He knew you," said Duncan before he dropped back to walk with Jessie and ask about her friends, distracting her from the conversation which George seemed intent on having.

"Yes but...me?" George said to Poppy, but lowered his voice. "I don't know what he's getting at. What does he think I did? Chased after his brother and killed him?"

"I don't think that's what he meant," Poppy said in an attempt to calm him down but to no avail.

"I hadn't seen Kyle for years and I kicked him out. You saw him leave, didn't you? Murdering him is a bit extreme for what he did at my place. Being sleazy doesn't have a death sentence. He left and that was the end of it as far as I'm concerned. Ralph would have more reason."

"Those detectives will be talking to Ralph again, I'm sure," said Poppy. "But I think he got it out of his system when he punched Kyle. He was pretty deflated when he left. You saw him. He even apologized for frightening Jessie."

"Someone looked in my window last night, George," said Jessie from behind them.

He looked at Poppy with a raised eyebrow. "Really?"

"Jessie probably had a dream and heard the lilac bush scraping," said Poppy, turning so her daughter heard.

"I didn't. Someone looked in. I saw them."

"What did they look like?" Duncan asked.

"A black shape. I was scared."

"I'm not surprised, but it won't come back, I promise."

"Did you hear anything at your place?" Poppy asked George.

"No. I sleep soundly, though. Nothing wakes me."

"Jessie usually does, too."

"She has a good imagination," said George. He drew Poppy ahead again. "It's not unusual for young children to have strange dreams. Just be careful what she reads and sees on TV. Having Duncan in the house could be unsettling for her, too. She knows Kyle was missing and now…little minds can imagine all sorts of connections."

"She likes Duncan," Poppy said. "And I was glad he was there last night, given what's happened."

"I wouldn't rely on him if I were you. Those brothers aren't the most responsible or reliable people. They always put themselves first."

"I didn't think you knew Duncan very well."

"I know enough to warn you about him. I'm speaking as a friend, Poppy."

"I know and thanks, but you don't need to worry about me."

"But can't you see what he's doing? He's already staying with you, and you barely know him. Wouldn't it be better if he moved to the hotel?"

"George…" Poppy started the sentence and stopped, trying to choose a tactful way of telling him to shut up and mind his own business.

"You have to think about Jessie," he said.

Enough! Who did he think he was to imply she didn't care about her daughter let alone dictate who she invited to stay?

"I always think about Jessie," she said evenly, keeping a tight lid on her anger. "You know I do and who I choose to have stay with me is my business."

"Of course. I'm sorry."

"We're friends, George, and I appreciate your concern, but I really don't need to be told what to do."

"Okay, okay. I said I was sorry."

Poppy and George walked in a prickly silence for the half block to the intersection with the main street.

"Mummy, can we go to the bakery? I want face biscuits for afternoon tea."

"There's still banana cake at home." Poppy

stopped at the corner to let Jessie and Duncan catch up.

"But I don't want that."

"Good," said Duncan. "I love banana cake and I can eat your share."

"No, you can't," said Jessie.

"I can and I will."

"No, don't. I want my share." Jessie began giggling as he rubbed his hands together gleefully.

"I just remembered I need to go to the supermarket," said George. "See you tomorrow."

He barely waited for a reply before turning to cross the street to the left. Poppy and Jessie turned right with Duncan close behind.

"What was that about?" he asked quietly, drawing level.

"He was upset when you commented that he was someone in town who knew Kyle."

"The only person, I would have thought."

"Me too. He got quite bent out of shape and thought you were accusing him."

"So. Do you believe me now when I say he's jealous?" He looked sideways at her as they walked, and his smile had just a hint of smugness.

Did she? George's behavior was certainly out of what she knew to be his character. She'd known him longer than she knew Duncan and hadn't picked up on any telltale signs of a crush. Steph and Lindy teased her about him, but they didn't take him as a serious contender. Surely they would have noticed something if there was anything to notice.

"Don't forget he'd be shaken up by this like everyone else. More so because he did know Kyle. Even if he wasn't all that keen on him, and was angry with him, he was still a friend of sorts. He might feel guilty for throwing him out."

"If he hadn't, Kyle might still be alive, you mean?"

Poppy heaved a sigh. "Maybe. I don't know."

"I still reckon he's your secret admirer."

"You're wrong."

"Uh uh. You'll see. I bet he tries to kiss you."

"Like you did?" Heat ignited in her chest and rose to her neck. He hadn't kissed her again.

"No, because you won't let him. And he couldn't kiss you the way I did, anyway."

Poppy's cheeks burned despite the cool autumn breeze swirling down the street.

Retirees Charlie and Janis came out of the chemist and stopped to offer Duncan their condolences. A few paces more and Fran from the Community Center stopped and said the same thing, then a young woman Poppy only knew by sight, followed by Amber pushing a pram, Joe from the Feed and Livestock store, and a couple of tradies fiddling with the downpipe on the wall of the real estate agency. They all turned and told Duncan how sorry they were. Reaching the crossing at the end of the block had taken twice as long as normal.

"Word gets around," Duncan said when they turned into Poppy's street.

"Sorry, I meant to walk back the same way we came. George distracted me."

She'd deliberately avoided the main street by walking parallel and crossing over a street past the school then around that block, to prevent Duncan becoming a focus of attention.

"It's okay," he said. "It's kind of nice."

Jessie ran on ahead stopping occasionally to pick

up brightly colored leaves.

"Everyone's shocked."

"It's…"

"What?" she asked when he didn't continue. She looked at him and was surprised to see him wipe a hand across his eyes.

"I wasn't expecting people to be so…kind, I guess. I don't even belong here. I'm a stranger."

"I think a lot of people feel bad that it happened in their town."

"Only one person is responsible though."

"But it's someone everyone now realizes they probably know."

"It'll make them more uneasy when the detectives start asking questions everywhere. They'll all be looking at each other and wondering."

"But no one will blame you for that."

"No, but I'll be the link to the crime, a reminder, won't I? The one whose brother brought something nasty to their nice safe town. Another weird rock musician from the city. That niceness can easily turn to resentment."

"Duncan." Poppy tucked her arm into his. "Don't start thinking like that. Don't make assumptions. Kyle was the victim, not the perpetrator. Currong isn't some hillbilly town. A lot of these people moved here from the city, too."

"I think I should leave as soon as I've done the ID. There's no reason for me to stay after that." He'd retreated into that stubbornly defensive reserve again, assuming he wouldn't be welcome for much longer and not waiting to find out.

"If you want." She gave his arm a squeeze then slid

hers free. "But you're welcome to stay with us as long as you like and whenever you like."

"Thanks."

She knew by the way he spoke and the resignation in his eyes she hadn't convinced him or even reassured him.

Jessie ran back with a bouquet of autumn leaves and presented them to Duncan.

"I found these for you," she said.

He took them from her. "Thank you very much. No one has ever given me a bunch of pretty leaves before."

"I can help you put them in a vase when we get home, and you can have it in your room."

She scampered away. Poppy watched him watching her. Did he realize how much he would mean to her if they told her who he was? And that she wouldn't care what he did for a living, how much money he made, who his relatives were, where he grew up, and where he lived? All she'd care about was that she had a father who loved her and spent time with her and was always there when she needed him to be.

Could he do that?

"If you leave in a few days, Duncan, will you come back? Ever? If you don't think you will, I'll never tell her the truth. If, eventually, you do decide to be in her life, when she asks you will have to explain to her why you went away and left her so soon after you met. I'm not going to make up excuses for you."

Duncan slowed as she spoke. His jaw tightened and she knew she'd hit hard. She meant to.

"Don't confuse two issues," she said in an effort to explain. "Don't mix up your assumptions about what the townspeople will think of you and your relationship with Jessie. One is random, completely unknown, and will pass one way or another and is irrelevant, the other is a fact and permanent."

"I understand that. I just…I'm not coping very well."

She grasped his hand and after a moment he gripped hers tightly.

"I know. The whole thing is dreadful. Impossibly hard. But look at her. She's such a ray of sunshine. She saved me, and she can save you, if you'll let her."

He looked at the leaves in his hand and then ahead to where Jessie was kicking her way through drifts of yellow and brown with chortles of glee.

"I'm terrified of messing up her life," he said softly.

"You? What about me? I knew nothing about babies or children when she was born. Nothing. My mother was no help whatsoever. She and my father had practically disowned me years before, and for the first weeks, until I got up the courage and the strength to ask for help from a support group, I was close to leaving my baby on someone's doorstep. I was so convinced anyone would do a better job than me. I had a couple of friends who dropped in occasionally and they kept me reasonably sane, but they knew less than I did about babies. Jessie was my responsibility anyway."

"But you survived. You're strong. And Jessie is a great kid."

"Only because I had to be strong. If it came to the crunch, I couldn't possibly have given her away, so I had no choice but to survive. And put her first."

"I've never had to do that."

"It's not hard when you're a parent."

She smiled and was glad he returned it. And kept hold of her hand.

"Duncan, you worry too much that people won't like you if they get to know you."

"I keep to myself. It's the best way of surviving," he said.

"Surviving what?"

"Life. I'm the only one I can depend on."

She knew what he meant. Evie was gone and she had no one.

"You can depend on me." She couldn't and wouldn't depend on him, not yet. Not for the big things.

"Can I?"

"I like you and so does Jessie."

"People like me well enough as far as that goes but you don't know me very well yet and Jessie likes everyone."

"That's true. About Jessie, I mean. But you won't let anyone get close so how do you know?"

He stopped walking. "Why are we talking about this?"

"It's important. And interesting."

"Not to me." He let go her hand and strode on to catch up to Jessie.

Chapter 18

On Wednesday afternoon Rudy Dietrich phoned Duncan to ask if he could go to Goulburn to identify Kyle's belongings. Thursday, at four thirty. He'd hoped it would be earlier but didn't argue. Rudy did tell him they were making good headway with the investigation but didn't give any more details.

"We don't want to take Jessie," Poppy said when he went to her office to tell her. "I can organize a play date for her after school."

"Thanks. I might head on home afterward rather than come back here."

"I don't think that's a good idea. We should go together in the same car. Stay here and leave on Friday." She pushed her chair back and came to him, to where he stood in the doorway not wanting to intrude.

He sighed. A large part of him wanted to stay but that would be prolonging the inevitable. Better to go, make a clean break and only return when and if it was necessary, which it wouldn't be. He had gigs at home and Rudy would keep in contact. He didn't need to be here getting in Poppy's way, raising her expectations. And Jessie's.

She was waiting for a reply, looking at him with that concerned expression she reserved for him. The eyes he'd initially thought green weren't. They had brown in the center and lighter flecks scattered through the emerald green, framed by black lashes, like her hair. Perfume wafted from her, faint but so identifiable.

"I need time, Poppy," he said softly.

She nodded and the disappointment was so palpable he reached to touch her cheek. Her arms slipped around his waist, and it was way too easy to lift her chin gently and press a kiss onto her soft lips. A farewell of sorts was in the back of his mind, but that vaguely noble gesture was soon eclipsed by a rush of passion so intense he could barely breathe.

Poppy gave herself to him with an abandon at once thrilling and frightening but in a dim corner of his brain he knew someone had to regain control or they'd be in even deeper water than they were already. More complication would be disastrous in such a fragile situation.

He reluctantly pulled away, breathing hard, body aching with desire for her but knowing it was the right thing to do. He brushed her cheek with light fingers, smoothing away a strand of hair.

"We can't."

She smiled. "I know but we will. One day."

He looked over her head, smiling. He wished.

"We already know we're good at it," she said and snatched a quick kiss before going back to her desk. "And that was in a cupboard. Just imagine…" Those green eyes gazed at him, and it was all he could do not to stride across and drag her to the nearest bedroom.

"Cut it out," he growled.

****

Jessie woke in the night with a plaintive cry of "Mummy."

Poppy sprang out of bed half awake and banged

her knee painfully on the corner of the bed as she went blindly to the door in the dark. She steadied herself, cursing and rubbing the sore spot. Footsteps sounded in the hallway. Duncan. By the time Poppy reached Jessie he was there by her bed, dimly illuminated by the night light.

"She's burning up," he said softly and moved aside.

"My throat's sore."

As Duncan had said, Jessie's face was flushed and hot, her hair sticking to her forehead with perspiration.

"Do you feel sick in the tummy, sweet pea?"

"No, my throat's sore," she whimpered.

"I'll get her a paracetamol."

"Mummy, stay. The bed's wibbly-wobbly."

"I'll be back in a moment."

"Nooo, stay. Sit on my bed." A hot little hand grasped her arm.

"Where is it?" asked Duncan.

"Medicine cabinet. The box is marked children's. Bring a damp washcloth too, will you, please?"

He hurried away.

Poppy made soothing noises. It wasn't the first time she'd tended a sick little girl. Usually whatever it was arrived suddenly, often accompanied by vomiting or diarrhea with or without the fever, and lasted a day or two at most. Also, usually, it was from school and there'd be other victims in her class.

Duncan reappeared, alarm in his rushed movements and tight voice. "Is she all right? Should I call the doctor?"

"No, we'll see how she is in the morning."

She helped Jessie sit and take her pill, washed

down with water which she drank thirstily. Poppy gently wiped the cool damp cloth over her face and neck.

"Don't go, Mummy."

"I won't."

"Do you have a thermometer?" Duncan asked.

"Yes. It's in the top drawer of the cabinet."

He went away, came back with it, and watched anxiously as she took Jessie's temperature.

"She'll be all right. It's not up much." She smiled at him. "Go back to bed."

"I'll wait."

"Sit down then," she said, and yawned. "What time is it?"

"Three fifteen."

"Ugh. She'll go to sleep soon." She patted Jessie's face and neck with the damp cloth. "Could you please run the cold tap over this again?"

Fifteen minutes later, Jessie fell asleep and Poppy and Duncan went back to their separate beds.

In the morning, the temperature had dropped to normal but the sore throat remained, along with a headache. Poppy rang the school and learned two other children in Jessie's class along with several in other classes, had had similar symptoms in the last week including today.

"It doesn't seem to be anything serious," Grace at reception said cheerfully. "A day or two in bed does the trick. Make sure you do the correct hygiene things. You sure don't want it as well."

"Thanks." Poppy put the phone down and reported to Duncan who was drinking coffee and yawning.

"I won't be able to go with you today. I'm sorry."

"That's okay. I'll manage."

"Promise me you'll come back here afterward."

He met her gaze silently.

"Don't you want to check on Jessie before you leave?" she asked.

"You know I do, but I can do that and say goodbye before I go to Goulburn."

"Up to you," she said and turned away to make toast.

"Poppy, don't do that."

"I understand and I said it was up to you. I'm not doing anything."

"Right. I'll call you when I get home."

"Good. Just make sure you do."

"I will."

"Promise?"

"Cross my heart. What are you, my parole officer?" But his smile took the edge off the query.

Jessie slept most of the day, waking periodically for a drink of water but not wanting food. By early afternoon she was a little brighter and the sore throat had improved marginally, so she managed to eat some strawberry yogurt. The cat curled up on the end of her bed which pleased her, and Duncan moved from the living room to sit in her room while he worked on his song because she told Poppy she liked to hear the guitar. "It makes me feel better," she said.

Looking at the pride on his face when Jessie told him, Poppy wondered if that alone would make him reconsider leaving this evening, but she wasn't asking again. As she said, it was up to him, and she wasn't going to start begging any man to stick around. Not even this one.

****

At three, Duncan told Jessie he had to leave to go home.

"When will you come back?" she asked.

"I'm not sure. I have to go to work tomorrow night and the next night and I have things to do at home next week."

"Okay," she said. "Don't forget to take your bunch of leaves."

"How about I leave them here for when I come back?"

"No, you have to take them and put them in your house."

"Okay. I will. See you later, alligator."

"In a while, crocodile. When your legs are straighter," she said with her sweet smile.

He lifted his hand in a little wave, fixing the image of her in his mind, and went to pack his things.

He put the overnight bag in the car along with his guitar. Back inside he stripped the sheets from his bed and put them in the washing machine.

Poppy came out from the office.

"Ready to go?"

"Yes. I'll call you."

"Promise." She gave a tiny laugh.

He smiled. "Yes, Ma, I promise"

He pulled her into a hug, breathing in her scent, absorbing it, memorizing it as he had Jessie's face. He kissed her quickly, consciously keeping it light, a goodbye, not a prelude.

She walked with him to the door and opened it. Duncan paused to take his jacket from the row of coat hooks by the door.

George was coming up the path.

"Hello," he said to Poppy. "I thought I'd pop in to see how Jessie is. I'm missing two of my class with the same thing."

He hadn't seen Duncan yet, in the dim light of the hallway. How pleased George would be to see him heading home and leaving the field wide open to make his advance on Poppy.

"She's okay, thanks. Better now than this morning," she said.

George looked over her shoulder and saw Duncan.

"Hello, mate. Still here?"

"Apparently," he said. He stepped out onto the veranda beside Poppy.

"He has to identify some of Kyle's things today," she said.

George assumed an expression of sympathy, but his eyes said otherwise. He wanted Duncan gone. "Where is that happening?"

"Goulburn."

"I was going with him," Poppy said. "But I can't now with Jessie ill."

"I can go alone," said Duncan. "It's fine."

"I don't think you should." She put her hand on his arm.

"I could go with you," said George. His eyes flicked to her hand and remained there.

"No, it's okay, thanks." Duncan spoke casually, stifling the sudden urge to put his arm around Poppy's shoulders just to annoy the crap out of George.

"That would be great," she said.

Duncan gave her a warning frown, but she ignored it.

"Sure. Now?"

"It's at four thirty so yes, I think so."

"Give me a minute and I'll be right with you."

"You'll have to take your car, George. I'm heading back to Sydney."

"Oh, right. How about I meet you there? Wherever there is."

Duncan gave him the address and George hurried home.

"What did you do that for?" asked Duncan.

"You need someone with you and George knows you."

"And hates me," he said. The feeling was fast becoming mutual. Would Poppy succumb to George if Duncan went away and didn't come back? Would she let him kiss her…

"He does not and even if he is a bit jealous, he'll put that aside in a situation like this," Poppy said indignantly.

"I doubt it. I really wish you hadn't told him." He gritted his teeth. He didn't need this interfering…he could go alone. He wanted to go alone if Poppy couldn't be with him.

"You need someone with you," she said again.

"I wanted you."

"I know and I wanted to go. I could ask him to mind Jessie instead but I'd rather not."

"No, don't," he said sharply. He didn't want George in Poppy's house making himself comfortable, near his daughter, caring for her. Making himself indispensable. "It'll be okay. At least I don't have to sit in the car with him."

She smiled and squeezed his arm. "You should go.

Give yourself time to find the place."

"Okay." He kissed her cheek. "Goodbye."

****

Misty rain fell in a miserable fog when he and George emerged from the redbrick building with Portia Mason.

"Thank you both," she said. "It's never easy, this finality."

Duncan nodded.

He held her sympathetic gaze firmly. "Find the bastard," he said.

"Oh, we intend to." Portia gripped his hand firmly. "We'll keep you informed. Safe trip."

"Thanks. "

She strode to her car.

"How about a drink before we go?" George said.

"I'm driving."

"A small one won't hurt, and you need it. You can have something to eat too. Come on. Leave your car here and I'll drop you later. We could walk but it's a bit wet."

George drove a couple of blocks to a pub he knew. The bar was dimly lit and almost empty with photos of local football heroes adorning the walls and a TV with the sound muted showing horse races.

Duncan sat at a table while George bought the drinks at the bar. A chalkboard announced the specials but he didn't have the stomach for food, not after that experience. Not that it had taken very long but in the end he was glad George had been there as well as Portia. Poppy was right about his ability to put aside personal feelings in such a difficult situation. The man was basically kind and generous. He'd had dinner twice with Duncan when he clearly would rather have not.

The torn and dirty clothes were unfamiliar, but George had already said they matched what Kyle had been wearing on that last day. He didn't know if the water-stained brown leather wallet was Kyle's but apart from the driver's license and credit card, the photo tucked into one of the pockets had brought a lump to his throat. He remembered the gig. It was at a music festival up on the north coast with a top band that had long since broken up. Kyle was at his best, center stage shirtless in the heat, low slung jeans, sunglasses, a massive grin, and a red bandanna, with Duncan in mid-flight beside him ripping out a solo.

He hadn't needed to see the close-up photos of the tattoos barely visible on the discolored dead skin. They were Kyle's of course, as was the watch.

One thing was missing, and he'd said as much to Portia. "He always wore a ring. It was silver with a pattern engraved on it. He bought it at a street market about ten years ago. I think it was supposed to be Egyptian. He loved it."

"We didn't find a ring," she said. "Perhaps he'd lost it or hadn't worn it on tour for some reason."

That didn't sound right to Duncan.

George placed two beers on the table along with a couple of packets of crisps and sat down.

"Here's to Kyle," he said.

"To Kyle."

Duncan took a sip. "Thanks for coming, George."

"No problem, mate." He broke open the crisps and crunched on one. "What happens now?"

"What do you mean?"

"Do they want you to stay in town? Are they

getting anywhere, those detectives?"

"They said the investigation was going well but they don't tell me much. I don't need to be in Currong. They'll contact me if necessary." He ate a crisp. "They've been very good."

"Must be hard to find any clues. It happened so long ago."

"It's amazing what they can find, according to Rudy Dietrich. I wonder what happened to his ring."

"I know the one you mean but I don't remember seeing it when he stayed with me."

"I was with him when he bought it. The guy who sold it reckoned it was Egyptian and had some ancient mystical symbol on it."

George smiled. "Maybe it did." He downed more of his beer, well ahead of Duncan who had only taken a couple of sips.

His phone chirruped with a text. Poppy.

—*Are you ok?*—

He sent, —*Yes. Having a beer with G.*—

—*Take care. Xxx*—

He stared at the xxx's, smiling.

"I think I'll go back to Currong tonight after all," he said. He ate more crisps. George smiled and opened the second packet.

"Maybe we should eat here."

"It's a bit early, isn't it?" He stood up. "Back in a minute."

"Another beer?"

"Not for me, thanks. I'll head off soon."

When he returned from the Men's George had a second beer in front of himself and more crisps.

"How's school teaching?" Duncan took a swallow

of beer and ate more crisps. Salt and vinegar. Bit addictive and designed to make you drink more. He'd pick up another bottle of water at that corner store on the way to the car. Maybe a few snacks so he didn't need to stop.

"I love it. Kids are like sponges."

"I wish I'd had teachers like you when I was a kid. I might have learned a bit more."

"It's not easy sometimes. Some kids have a lot of problems."

"Yeah, that was Kyle and me."

"How did your father take the news?"

"Didn't give a toss."

George shook his head. "That's tough."

"I've given up trying to do anything for him."

"Did Kyle drop in to see him?"

"No. Not much of a family, is it?"

"Is that why you're so keen on Poppy and Jessie?"

"What?"

"Aren't they a little family in need of a man?" The smile was glued in place, unnervingly so.

Duncan laughed softly. "I dare you to say that to Poppy." He could see the fire flashing in her eyes as he pictured her reaction when he told her.

George leaned forward and lowered his voice. "She's my friend. We're pretty close and she asks my advice a fair bit."

Duncan nodded. The implication was clear. The reality wasn't but no way was he getting into a discussion on the subject of Poppy. He drained his beer.

"I have to make a move, George."

"Okay. It's a long drive." He looked at Duncan meaningfully.

Let him wonder. Currong or Sydney. He hadn't decided himself.

"Stay and finish your beer." He stood and slipped his jacket on. "Thanks for coming with me."

George leaned back and held out his hand. "Safe trip."

Duncan walked back to the parking lot carrying a bag with the water, an apple, and two muesli bars from the corner store. The rain had stopped, and the last glimmer of the setting sun was showing red against the darkening sky to the west. He should do as planned and head home. He'd really only mentioned returning to Currong to annoy George, and because Poppy's text had come in.

He drove back to the main street and headed north. If there were no hold-ups and the rain stayed away, he should be home just after eight. Then he'd call her and say, "Told you so." He smiled at the prospect of hearing her laugh.

Chapter 19

Poppy tried calling Duncan later that evening but got the recorded message. If he was still driving, he may have turned the phone off rather than use the hands free. The TV weatherman said there was rain all across the Southern Highlands and in Sydney so it would be safer for him to concentrate on the road.

She called George to check when he'd left Duncan.

"We had a drink in a pub afterward. That was about five fifteen, I suppose. I didn't look at the time. We stayed maybe twenty-five or thirty minutes. Duncan left before I did. I ate there."

"Was he all right to drive?"

"Yes. He was conscious of driving and only had one small beer. Light beer, actually. We took my car there because it was raining earlier. It was only a few blocks and he walked back to his. He should be home by now but there could have been hold-ups."

"Yes, I guess so. Thanks, George. How did it go?"

"It's pretty grim. There's no doubt it was Kyle. His driver's license and credit card were there, and Duncan identified a photo of the two of them. They showed him a photo of the tattoos, too."

"How awful. I'm glad you were with him."

"Me too. How's Jessie?"

"Much better but I'll keep her home tomorrow."

"Good idea."

"See you later."

Poppy disconnected with a vague sense of unease. It was nearly nine o'clock. Had something happened to Duncan on the drive to Sydney? Accidents were relatively common on that highway with drivers lulled into speeding by the long distance devoid of towns, generally light traffic, and good surface. Bad weather and poor light made it worse. She dialed the local police station.

Constable Alice answered. She of baking fame, having won Best Scones in the last three Currong Shows much to the extreme annoyance of the older local cooks who thought a blow-in should never be granted that honor. Even if she was a country girl from Orange, she wasn't a local country girl.

"Alice, it's Poppy French. I…" What was she ringing for? Was worrying about a man driving to Sydney a legit reason for calling the police?

"Hi Poppy, what's up?"

"I'm not sure I should be wasting your time but…um…"

"Poppy, whatever it is, you thought it was worth calling us so say it. You're not wasting my time."

"Duncan Barnett went to Goulburn today to…to…"

"I know," Alice said gently. "It can't have been easy for him."

"George went with him because I couldn't go. Jessie is sick with that virus going around school and she stayed home." She stopped, aware she was babbling.

"What's the problem?"

"He was going straight on to Sydney from

Goulburn and he promised to call me when he got home but he hasn't and he's not answering his phone. I texted him earlier and he said he was in a pub with George. George said they had a drink afterward, but that Duncan didn't drink much. He left to walk back to his car. George stayed and had dinner."

"What time was that?" Her voice altered subtly but to Poppy, the change was clear. She was on alert. Why?

"Um…about six, I suppose."

"Okay, thanks for calling, Poppy." Alice's voice had regained the smoothly reassuring mode she had expected and that she now realized was partly why she'd phoned. "Try not to worry. There could be something happening on the highway. Road works at night—anything."

"Will you let me know if…if…there's been an accident?"

"I will."

Poppy checked on Jessie again before she went to bed. She was sleeping peacefully with barely a trace of the bug that had arrived so quickly last night. Her energy levels were down this afternoon so Poppy would keep her home tomorrow anyway. Just to be sure.

It was well past midnight before she drifted off, but she woke before dawn to the twittering of sleepy birds wondering if it was time to get up.

No word from anyone which was good news and bad news. If there'd been an accident she would have heard and because she hadn't, didn't necessarily mean he was in trouble. His phone battery could be flat. He might have arrived home to a burst water pipe or a gas leak and been distracted. Or he could simply have forgotten or if he did remember, think that he'd get around to it later.

Poppy threw back the doona and went to stand in the shower, remonstrating with herself for being so obsessed with the man. She hadn't done this sort of thing since she was sixteen and waiting for Jayden Belmont to phone and ask her to some dance or other that was highly important to the population of her high school at the time.

It wasn't just the fact that she wanted to hear his voice and know she was on his mind. She was worried. Kyle had disappeared and now Duncan. She hadn't imagined Alice's reaction. She was concerned too, but tried to conceal it. Two brothers going missing in the same town, both strangers and only here by chance with no links to the place except for George and now herself. Too odd to be a coincidence, wasn't it?

Except Duncan hadn't been in town. He was on the highway driving home and she didn't really know he was missing.

Just before eight George phoned. Angry was an understatement. He was furious.

"What did you say to the police last night?" he demanded before she could say anything beyond hello. "Why call them in the first place?"

"Because I was worried." Her fingers tightened on the phone. "I told them what you told me," she said through the rising anger. "That you went with Duncan to Goulburn, you had a beer together, you stayed, he left. What's wrong with that?"

Heavy breaths sounded in her ear before he replied. "I've just had a cop here at the crack of dawn insinuating that I had something to do with him not getting home on time. What the hell? I didn't see him again after he left. I had dinner and drove home."

"I know, you said so and I believe you."

"I've had it with those bloody Barnetts. I was just trying to help you out and now I'm all but accused of…"

"What did they say? Has he turned up?" They would have told her, wouldn't they? "George? Has he?"

"I don't know, and I really don't care."

He disconnected.

Poppy stood with the phone in her hand, shocked and shaking. Was that really George? Where was the calm, friendly, kind man who lived next door? Why was he so upset? Maybe this whole thing was getting to him too. But why was he blaming Duncan?

What made him think he was being accused of something? Accused of what? Was that why Alice had reacted the way she had? Was George under suspicion?

She sat down hard on the kitchen chair as the implications of that wound through her head. Both brothers disappeared and George was the last known person either of them had seen. What possible reason could he have for disposing of Kyle, let alone Duncan?

Something from their past? But he and Duncan had no past.

Had Duncan accused him of killing Kyle?

She shook her head. That was totally preposterous. She and Duncan had discussed Kyle's disappearance many times and never had George's name been tossed into the mix as a possible suspect. Even if something did occur to him as suspicious Duncan was hardly likely to accuse George of killing his brother while they were having a drink in the pub. He'd say goodbye, get in his car, and call Rudy Dietrich. So, not that.

The only thing Duncan had accused George of was jealousy and that was a flimsy motive given her relationship with George. And she had no relationship with Kyle.

Poppy got up and made more coffee. She'd just poured herself a cup when the phone rang.

Duncan!

"Thank God!" she said. "What happened? I've been so worried."

"Sorry, I didn't call." His words were slow and slightly slurred. Was he drunk? On drugs? Was that why he hadn't rung?

"Are you high?" Her voice came out sharp and accusing.

"High?"

"On drugs. You sound like it. Or drunk?"

"No…not…I don't know what happened. My head feels really…thick."

Remorse kicked in. Maybe he had a version of what Jessie had. "Do you feel sick? Like Jessie?"

"No…just really…I don't know, as though my head's full of…I can't think straight, and I feel really weak."

"Where are you?"

"In my car in a lay-by."

"On the highway?" Had he been there all night? What was going on?

"Yes."

"Did you sleep in your car?"

"I must have. I remember driving out of Goulburn and somewhere…I felt really tired. It hit me like a ton of bricks." His voice was stronger now. "There was a rest stop and I just managed to pull off the road and park. After that…nothing. I just woke up a few minutes ago."

"Were you drugged?"

"I think so…"

"I called the police when you didn't ring me. I thought you might've had an accident."

"I would have if I hadn't been right near the rest stop. I was doing 110. Lucky."

"You could have been killed." Poppy could barely get the words out so immense was the realization, followed fast by the next one. "Was it George?"

"I…don't know…I can't think properly yet."

"Don't try to drive. Stay where you are, and I'll call the police. You should come back here."

He didn't argue.

"Poppy?"

"Yes?"

"Be careful."

Poppy dialed the police with fingers shaking so much she had to start again to hit the right numbers.

****

Duncan opened the car door and breathed in the fresh eucalyptus scented morning air, the perfume made stronger by the recent rain. Weak sunshine clawed its way through the clouds but didn't hold much warmth. He drank half the bottle of water he had in the center console then opened the door and stood unsteadily, gripping the top of the car, waiting for his head to clear. Talking to Poppy had anchored him, her concern real and very comforting.

Going back to Currong for a while to get his head straight and talk to Rudy and Portia would be okay but he had to be back in Sydney for the gig tonight. A couple of hours, Poppy's coffee, and some food and he'd be fine.

Another car pulled in. The driver got out and sauntered across to the small toilet block. Minutes later he returned and drove away raising a hand to Duncan as he passed by.

The rest stop area was long enough to accommodate a couple of big trucks and curved in a shallow arc, screened from the road by wattles and other native shrubs. A picnic table with attached bench seats stood near where he'd stopped the car. He couldn't honestly say it was parked but he'd managed to get well into the rest stop in the darkness and out of the way of incoming cars or trucks which was something to be thankful for.

Duncan took his own trip to the toilets walking slowly and carefully on legs that felt as unstable as rubber bands. He sat at the picnic table and tried to assemble his still fuzzy thoughts into coherent order. Whatever he'd been given had knocked him out cold for over twelve hours. Was it intended to kill him? Or was it supposed to make him have a tragic accident? Either way he was lucky to be alive.

Poppy assumed it was George but not knowing what he'd been given and the timeframe for it to take effect it was difficult to definitively say he was responsible. But if not George who? Poppy? He shook his head to rid himself of such a ridiculously vile and painful thought. Never. She wouldn't. She had no reason whatsoever. But did George? Was jealousy enough?

Or had he simply been hit with a super version of the virus that had hit Jessie? It seemed unlikely given the symptoms but since Covid who knew what viruses lurked about and in what forms?

Twenty minutes later a highway patrol car swung into the rest area and stopped in front of Duncan's car. Two female officers got out.

"Duncan Barnett?" the blonde one asked.

"Yes." He stood up, stronger now with a clear head thanks to the snack bars he'd bought. "Thanks for coming."

She introduced herself as Constable Faye Truscott. "How are you feeling, sir?"

"Better now, but I was pretty fuzzy earlier."

"We've been asked to drive you back to Goulburn where DI Dietrich is waiting to interview you."

"What about my car?"

"I'll drive that, sir," said the second constable.

"Okay, the keys are in the ignition."

"No problem."

****

Rudy Dietrich listened intently even though to Duncan it seemed there was nothing much to tell.

"We'd like to take a urine sample and a blood test if you agree," he said when Duncan had finished giving him his story.

"Why?"

"We'd like to know exactly what you were given."

"Okay."

"Good. We can do it now. The sooner the better."

"Do you think George Caramani did this?"

"It's hard to think otherwise but we have no evidence to connect him to this or what happened to Kyle."

"Kyle?" Duncan swallowed. "You don't think

George killed my brother, do you?"

"It's one avenue of inquiry. But this is strictly confidential, Duncan. I'm only telling you now because of what just happened so you can be alert. I'd advise you to go back to Sydney as soon as you feel ready to drive."

"I was going to go back to Currong for a while but if you think I shouldn't… What about Poppy? Is she safe?" How could he run away and leave her and Jessie in danger?

"I don't think there is any reason to think he, or anyone else, will harm her or the child. They've lived next door to each other for months and seem to get on well by all accounts. Kyle was the catalyst for this, but she wasn't involved with him at all so is unconnected to whatever motivated the attack on him."

Duncan hoped he was right. His reasoning was plausible but who knew what went through an unhinged mind?

"What about that footprint you found in Poppy's yard?" They hadn't come back to take a cast of it but the constable had taken photographs.

"That's another piece that we can't put into place at the moment. Not until we have grounds to suspect someone of the trespass."

"All right. That makes sense." Frustrating but then the law was most of the time.

"We won't stop our investigation, Duncan, even though it may look as though we have. We want him, the murderer, to think he's safe. In regard to what happened to you last night don't tell anyone. Poppy won't talk either. I've talked to her about it. If anyone asks, she'll say you've gone home."

"But she rang the police last night."

"That's fine, a natural thing to do and the locals spoke to Caramani this morning about when he last saw you."

"How did he take that?"

"It upset him. Poppy told Portia he rang her straight after they left and abused her for telling the police, and that they accused him of harming you."

"My God. Did they accuse him?"

"No, he made that inference from the questions. He's rattled but until we can prove something there's nothing we can do."

"That visit will get around town."

"All he needs to do is tell the truth. That is, Poppy was worried you were late, so she rang him first then Alice at the station to check on accidents. You were held up on the way but now you're at home."

"I should leave, shouldn't I?"

"We'll just get those samples first."

"Can I call Poppy?"

Rudy smiled. "She's more than a friend, isn't she?"

Duncan hesitated, then nodded. "I hope so."

"Good choice." He looked at Duncan for a long moment. "Nice little kid, too. I wonder who the father is?"

He turned and opened the door but not before Duncan caught the smile widening on his face.

"I'm a detective, mate," he said, and patted Duncan on the back as he went past.

Chapter 20

Poppy spent the day working, with occasional visits to Jessie who stayed in bed until mid-morning then got up and watched a video in her pajamas, ensconced on the couch with a blanket and the cat.

Duncan had called to tell her he was going home rather than coming back to Currong. He didn't elaborate as to why, but she strongly suspected Rudy Dietrich had something to do with the decision because the detective had told her not to tell anyone what had really happened.

She knew Duncan had a gig that night so it was natural, obvious, to go home as planned. There was nothing to keep him in Currong. She knew that, but it still hurt.

Having him around had begun to feel comfortable. Easy. He did his thing while she did hers. He didn't interrupt her at work and the gentle sound of the guitar and occasional snippets of his singing were an unobtrusive background. She caught herself listening to the silence waiting for the guitar to start up again and when it didn't, pushed away the disappointment.

Portia Mason arrived and asked her a few more questions. Had she noticed Kyle wearing a silver ring at any time? Yes, she had. The first time they met. She noticed because it was quite a striking design. Was he wearing it when she last saw him? She couldn't remember.

Had she actually seen Kyle in the car that left George's place that afternoon? That gave her pause. Had she seen the driver? She heard the engine, looked up, and saw the car accelerate away. The passenger side faced her so she couldn't definitely say who was driving. She had to say no she hadn't seen Kyle. She'd assumed he was in the car because it was his.

"Should I be worried?" she asked as the unspoken implication hung in the air between them.

"We don't think you have anything to be concerned about and this is really double-checking the original investigation into his disappearance. Don't hesitate to call us if you think of anything else or you have any concerns. Try not to worry, Poppy. We have no clear evidence to pinpoint anyone in particular."

"Just suspicions?"

Portia nodded. "But we're keeping open minds."

Poppy thanked her and closed the door but the undercurrent of alarm wasn't going away any time soon. Portia hadn't said as much but it was all too clear to Poppy that she was living next door to a man who was the number one suspect in both a murder and an attempted murder. Until they were sure, she'd just have to do her best not to act unnaturally or upset him. Not let him see how deeply frightened she was of him.

At about four that afternoon, George arrived on the doorstep bearing a large bunch of deep red roses and wearing a shamefaced smile. Poppy didn't open the old wooden screen door even though the catch was feeble and no protection at all. For the first time since living in the house she decided to replace it with a security screen. His abusive call and angry words still burned like acid in her mind adding to the underlying fear.

"I've come to apologize," he said. "Phoning you this morning was completely unforgivable and I'll understand if you never want to speak to me again." He held out the flowers. "I'm sorry, Poppy."

Jessie appeared by her side, stickybeaking as usual.

"Hello, George. Did you bring my Mummy flowers?"

"Hello, Jessie. Yes I did. Are you feeling better?"

"Yes, thank you. Why did you bring them?"

"Because I was a bit rude to her and I came to say I'm sorry."

A bit rude? Her teeth clenched so hard she realized she might break something. She relaxed her jaw.

"Why were you rude?"

"I was a bit upset and cross." There was the bit again. Try extremely or unforgivably.

Jessie looked up at her expectantly. "Why don't you take the flowers from George? He said sorry."

"Yes, you're right."

She opened the screen and stepped out. "Stay inside, Jessie, it's too cold out here and you've been sick," she said sharply as she pulled the front door almost closed. Jessie peeped through the gap.

George offered the flowers again and she had no choice, under the watchful eye of her daughter, but to take them with a forced smile.

"Thank you. They're lovely." She sniffed one of the blooms. Scentless as they always were from the florist, unlike the home-grown beauties in her garden. "But you shouldn't have." He really shouldn't have. Her stomach churned.

"Friends?" he asked hopefully.

She nodded curtly. "Friends."

But they wouldn't be. Not now, not ever. Even if Portia hadn't called by with her revelatory questions, he'd effectively trampled on any chance of that this morning.

"Have you heard anything more about Duncan?"

"Yes, briefly. He rang just after you called. He's fine. Got held up last night that's all."

"You should have let me know…"

"Should I? After what you said?" she snapped.

"Oh…no…I suppose not. Sorry. I'm glad he's okay. Really, I am."

"Good."

"I was thrown when that policeman turned up and started asking questions. I hadn't had my coffee and there he was being quite aggressive. Almost accusing me."

"Of what? There was nothing wrong with Duncan." But he'd be assuming there was, wouldn't he? Hoping.

"No. I overreacted." George smiled thinly. "I suppose Duncan won't be coming back for a while."

Poppy shook her head. "I doubt it. No reason to."

"Does that upset you?"

"Why would it?"

"You two seemed to be getting on well together."

She shrugged. "Yes, well. Why not? I get on well with most people."

"Right. Okay. I'll be off home."

"See you later. And thanks for the flowers."

He turned to go then stopped halfway down the steps.

"Maybe we could have dinner together one night.

There's that new restaurant near Crookwell that's supposed to be very good. A chef from Sydney opened it recently."

Oh God. She swallowed, thought fast.

"I've heard of it. Perhaps Steph and her boyfriend could come along. That'd be fun."

If that annoyed him, he didn't show it. "Let me know."

"Okay. Thanks."

Poppy went inside and closed the door, her heart galloping like a bolting horse. The roses were a bouquet of toxic weeds in her hand, but she couldn't throw them out the way she wanted or Jessie would ask questions and without a doubt tell George. She could hear her now piping up in her penetrating little voice. "Mummy threw your pretty flowers in the garbage."

"Where are we putting the lovely flowers?" Jessie asked.

"We need a big vase first. Where do you think is a good spot?" Apart from the compost heap.

"That was nice of George wasn't it, Mummy?"

"It was."

"Mrs. Morton said it's important to say you're sorry when you've done something wrong."

"She's right about that but I don't think Maurice knows yet, do you?"

Jessie giggled. "Naughty Maurice."

He'd jumped up onto the table while they were having dinner one night and tried to eat from their plates much to Jessie's delight and Poppy's dismay. He also liked to knock things off her desk if he wasn't getting the attention he thought he deserved.

She arranged the flowers in the vase. A man had

never given her roses. In fact, she doubted she'd ever been given flowers by any man, ever. What a way to break that drought. She firmed her mouth. Maybe she and Duncan were wrong about George. She really hoped so.

What was she going to do about the dinner invitation? Would she have gone out with him on such an obvious date pre-Duncan? Maybe. Why did he ask now? Hadn't she made herself clear to him? Friends was as far as she was prepared to go. Wasn't he going to take no for an answer? What would she do then? What would happen if he became angry with her? She'd seen his unfettered rage this morning.

For the first time in years she'd blatantly lied. Steph didn't have a regular boyfriend, but she'd conjure one up and think it was a hoot. If George pressed for a reply, she'd have to say yes or risk his jealousy and that shocking anger growing to an uncontrollable level— turning on her.

After Jessie was tucked up in bed Poppy phoned Steph. Typically, she laughed like a drain when Poppy gave her the sanitized version of her problem. No mention of Duncan's theory of jealousy, no mention of anything beyond what to do about a dull guy asking her out. No mention of suspicion.

"I knew it!" she crowed. "He's not going to give up on you."

"That's what I'm afraid of."

"He's not asking you to marry him for God's sake, Pop. He's asking you out to dinner. That's what people do. They go on dates. Except you. You've forgotten how it's done."

"But what if he thinks I'm more interested than I

am?"

"If you make it clear that's how you feel—and suggesting me and my imaginary boyfriend come along is a pretty clear indicator of that, I can tell you—if he gets the wrong impression that's his problem, as long as you're honest about how you feel."

"I have been."

"Then it's his problem."

"What if he doesn't believe me and keeps asking me out? Then it's my problem bigtime."

"You say no thank you firmly and politely."

"And if that's not enough?"

"You call the cops because he's a stalker."

"My God, Steph." George was way more than a stalker but had that footprint in the garden belonged to him? Was he already stalking her? Peering through the windows to see what she was doing with Duncan? Frightening Jessie?

She pressed her hand against her mouth to stop a whimper of fear. No. That was impossible! That was a wild assumption. Based on half a footprint and a sleepy little girl's claim.

Steph was still wittering on.

"It won't come to that. We're talking George here, remember? Now tell me all about Duncan Barnett. How come I didn't know he was staying with you?"

The abrupt change of subject derailed the crazy line her thoughts had taken. "You do know."

"Only because I heard it from Mel when she was doing my hair yesterday. She asked me and I had to pretend I knew but wouldn't gossip about you. How embarrassing is that? My best friend doesn't tell me she has a good-looking guy staying with her and not just overnight. Several nights."

"How do you know he's good-looking? You've never met him."

"Robbie Benson was in the next chair, and she saw you both at school collecting Jessie. She said he's drop dead gorgeous. Mind you her husband looks like Gollum on a bad day, so her judgment is skewed but you get the general drift."

Poppy couldn't help but laugh. Trust Steph to jerk things back into perspective. She was right. She should stick to honesty and say no thanks to George as she had before.

"Why do guys make it our problem when we don't want to go out with them or don't like them as much as they want us to? I don't want to be responsible for someone else's crush and making them feel bad if I turn them down."

"Are we talking about George or Duncan?"

"George. It's not fair."

"No, but it applies to women too."

"Guys don't seem to care as much about hurting a girl's feelings when they dump them."

"That's true. They just move on and expect us to do the same. You avoided my question, by the way."

"What question?"

"Duncan Barnett. What's going on there?"

Poppy hesitated. Steph would be livid when she found out that the truth about him hadn't been shared but she couldn't possibly tell her, not before Jessie.

"Pop? Come on. I tell you everything. I told you about my cat and Yuri and that one-night stand disaster with that newspaper bloke from Goulburn."

"I know but there's nothing to tell. He was very

broken up when he got the news about Kyle, so I let him stay here."

"Why didn't he stay at the hotel or with George?"

"We get on well and Jessie likes him. He needed to be with someone. I was around when he got the news and George wasn't."

"Okay…so…is there more? There has to be."

Poppy took a deep breath. "There might be if he lived here but he doesn't."

"Dammit. Why is there always some basic flaw?"

"Indeed."

"I'm so sorry." Her sympathy was genuine and warmed Poppy's heart. "It's hard enough to find a decent man you like without that as well. Is he coming back?"

"Not that I know of. Unless something happens in the murder case, but he's not involved in the investigation so there's no reason why they'd want him here."

"Would you go to Sydney to see him?"

"Steph, that's not going to happen, is it?"

"It could if you want it to."

"He has some things to work through."

"Like what? He's not married, is he?"

Poppy gave a mirthless laugh. "Hardly. No, that's one of the issues."

"Aah. A commitmentphobe."

"Not exactly. He feels he's not worthy in some weird way. He and Kyle had a rotten family and they basically brought themselves up. He's learned he can't rely on anyone else and that he's not a reliable person. But I think he is."

"And now he's all alone. That's so sad."

"Yes, and it's hard to break through to him. He'd love to have a family, but he thinks he'd ruin it and he's better off alone."

"Poor man."

"Yes. I'm not going to push him though. I'm hoping that he'll start to miss us more than he thinks he will. I don't want to be a George."

"Oh God no. So, what are we doing about the date?"

"We're waiting to see if he brings it up again. I'd only go in a group though."

"Fine, let's do it. I'd love to go that restaurant. I'll bring Yuri."

"Okay."

Yuri was a very popular lecturer in soil enrichment and conservation techniques at the Ag College where Steph worked in Student Admin. A burly, enthusiastic man with a loud infectious laugh and lots of anecdotes which he told in a Slavic accent, he was good company and would save the evening from sinking into awkwardness. He and Steph had had a brief affair that she said was fun but neither expected more than that and now, fortunately, they were good mates. Just as well as they worked in the same place.

"Next weekend?" Steph asked.

"All right. Let's get it over with."

"I don't know why you're making such a big thing out of it," she said.

Steph mightn't but Poppy did.

****

Poppy didn't see George over the weekend which was a vast relief because she kept expecting him to appear on the doorstep and press for an answer. After the stress of worrying about Duncan, Portia's questions, George's unnerving visit, and the consequent onslaught of all consuming fear, the uneventful weekend went a long way toward a return to normality. Events fell into perspective and by Sunday she'd decided her reaction had been overly dramatic, bordering on hysterical. She had nothing to fear from George, Portia had said as much, so she'd stick to her plan of friendly neighbors, but not too friendly. He must accept that he'd overstepped badly with that phone call, and roses with an apology weren't going to cut it. Any coolness on her part would thus be natural.

Another relief was that Jessie had made a full recovery. She woke bright and cheerful on Saturday morning and crawled into Poppy's bed.

"What will we do today?" she asked.

"If it's not too windy and cold we could go for a bike ride."

"And have a picnic?"

"Not a picnic, but how about we ride to the Happy Bites Café at the plant nursery out near the showground and have hot chocolate?"

"Yes, let's."

"And we can buy pansies for the front garden near the letterbox."

"Can Maurice come? He can ride in my basket."

"No. He wouldn't like that. He'd jump out and run away."

"And get lost."

"Yes, or hurt himself. Come on, let's get up and get going. We've slept in."

Poppy sat up and put both feet on the floor, but Jessie didn't move. "We should have a bike for Duncan when he comes to stay with us."

"Would you like him to stay with us again?" Maybe the time of the big reveal was drawing nigh.

"Yes. I like him this much." She held her arms out. "I like it when he sings songs with me."

"He thinks you're a good singer."

"I am. Can I learn the guitar?"

"You might be a bit small."

"I can ask Duncan."

"All right." Poppy smiled and dropped a kiss on her head. "Time to get up, lazy bones."

She wasn't the only one missing him but was he missing them? And if he was would he admit it?

The bike ride was fun and successful and after lunch they planted the pansies. George waved hello from his front garden but thankfully didn't come over. Helen from the other side dropped in to tell Poppy she was heading north for her annual migration to warmer climes in a few days' time.

"I'm like the birds," she said to Jessie. "I fly north to avoid the winter cold."

"Except you drive your car," said Jessie.

"I do." Helen laughed. "You're a smart young poppet."

"Drive safely," said Poppy. "We'll collect the mail and keep an eye on the house."

"Thank you. And if you could water the pots on the veranda that would be lovely."

Sunday meandered by in much the same way, the casual routine and Jessie's usual chatter and questions restoring Poppy's energy and equilibrium. She hadn't heard from Duncan but didn't expect to. He was back at work, slotting into his regular life the way they were.

Except now there was a gap she hadn't been aware of before and a month ago would have denied its existence. A gap only Duncan could fill.

Chapter 21

Rudy phoned Duncan with the results of his blood and urine tests.

"High concentrates of lorazepam which is a sedative," he said. "Enough to knock you out but not kill you."

"George," said Duncan viciously. "The bastard wanted to kill me. Make me kill myself by crashing." He would have slipped the drug into his drink when Duncan went to the toilet.

"Do not do anything about it, Duncan. Don't confront him. We have this under control."

"Do you? It doesn't seem like it to me. I could be as dead as Kyle."

"Promise me you won't interfere in the investigation."

Duncan gave a grudging agreement and hung up with fury writhing like a snake in his belly. George wasn't getting away with this. He might be clever and think he'd got away with his crimes, but he hadn't, and he was going to pay.

****

Without making it intentional Poppy managed to avoid seeing George until the following Friday. She wasn't sure why that was because Jessie reported seeing him at school which meant he wasn't away or ill, but for some reason their timing hadn't coincided. Was he avoiding her? Whatever the reason it was a breathing space she welcomed.

Strong winds had buffeted Currong for most of the week bringing down a branch in the back garden and leaving another broken and hanging precariously just out of reach of Poppy's saw. Unwilling to climb the ladder without someone to steady it in the soggy, uneven ground under the tree she thought of asking George but quickly discarded the idea. It wasn't going to do much damage if it fell but it was annoying.

Helen had left on Tuesday, her car loaded up for the long drive, so Jessie diligently went next door all by herself to collect the letters when she came home from school. On Friday she was a little longer doing her job than normal, so Poppy went out to check even though she'd been watching through the office window as she finished her work for the day. Helen's letter box was obscured by an evergreen shrub, but bits of Jessie's hot pink puffer jacket were visible through the leaves.

She was talking to George. As Poppy went down the steps the pair came into view with Jessie saying, "It's a very important job so I have to be very, very careful and put the letters straight into this bag." She held up the cloth carry bag. "And then we put them in a special green bag so they don't get lost and when there are enough Mummy goes to the Post Office and puts them all in a special Red Bag and sends them to Helen."

"It is a very important job," said George. "How many letters did you collect today?"

"Two. Helen doesn't get lots of letters. Yesterday she didn't get any."

"Hi, Poppy." George smiled at her. The smile she was used to, the kind, patient, interested one he used around the kids at school and with Jessie. If she hadn't seen the other version and didn't know what she knew, she would have slipped right back into the old, easy friendship. Now, she would do the superficial version, mainly for Jessie's sake, but also to keep George onside.

She returned the smile. "We haven't seen you much this week," she said.

"No, we're right into rehearsals for our part in the Currong Festival."

"I'm singing in the choir," said Jessie.

"Of course. How could I forget?"

The Currong Festival was an annual event at the beginning of spring when everyone joined in the weekend of activities. The primary school always did a Friday evening performance for the opening ceremony and Jessie had brought home a newsletter last term asking for parental help from those who could paint, sew costumes, or help in any way with the musical event the senior school was putting on.

"Being a musician, I've been roped into organizing all the music."

"Gosh, no wonder you've been busy." He didn't seem annoyed by the extra work. Quite the opposite.

"We have extra choir practices at lunchtime on Wednesdays," said Jessie. "I'm a good singer. Duncan said so."

Poppy's attention flicked quickly to George's face, but he smiled at Jessie and she couldn't read anything but his usual response to a child.

"He's right. You are."

He turned to Poppy. "Have you heard from him? Is he okay?"

"I expect so but no, I haven't heard."

He nodded. "Well, I'm looking forward to a night off tonight with a beer and the TV. See you later." He raised his hand in farewell and sauntered away.

Poppy and Jessie went inside to deal with Helen's mail.

He hadn't mentioned the dinner date. Was he too busy and tired to think about going out? He'd certainly looked exhausted and wanted to stay home this evening. He might have forgotten or was he waiting for her to bring it up? She wasn't going to. The more she thought about it the less she wanted to go out with him in a group or otherwise.

Steph had told her to get over herself and not over think it, but she was renowned for spontaneous actions almost immediately regretted. And she had no responsibilities in the form of dependents, apart from Peach the cat who wasn't in a position to object, offer moral guidance, or guilt trips.

Poppy went around the house closing the curtains and making sure the doors were locked and the windows properly closed. Winter was creeping up slowly but surely and the nights were already cold. She'd turned the heating on much to Maurice's delight having quickly discovered where the new warmest spots were.

Friday night was homemade pizza night which involved making the base dough, the tomato sauce, and choosing toppings. Poppy had just slipped the finished products in the oven when Duncan rang.

"Hi there," she said. "How are you?" Nerves fluttered to life in her stomach, robbing her lungs of air, tightening her throat.

"Okay. Busy. I have a gig later tonight." He sounded calm, casual.

She drew a deep breath, closed her eyes briefly. Focused.

"That's good."

"Yes it is. I wanted...I haven't heard from you. Sorry. I don't mean that you should have called me..."

"It's okay. I'm...we're not..." How did that sentence end?

"I should have called earlier. How are you? Any trouble with George?"

Worried about her, worried about Jessie. Protective despite his self-doubt.

She glanced toward the kitchen door. Jessie was in the living room choosing the video they were to watch with their pizzas. She lowered her voice just in case. "No. He's been busy with school stuff, and I saw him this afternoon for the first time all week. I think he's being cautious around me."

"Have you seen anything of the detectives? Heard anything new?"

"No, Portia asked me some more questions. About Kyle's ring and whether I actually saw him in the car when he left."

"And did you?"

"No. The driver was on the far side from me. I assumed it was him from the car and the way it took off down the street."

"Fair enough. What about the ring?"

"He had it on at the gig. I noticed it when George introduced me because it was so interesting."

"I was with him when he bought it. He never took it off, but he wasn't wearing it and they didn't find it at the scene or in his car or his bag."

"Maybe he left it at George's."

"Unlikely. He loved it. Did he have it on when you saw him that last time?"

"She asked that too, but I honestly can't remember. There was so much going on. Ralph might know."

"They'll have asked him, and Sarah."

"What does it mean? Is it important?"

"It's a missing piece and Dietrich doesn't like things like that. Same as the footprint in your garden. It could be connected, or it might not, but he can't discard it until he knows."

"Who are you talking to?" asked Jessie. "Are our pizzas ready?"

Poppy turned. Jessie stood in the doorway with indignant hands on hips.

"It's Duncan."

"I want to ask him about my guitar." All eagerness now.

"Jessie wants to ask you something," she said to Duncan. She handed over the phone and checked the pizzas—not ready yet—then got plates from the cupboard and green salad from the fridge.

Having asked her question, Jessie was listening intently and nodding. A big smile suddenly spread across her face, and she handed the phone back to Poppy.

"Duncan says I should learn to play a..." She frowned. "A ukeylayly because it's small. Some of the big kids have them at school. Can I?"

"A ukeylayly?" she said to Duncan, smiling.

He laughed. "Ukuleles are ideal for kids. They're small and light."

263

"Okay, how do I get one? I know nothing about them." The obvious solution was to ask George but that wasn't appealing at the moment.

"I do. Let me give her one."

"Are they expensive?" she asked. "She's only five. Is she old enough to start?"

"I think so. She's keen so why not encourage her? They can be expensive, but beginner ones are about forty dollars. They come in different colors, but I guess pink is the only choice."

Poppy laughed. "Yep. That sounds perfect. Thank you."

"My pleasure. I could probably bring it next Sunday and show her some things to practice. Maybe stay overnight?" The last had a hopeful tone to it.

"Sounds good. I'd better go. We have pizzas in the oven. See you next week."

"I'm looking forward to it."

"Me too."

She disconnected.

"Is Duncan coming to stay?" asked Jessie.

"Yes, on Sunday next weekend, and he'll stay overnight."

"Goody." She clapped her hands. "When can we get my ukeylayly?"

"Duncan will help us."

"I can learn from George. He teaches music after school."

"I think we'll let Duncan show you first before we bother George. Remember he's very busy with all the extra rehearsals."

Maybe it was time to break the news. Duncan hadn't hesitated with his offer and he'd taken Jessie's question seriously when he could have brushed her off as too little. All through the movie, yet another viewing of Toy Story, Poppy pondered the decision to reveal Duncan's identity and when the best time would be.

After she told Jessie their lives would be changed forever. It was like being poised on a cliff overhanging a pool where one small step would send her plummeting into the water below. Anything could happen when she hit the surface. She could break her neck on a submerged rock, damage her spine, drown, or survive and swim safely to the edge proud of her achievement, mentally stronger and braver than she'd been before she took the plunge.

She looked at the head of dark curls nestled against her side. She loved Jessie more than anything in the world and wanted only the best for her. Bringing her father into her life was part of that, she knew, but taking the final step into the unknown, saying the words, was the most difficult thing she'd contemplated doing in her life.

But it wouldn't be just three lives that were affected. What about George? How would he react? It shouldn't figure in her decision at all and wouldn't have normally, but now wasn't normal and it did. He'd tried to kill Duncan.

Jessie would be incapable of keeping her news to herself and it would be all over the school and the town in five minutes. Duncan being named and proudly claimed as her father would be a terrible shock to George. Would it tip him over the edge into unknown territory? No matter how much he tried to hide it she knew what he truly thought of Duncan and how right Duncan had been about the poisonous vein of jealousy he harbored. The quality of the anger lurking just below the smiling surface was frightening. She'd been on the receiving end and that had been over the phone. What if it was face to face?

No. She wouldn't tell Jessie. Not yet. When Duncan came, she'd explain how close she'd come and her reasoning for holding back, and he'd understand why. Unproven or not the chances were high he'd come very close to being George's victim. One of George's victims.

She shuddered. Was that really the truth?

"What's the matter?" Jessie twisted to look up at her.

"Nothing. Look, Maurice isn't even watching. He's asleep."

"That's his most favorite thing. Now sshh, Mummy, we have to watch the movie. This is my best bit."

"Okay. Sorry."

****

Duncan worried about Poppy and Jessie even though Rudy had assured him they were safe from George's vitriol when he phoned him on Saturday morning asking for an update. George's white-hot anger had subsided to a smoldering ember but a spark could set it off again, he knew.

"We brought George in for fingerprints and DNA. For elimination purposes."

"Did he agree to that?"

"Yes. If he's innocent, why not? It would look very odd not to want to help with the investigation. People would wonder why, and he knows that. He also knows that we can't prove anything from finding his prints in

Kyle's car."

"And did you find them in his car?"

"Nowhere we wouldn't expect them to be if, as he said, he moved it out of the driveway so he could get his car out. I can tell you, that ring has me bothered," Rudy said.

"You should search George's house and car." Why on earth weren't they doing that?

"We need a good reason to get a warrant and we don't have one."

"Can't you ask him to let you in? If he's not involved it shouldn't be a problem."

"He won't. He said he's given us his prints to check Kyle's car but anything more makes him look like a suspect. He also said when Kyle disappeared the local police came and had a look and found nothing. He'd cleaned Kyle's room months ago and washed the linen so there's nothing to be gained.

"That's as far as his helpful citizen act goes. He was furious when the constable asked him straightforward questions about when he last saw you in Goulburn, and he took it out on Poppy. I don't want to antagonize him until we know we'll find something. If we went in and it was clean, we'd blow any chance of proving he was involved."

"But sitting around waiting isn't getting you anywhere." Were they actually doing anything? It didn't feel like it.

"We're making progress, Duncan, believe me. I can't reveal the details to you—you know that."

Duncan put the phone down after the call not completely satisfied with what amounted to a brush-off but there was nothing he could do. Rudy was right about not upsetting George. He'd had plenty of time to find that ring if he hadn't realized it was missing until…

Oh shit! He'd told George something that could have been the key to implicating him. He smacked his hand against his forehead. Idiot. He shouldn't have blurted out the question, shouldn't have asked where the ring was. He should have waited and asked Portia when they were alone. No wonder George had been so keen to go to Goulburn with him in Poppy's place. He wanted to see exactly what evidence they had.

If the ring was in the house, he could easily have searched and found it and said Kyle had left it there. Same with the car. But he hadn't done that yet, which meant either he hadn't found it and was freaking out that the police would, or he'd hidden it somewhere where he knew they'd never find it. Maybe that's why he was so angry that morning when a policeman turned up on his doorstep—he thought he was being busted. He might have been in the midst of a frantic search.

"I bet he's hidden it somewhere," he said aloud, clenching his fist in a gesture of frustration. George wouldn't want to draw any more attention to himself and not want to do the detectives any favors by suddenly finding it especially when he told them he'd cleaned the room months ago. Was this a mistake by George that could be the first crack in the case?

Duncan phoned Rudy and outlined his theory. Rudy listened and agreed. They'd come to a similar conclusion, he said. But they were also looking at his past in some detail, looking for motive. Somewhat deflated, Duncan hung up and went down to the beach for a walk. Motive was something he hadn't come up with apart from jealousy. But George wasn't jealous of Kyle.

The wind was blustery and cold, not conducive to strolling and not safe for swimming although braver surfers than he were taking advantage of the large blue-gray waves that pounded in to break into masses of foam and run up the smooth glistening sand.

He buttoned his coat and shoved his hands in his pockets. By George's past Rudy must have meant where that intersected with Kyle. He'd heard from a few musos that the police had asked them about Kyle and George, particularly those who'd played in the same bands at the same time as both of them. Not everyone was still in Sydney and no one Duncan talked to had anything to offer beyond vague comments about Kyle being "pretty out there" back then.

The police may have had better luck gathering information, but Rudy certainly wasn't sharing it with Duncan. He had nothing but speculation which took him in circles. Something had to change. George had to be goaded into doing something rash but that could mean exposing Poppy and Jessie to his wrath and was therefore impossible.

He reached the end of the path and turned to retrace his steps. After lunch he'd pack his gear into the car. Tonight's gig was a wedding at Bilgola up on the northern beaches, a solid hour and a bit more of driving depending on traffic. He'd have to leave by three thirty at the latest, preferably closer to three, and he wouldn't be home until after one in the morning after a five hour gig. Tiring, but the money was excellent as it bloody well should be for the time and effort involved.

On Monday he'd go shopping for a pink uke. The

thought made him smile. He'd need a beginner book too, suitable for a young kid. Jessie had definitely inherited the Barnett musical genes. Kyle would have been proud of her. He liked kids and had confided once that he and Meghan planned to have babies, but it hadn't happened. She wasn't ready, he said, but Duncan remembered thinking maybe she figured by then that Kyle wasn't reliable father material. Same as himself. But Kyle never had the chance to prove himself with the approaching new baby, Fiona's baby.

Duncan had a chance with Jessie, and he was going to do his best against all the genetic odds stacked against him.

****

Duncan arrived at Poppy's mid-afternoon the following Sunday. He wasn't worried about what George might think but Duncan remembered he played tennis on Sunday afternoons. That was a relief and meant there wouldn't be a confrontation as soon as he got out of the car. He didn't trust himself to keep it civil, but the sight of Poppy and Jessie coming out onto the veranda to welcome him before he'd turned the engine off made thoughts of George disappear like muck down a drain.

Poppy kissed him on the cheek, her lips leaving his skin tingling with the anticipation of more adventurous kisses to come. He'd been so preoccupied with Kyle and Jessie, the elemental force that was Poppy had receded in his mind, but the incredibly sexy woman smiling at him with warmth in those green eyes stole his breath away.

Jessie bounced up and down in excitement when she spotted the ukulele in its soft cover, hanging over his shoulder.

"Hello, Duncan. Is that my ukylayla? Can I see it? Will you show me how to play it?"

"Let Duncan come inside before you monster him," said Poppy. "She's been looking out the front window since breakfast even though I said you wouldn't be here till after lunch."

"That's fine. We might as well do this before one of us explodes."

Poppy laughed. "The spare room's all yours."

Jessie followed him down the hallway with the cat following them both. He put his guitar and overnight bag on the floor and laid the uke down on the bed. Poppy watched from the doorway.

"Before we get started," he said. "You have to treat your instrument like your best friend. Your ukulele isn't just a piece of wood and it's not a toy. It's a real musical instrument and must be treated with respect. When you're not playing it put it back in its cover so it doesn't get dusty or damaged. Don't leave it somewhere the cat can knock it over or where someone might sit on it or trip over it. Understand?"

She nodded solemnly, eyes shining as she glanced at Poppy and smiled.

"Now, watch how carefully I take it out of the cover."

Jessie gasped with delight and clapped her hands when she saw the little pink instrument.

"Wow," said Poppy. "Isn't it beautiful?"

"Yes, I love it." Jessie threw her arms around his middle and gave him a massive hug. "Thank you, Duncan."

He placed a hand gently on her head. "You're

welcome, sweetheart."

He looked at Poppy and her eyes glistened with unshed tears as, he suspected, did his.

"Let's get started," he said. "I'll tune it for you, but you'll learn to do it yourself later."

Jessie sat on the bed, and he proceeded to demonstrate how to hold it and how to pluck the strings. The tutor he'd bought had simple instructions and big diagrams as well as a CD to help the student practice. She was a quick learner and surprisingly her fingers were flexible and strong enough to play the simple positions that were the first lesson.

So engrossed was he that when Poppy appeared and told them it was afternoon tea time he was amazed that they'd spent nearly thirty minutes laughing and playing together.

"Well done," he said. "We can have another lesson tomorrow, but you need to take a break now or your fingertips will get blisters and be too sore to play. After a while they'll toughen up like mine. See?" He held out his left hand so she could feel the calloused fingers.

She carefully put the instrument in its case under his watchful eye.

"What's for afternoon tea?" he asked.

"Mummy made scones and I helped."

"Great, let's go."

Drinking tea and slathering scones with blackberry jam and cream was the most relaxed Duncan had been for weeks. He shed the ever-present thoughts of the evil living next door and the frustrations of the slow moving case like a heavy weight, and he sensed a similar relaxation in Poppy. He was pretty sure she trusted his intentions toward Jessie, and he was determined not to push her now that he had an inkling of how it felt to be responsible for a child's wellbeing.

He'd had no idea how that became so important in a parent's life. Intellectually he understood, of course, when people had babies and said how much they loved their child, but he'd had no idea of the visceral nature of the love Jessie engendered. It went far beyond anything he'd ever felt before. Those times in his life when he'd fallen for a woman and thought his love was all encompassing turned out to be simply lust and hadn't lasted more than a few months. That initial emotion wasn't even a shadow of what he felt for the chattering little girl at the table. This growing love was on a whole other level, came from a completely different place. He'd protect this child with his life, he had no doubt.

And then there was Poppy, the mother of his daughter and precious for that reason alone. There was no doubting the electrifying physical attraction between them and neither tried to deny it but he knew, and she definitely knew, that sexual attraction wasn't enough to sustain a long-term relationship.

What he felt for Poppy was a confusing mix of attraction and admiration. And a type of love. He wanted to be with her but wasn't sure if that was because of the ideal of the happy family, the loving mother, she represented or if it was a desire to be the sole man in her life, regardless of their daughter. Did he want to love and be loved by Poppy? At the moment he didn't know. He wanted Poppy to like and trust him and he thought he might have reached that place. At the moment he was just happy to be here. To be welcome in their lives.

Chapter 22

Poppy asked Duncan to help her in the garden after they'd finished the scones so even though he didn't think he'd be much use he went with her while Jessie stayed inside drawing yet another picture for him. Poppy took him across toward the back corner.

"I want to cut that dead branch off but it's too high for me to reach and I can't get the ladder in safely with that groundcover. Could you do it, do you think?"

He looked to where she pointed. The tree was some sort of deciduous thing, big and old with thick branches sprawling wide in the corner where her fence met George's and the neighbors' fences over the back. The branch in question was partially broken and hanging at an odd angle. "What is it?"

"A walnut tree. It's been here forever but we've had some strong winds lately and bits of it are breaking off."

"I'll give it a go, but it'd be easier with a ladder."

"We can try. I didn't want to do it on my own. It'll be safer if I steady it. The ground is so soft."

"Don't you have a chainsaw?"

"No. And it's hardly worth it for that." She gave him a mildly scoffing look that said city slicker. "It won't take long."

With the ladder in place and saw in hand Duncan climbed a few rungs and began sawing where Poppy directed. He was glad she held the ladder because his weight made the legs sink unevenly.

From up high he had a good view into George's yard. A fallen branch lay on the ground across the other side of the stretch of unmown grass, the leaves brown as though it had lain there for some time. It wasn't as well kept as Poppy's garden, and George hadn't planted vegetables in the plot marked out along the adjoining fence. The grass needed mowing and the flower beds had weeds. He needed to get outside and do some garden maintenance. It looked as though it had been well planned out once and would come good with a bit of work. Not that Duncan was any sort of expert but his own small experiments with herbs on the balcony had given him a taste for growing things.

The branch yielded to the saw and came down safely guided by Poppy. He climbed down. She dragged the branch clear, and he took the ladder and the saw to the shed.

"What are you going to do with it?" he asked.

"Cut it up and take it to the dump. I don't have a wood fire."

"You know a garden is a good place to hide something," he said casually. "I had a good view of George's yard from the ladder. It's very overgrown."

"You mean the ring? Why would he hide it there? All he'd need to do is throw it in the lake or drop it somewhere miles away. Even throw it down a drain on the way to school."

"But that's too public, especially now with the police asking questions around town. People are out and about all the time. You don't know who's watching. A back garden is private, and you'd need a

Elisabeth Rose

metal detector to find anything in that jungle."

"Did you see any freshly dug up spots, Sherlock?" She was laughing at him.

"No, of course not. He's not stupid. There's a vegetable plot on the fence but he hasn't done anything with it. Not like yours."

Poppy had a large, neatly dug patch with silverbeet, peas, and beans in neat rows and some other new little green plants coming up.

"You're not digging up my veggies to look," she said sternly.

"It never entered my mind," he said. "But now you mention it, it's the perfect place. Soft, newly dug. Easy to poke a stick down deep and drop in the ring."

"I dug that fairly recently, so if it's there I'll find it when I dig in spring. It's such a shame about next door," she said. "The Prestons spent a lot of time out there, but I guess George doesn't know much about gardening."

"Maybe I should have a poke around tomorrow morning," he said.

"No, you should not!"

"Why not? He'll be at school. He won't know."

"It's useless. You said so yourself."

"It's not. The police aren't allowed to have a look, but I can."

"What if someone sees you?"

"I'll say the cat hopped over the fence and we're looking for him."

"And what if you leave footprints? That long grass will show up were you walk even if you don't step in a muddy patch."

"The way he did?"

"We don't know that."

"We do. Who else would be snooping about your house in the middle of the night?"

Poppy exhaled loudly but didn't say anything. She didn't need to. She thought exactly the same as he did.

"Rudy told me they'd taken his fingerprints and DNA to eliminate them from Kyle's car."

She frowned. "When did he say he was in Kyle's car?"

"I don't know but George told him he had to move it to get his own car out."

"That can't be true. He had no time. Kyle went straight to the pub with the band when he arrived in town and George walked to the gig, so his car was at home that night. Kyle got to the house with Sarah after George had gone to bed and George didn't get home from school until the fight started at about four."

"Did he drive to school that day?"

Her forehead wrinkled in thought. "Damn. I don't know. It's so long ago. I can't remember if I saw his car that day, but I don't walk past his house when I walk to the shops or the school. I know we didn't walk together in either direction because I didn't see him until the afternoon. And of course he'll say he did drive and had to move the car in the morning."

"I'll tell Rudy anyway. Someone might remember."

"I've been thinking," she said a few moments later. "I was going to tell Jessie about you and then I realized she'd immediately tell everyone at school."

"And?"

"I didn't know how George would react. He scares me sometimes. At the moment he's okay and

277

superficially we're back to normal but that phone call when I thought you were missing was seriously unhinged. I…we have to protect Jessie."

"Yes." He gripped her hands. "I know what that means now. I remember when you were worried I'd take her from you. You looked like a lioness for a moment…"

She held his gaze. "And now you feel the same."

He nodded.

"What will we do?" she asked. "I want this to end as much as you do but I can't see how snooping about in his yard will help. You'd never find anything."

"Okay, point taken, but we have to goad him into doing something rash. Would he hurt Jessie?"

"I doubt it but I honestly don't know. What are you thinking?"

"What if we let her tell everyone I'm her father? Could she go somewhere safe overnight? A friend's house?"

"Duncan, she's not going to want to do that while you're staying here, is she?"

"No. Okay, I'll have to think about it."

As they walked back to the house, Poppy said, "Thanks for helping with the tree."

"No worries. Anything else you need? Jars opened, light bulbs changed, fuses fixed. Manly stuff?"

"Ha-de-ha." She grinned at him. "You can peel the spuds for dinner."

"Okay, what's for dinner?"

"Roast lamb. I'll have to get it started soon."

"Great. Where did you learn to cook so well?"

"Mainly from Evie. It was fun staying with her. She taught me lots of things."

"You were lucky to have her."

"I was."

"And now you're teaching Jessie."

"I hope so."

"You are. I can see it happening. That's one of the reasons I'm so worried about interfering in her life, since you're doing so well."

"Don't start that again," she said. Even though she smiled the words held an underlying sharpness. "Small steps. You're doing fine. Think of it more as enriching her life. You bring with you things I can never provide."

"Music?"

"Yes, but she could have music lessons. It's what you bring with your music that's so valuable. It's a different view of what's possible, an artistic approach. I'm more academic."

Valuable? He'd never had anyone say he was intrinsically valuable. It was similar to what he'd thought about Kyle.

"Thank you," he said. "I just hope I'm worthy of that value, as a man, I mean. Kyle had a terrific talent, but as a man he was a disaster."

"You're not a disaster, Duncan."

She opened the back door. In the laundry she took her muddy boots off and washed her hands in the sink. He did the same and followed her through to the kitchen where Jessie sat at the table surrounded by paper and colored pencils.

****

Preparing dinner with Duncan was fun—discussing how many potatoes to peel, who liked sweet potato and whether to have peas or broccoli, whether the road

279

works would ever be finished on the highway and what was top on their respective bucket lists—mundane, ordinary chat but an experience she hadn't had for years and never with a man. Group housemates weren't the same. Poppy produced a bottle of red wine and when the roast was in the oven she sat with him at the kitchen table enjoying the unfamiliar but comfortable sensation of sharing a Sunday evening.

Apart from their obvious link, Poppy liked spending time with Duncan. He'd relaxed more and more in her presence, and she knew he wasn't going to steal Jessie from her or make unreasonable demands. The admission he'd made about protecting his daughter had been a revelation to her and one that made her certain she'd done the right thing by telling him.

Jessie had drawn a picture of her pink ukulele with herself and Duncan. He admired it and when she asked him to draw a picture for her, he surprised both Poppy and Jessie by drawing a cartoon of Maurice washing himself.

"Do another one." Jessie leaned on the table next to him, watching closely as he sketched her with her uke.

"Where did you learn to draw like that?" asked Poppy.

He shrugged. "I've always done it, but I haven't drawn anything for a while. I used to get into trouble at school for drawing cartoons of the teachers in my textbooks."

"I'm not surprised," said Poppy.

Someone knocked at the front door. George? Duncan met her gaze and made to rise.

"I'll go," said Poppy. "It could be anyone."

It could be anyone but all the same her heart

thumped liked a war drum as she opened the front door.

"Hi, Poppy. I saw Duncan's car here and thought I should pop in and see how he is. I brought a bottle of wine. Thought we might have a drink."

George, smiling, flourishing the bottle in his hand. No way was she drinking that.

"Hi, I thought you'd had enough of the Barnetts." She said it as casually as she could but it was a fair question and he couldn't expect her to forget his nasty words so quickly.

"I shouldn't have said that, Poppy. It was unfair and I'm sorry." He shook his head and sighed. "I guess it was all a bit much to take in. Identifying Kyle's belongings then the police turning up and Duncan missing…I'm sorry."

Poppy stared at him, undecided. What would Duncan think if she invited him in?

"I don't want to interrupt anything," he said. "Sorry. I'll go."

"Come in, George." Duncan, behind her.

George looked at Poppy. "Are you sure?"

"Okay, come in," she said, knowing it sounded grudging.

George shook Duncan's hand. "Glad to see you're okay, mate. What happened?"

Poppy closed the door behind them, teeth clenched. What was Duncan doing? Was this part of his plan to goad George into some sort of action? In her house with their daughter right there in the firing line? How dare he? So much for his "I'll protect her with my life" statement.

She was not drinking wine with George, and she was not inviting him to stay for dinner.

"Go into the living room," she said. The kitchen was too intimate and cozy, rich with the smell of baking and the table covered with Jessie and Duncan's artwork. Not for George. The intruder.

"So tell me what happened after you left Goulburn last week." George relaxed into his chair, with an interested expression. "Why did Poppy think you were missing?"

Poppy sat on the couch and Duncan sat beside her, closer than he normally did.

"You know why," Poppy said. "I overreacted when Duncan didn't phone when I expected. It was a nasty night for driving and I thought he might have had an accident."

"I didn't," said Duncan. "There were road works, and someone had gone into a tree near Mittagong. No idea how they managed that. Must have gone to sleep or something. It was a bloody awful trip, actually. I wished I'd come back here instead."

Duncan smiled at Poppy, his gaze lingering on her face like a caress.

"Why didn't you call her?"

Duncan looked at George, eyebrows raised. "I'm not a child. I didn't think I needed to check in. I called in the morning."

"Rather inconsiderate, don't you think? Worrying her like that."

"Can't help that." Duncan shrugged. "She got over it, didn't you, Pop?"

She nodded, incapable of speech.

"How about a glass of wine?" said George. "This is supposed to be a pretty good drop. From the local winery."

Duncan picked the bottle up and read the label. "I'm not big on white wine," he said and put it down.

"I can pour you a glass, George, if you like," said Poppy.

"No, that's fine. I just thought it could be by way of a peace offering." He smiled from her to Duncan, but the strain was beginning to show.

"What have you done that you need to make peace?" asked Duncan.

"Call it a cover all bases offer." George laughed. "There's sure to be something to atone for apart from upsetting Poppy."

"No doubt," said Duncan.

"Excuse me," Poppy said. She escaped to the kitchen where she was able to draw a couple of deep breaths and regroup.

Jessie sat at the table copying Duncan's drawing of the cat. "Duncan said I had to stay here," she said. "Why can't I say hello to George?"

Poppy kissed the top of her head. "Because it's adult talk."

"Is George staying for dinner?"

"No."

"Good. I want it to be just me and you and Duncan."

"So do I."

Poppy took the baking dish out of the oven and turned the meat over, added the par boiled potatoes, then slid it back in.

"That smells yummy yum," said Jessie. "Maurice thinks so too. He wants his dinner."

"It's a bit early but I suppose we could feed him. You get his food."

Poppy rinsed the cat's bowl and then spooned in fishy dinner cat food with Maurice sitting at her feet anxiously. She handed the bowl to Jessie who took it to the laundry chatting to the cat as she went.

"We won't be very long, Jessie," Poppy called.

"Are you still doing adult talk?"

"Yes."

When Poppy resumed her seat in the living room George said, "Something smells wonderful."

"Thank you," she said.

"We have some news, George," Duncan said. "And I'm glad you dropped in because Poppy wanted you to be the first to know."

She shot him a startled look and he took her hand and squeezed it, then kissed her cheek.

"We're engaged to be married," he said.

"What?" George cried. "That's…that's…you hardly know each other. Poppy? You were always dead set against marriage. You told me."

The grip on her hand tightened, then relaxed, warning her.

"She had to meet the right man," said Duncan with a smug smile. "Isn't that true, sweetheart? You can't fight it when it's right."

She nodded, speechless. Marry Duncan? Where had that come from? Why say that of all things?

"And what about you?" George gasped for air like a stranded fish, his face red. "With your reputation…What makes you think you're the right man for her? Poppy, have you any idea who he is? This is…I can't believe you'd do that."

"I didn't think I would either," Poppy said. "But as Duncan said, the right man never came along. Until now."

"But why him?" The unspoken question hung in the air—why not me?

"We've discovered we have a lot in common," she said.

George stared at her, shattered. If Duncan wanted a reaction, he got one.

"Aren't you happy for us?" Duncan asked. "For Poppy?"

"Yes…I…I'm sorry. It was a shock. Congratulations."

"Thank you." She managed a tiny smile. "It was a bit of a shock for me too. I never thought I'd find someone, but we have you to thank, George, for introducing us."

"That's true. I'd forgotten." Duncan slid his arm around her shoulders and hugged her close while George watched with a stony expression. "I'll have to find a ring to make you officially mine. It's all happened a bit fast."

"I'm happy to wait."

"Speaking of rings. George was asking about Kyle's ring while you were in the kitchen," said Duncan.

"The missing one?"

"Yes."

"I have no idea what's happened to it," said George. He coughed, cleared his throat, visibly pulled himself together.

"He was wearing it at the gig," said Poppy. "I noticed it because it was such a beautiful design."

"Did you? I know the ring, but I don't remember seeing it at all, but then I didn't see much of him really."

"I think he was wearing it when he was fighting with Ralph," Poppy said. A deliberate lie.

George shrugged. "I have no idea and I told the police that."

"Not very observant," said Duncan.

"Maybe, but there was no reason to be particularly observant was there? It's easy in hindsight to say you should have noticed this or that."

"True enough," said Poppy.

"I'm glad you agree," George said with a touch of acid.

"I do agree. Have I disagreed with anything you've said?"

"I get the distinct impression you're both trying to catch me out in some way."

"Why on earth…why would we do that?" Poppy exclaimed.

"I don't know but that's how it feels. As though you think I'm involved with Kyle's death. I'm not and I really resent the fact you think I am. I thought you were friends, both of you, and now you're siding with the police. I wouldn't be surprised if you've told them lies about me."

"What sort of lies?" Duncan asked calmly. She threw him an alarmed glance, but he wasn't looking her way. He was focused on George.

"All this stuff about that damn ring. What's so important about it?"

"It was important to Kyle," said Duncan. "I'd like to have it."

"If it was so important to him, he should have taken better care of it."

"The police might think the killer took it as a trophy," said Poppy.

"A trophy? For God's sake, isn't that a serial killer thing?" George spread his hands wide then let them drop with a slap onto his thighs.

"Maybe. I don't know enough about it."

"Exactly," George said disdainfully. "Neither of you know anything and neither do those so-called detectives."

"They know a lot more than they let on to the public, or me," said Duncan.

"That's what they tell you to keep you happy. You're the bereaved family member and they don't want you making waves and complaining that they're not getting anywhere."

"They are getting somewhere. In fact, I think they're close to making an arrest."

"Hah! And pigs might fly. I heard they've gone back to Sydney. Given up."

"We'll see. But Rudy Dietrich is a lot smarter than you give him credit for."

"Calm down, you two," said Poppy forcefully.

Duncan would go home tomorrow, and she'd be left with an angry, resentful George to contend with when she'd deliberately tried to keep the relationship on a stable footing. And now she was supposedly marrying Duncan. How could she keep that from spreading around town? He had no idea what a stupid move that fake engagement was.

"I came over here to see how you were," George said to Duncan. "And this is what I get. Accusations."

"Stop it." Poppy glared at George. "I'm sorry you feel that way, but it's been upsetting for all of us."

"Excuse me." Duncan got up and strode from the room.

George leaned forward and said softly, "Poppy, I can't imagine why you would want to marry Duncan of all people but remember I warned you about him. You can't trust him. He'll turn on you as easily as he turned on me. Kyle was the same."

"I didn't know Kyle so I can't compare them."

"I do know them both and trust me, they come from the same bad place. You're making a hideous mistake. Please, please, don't do this. Don't marry him."

"George," she was almost whispering. "Do you think I'm in danger? From Duncan?"

He hesitated. "Not in danger the way Kyle was, no. I mean he'll treat you badly. He doesn't respect women. Kyle did things...manipulated and damaged people for his own gain."

"Do you think that's why Kyle was killed? Someone he did something to had had enough?"

"I think so." He nodded. "I'd say that was what happened."

"Someone from Sydney followed him here, do you think?"

"It has to be, doesn't it?"

"I suppose so." Poppy sighed. "It's too awful to think about."

George leaned back in the chair, his eyes narrowing to slits. "Are you happy having Duncan around Jessie? If you marry him, he'll be living with you both. Closely."

"Of course. Why not?"

"Just asking."

"What are you implying? That he's a pedophile?" She almost laughed. Even for George in his heightened state that was preposterous, and infuriating.

"You can't be too careful with children."

"Okay, George. That's going too far. I know you're upset about the engagement but accusing him of that? No." She shook her head vehemently and stood up. "No way."

"What are you accusing me of?" Duncan stood in the doorway.

Poppy looked at George, eyebrow raised.

"Nothing," he said. He rose and went to the door. "Take care, Poppy."

"Don't worry about me, I'll be fine and so will Jessie."

He grasped her hand. "I'll make sure you are."

The look in his eyes robbed her of words but she managed to smile and say, "Goodnight," as she opened the front door.

"Take the wine, George."

Duncan held out the bottle, but George shook his head. "I brought it for you. You can celebrate with it."

"Thanks," Poppy murmured and raised her hand in a feeble farewell wave before closing the door and collapsing against it.

"That was interesting," Duncan said.

"What? That was crazy. We're getting married? What were you doing?"

"Getting a reaction."

"Well that worked. He asked me if I thought it was safe to have you around Jessie." She glared at him as the implications sank in.

"The bastard. Is that what he didn't want to say to

my face?" Anger replaced the satisfaction.

"Yes."

Jessie came out of the kitchen. "Has George gone?"

"Yes."

"Was he angry?"

"No."

"He sounded angry. He was shouting."

"He wasn't angry." Poppy frowned at Duncan over Jessie's head.

"And he wasn't shouting. He was just talking loudly," Duncan said.

"How's our dinner getting on?" asked Poppy.

"I don't know, but I'm really, really hungry."

"Me too." Duncan headed for the kitchen. "We need to put the peas in the saucepan."

Poppy went to the living room and retrieved the bottle of wine. It was a good wine—she'd had it before. She examined the top. The screw seal was unbroken and now she thought about it, George was far too smart to drug Duncan again, and would he want to drug her? His last words were terrifyingly protective. Duncan was the one who needed to be extra careful but there he was deliberately poking the bear.

Married? To Duncan? Insane.

She put the bottle in the cupboard with a couple of other wines she'd been given as gifts.

Chapter 23

Duncan was pleased with his spontaneous announcement and pleased Poppy had immediately played along. He hadn't had a clear idea of how he could shock George into action but playing on his jealousy seemed the best avenue and the engagement announcement had come to him in a burst of creative genius.

Poppy didn't think so. She couldn't let fly in front of Jessie, but she was storing it up for later. That was obvious by her crisply polite responses and stiff shoulders.

Duncan focused on Jessie and together they cleared the table and set it for dinner, carefully stepping around the cat who insisted on getting under their feet despite being told sternly by Jessie that he'd had his dinner already. The glasses of wine they'd been drinking when George interrupted them were unfinished and the bottle still over half full. He topped up the glasses and handed one to Poppy.

"Cheers," he said.

She took the glass with a frown but touched it to his and took a sip.

"You need to be careful," she murmured, her back to Jessie as she bent to take the roast from the oven.

"I will."

After dinner, the dishwasher sloshing and Jessie in

bed, Duncan sat with Poppy at the kitchen table. She'd carefully closed the door to avoid disturbing Jessie, so he knew he was in for a pasting.

She launched straight in.

"Have you any idea how fast that stupid statement of yours will spread around town?"

"Does it matter?"

Was that really her biggest worry? He doubted that; she was just warming up.

"Yes, it damn well does. It's all right for you because you don't live here. I do and now everyone will be contributing their ten cents worth on why I would marry you and how desperate I must be and how no one thought I'd ever get married and isn't that good and poor George and on and on." She drew a breath.

He braced himself for the rest of the barrage. Let her get it out of her system before he explained his reasoning.

"And what about Jessie? How's that gossip going to affect her? She's going to be excited about finally getting a father and ask me why we didn't tell her. And what about my relationship with George?"

His eyes snapped to her face. "You don't have a relationship with him. Do you?"

"Oh God. Don't you start with the jealousy. I can't handle it." She clenched her hands into fists and gestured impotently. "Men. Always about them."

He sat forward, surprised and mildly alarmed by her reaction. "You realize, Poppy, that it isn't true, that we're not engaged and don't intend to be?"

"Of course I do." Her eyes shot fire bolts at him. "I don't want to marry you or anyone else."

"Neither do I so what's your problem?"

Was that really true? The idea had to have come from somewhere in his subconscious.

"I've just told you. Aren't you listening?" She sighed. "Why did you have to tell him that of all things?"

Thankfully the pitch of her voice had dropped to a more normal level along with the decibels.

"Because he's obsessed with you and it was guaranteed to needle him, and it did."

"So what do you think he's going to do? He's already tried to kill you once. You must be completely mad. Did you hear what he said to me when he was leaving?"

"No." He'd lingered to pick up the bottle of wine as they left the room and arrived at the tail end of that exchange.

"I told him not to worry about Jessie and me that we'd be fine, and he said, 'I'll make sure of it.' He's really on the edge."

"That's what I wanted."

She shook her head. "I don't believe you think this is a good thing! You didn't see the crazy look in his eyes. I'm frightened and you should be, too. He's a murderer, Duncan."

"I'm not frightened. I'm furious and I'm ready for whatever he tries next."

"Who do you think you are? A superhero?" She took a mouthful of wine. "You're not the only one affected. We should tell the police."

"If he tries anything we will. That way they can catch him in action."

Her face registered what she thought of that. Horrified.

"That's totally ridiculous. I'm going to arrange for Jessie to stay with her friend." Poppy pulled out her phone.

"If you do that, he'll know something's up. We should keep things as normal as possible. She'll be safer here with us, and I doubt he'll harm her or you. He wants to eliminate me."

Poppy hesitated then put the phone on the table.

"You still haven't told me what you think we should tell Jessie," she said tightly.

Jessie. He hadn't given her a moment's thought at the time. Poppy was right. He'd only been focused on himself and what he wanted. Hadn't thought it through.

"I don't know."

"No, you don't." Disgust dripped from the words.

Silence settled uncomfortably, tainting the cozy room with a miasma of unease until Duncan said, "Will George tell people, do you think? Won't he be too embarrassed?"

"He's angry. He'll tell. He'll give his opinion and he'll spread those implications about your intentions toward Jessie." Her tone was clipped. "And because he's George people will believe him."

"Christ. We have to get in first and tell her I'm her father."

"Will that help?" She eyed him skeptically. He didn't know. He was floundering under the weight of what he'd unwittingly unleashed.

"It'll make an engagement more understandable."

"Not to people who know me, which is half the town."

"But won't they think George's opinion could be partly sour grapes?"

"Possibly, but that sort of mud sticks. After all, I've only just met you. What do I know? George has known you much longer."

"Maybe but not well, only as an acquaintance. We know each other better."

Poppy emptied the remains of the wine into their glasses. "Do we?"

A gaping hollow opened in his stomach like one of those sink holes where everything suddenly disappears into a bottomless chasm. Did she actually believe George had a point? That he was a child molester? Or a man who bashed women? Both?

"Perhaps I should leave," he said.

"Good one. Clear out and leave me here with the mess." She met his gaze, her expression fierce.

"It was only a suggestion in case you were too polite to tell me to piss off."

"I'm not too polite for that." She half smiled. "And before you do go, get Brian at the garage to check your car over. Brakes and whatever. Just in case."

"Poppy, tell me you don't think…Do you have doubts about me…with Jessie?"

He swallowed, his breath shallow with dread. Surely she trusted him. There was no suggestion anywhere, ever, in his past or now, no suspicions or accusations. Nothing. Children barely featured in his life until Jessie landed with earth shattering effect. He was terrified of what she would say. Far more than anything George could do to him.

Suddenly she transformed before his eyes, became the woman who had comforted him, twice, who cared and worried enough to call the police when he was thought missing last week. The woman who kissed him as passionately as he kissed her. Who implicitly promised more.

She stretched her hand across the table to grasp his. "Of course, I don't think that. If I did you never would have set foot in this house. I was furious with George and told him he'd gone too far."

Relief flooded his body, washing away the doubt and filling the hollow in his stomach. He held her hand with both his. "Thank you."

"I think I should tell George tomorrow that the engagement is off," she said, her eyes focused on his.

"Probably that's the best thing to do." Why did it feel like a rejection?

"I'll catch him first thing and say we've reconsidered."

"That his reaction made us realize we acted a bit fast."

"Yes." She smiled and this time it was her proper smile. "That must be the shortest engagement on record. Beats those celebrity fiascos by a good couple of hours I reckon."

He didn't release her hands and she didn't try.

****

Poppy knocked on George's door at a quarter to eight the following morning. She dreaded seeing him, but Duncan agreed it was the best way to defuse a situation that could easily go wildly out of control and cause untold harm. The door opened.

"Good morning," he said with a distinct chill in his voice. He didn't look well, his face paler than usual with dark rings under his eyes.

"Good morning, George. Are you okay? You don't look too good."

"I'm tired that's all."

She wasn't here to feel sorry for him or offer to bring chicken soup.

"I've come to tell you that I've, we've, decided to call off the engagement. It was too soon, too rash. You were right. We need to get to know each other better."

He studied her for a long moment during which her heart thudded so hard she was sure he'd be able to hear it.

"I was surprised when Duncan told you," she said when he didn't speak. "We'd agreed to keep it secret until we told Jessie."

"I'm glad you came to that conclusion. It's the right one, I'm sure." Pompous bastard, but she kept her temper in check. He wasn't getting away with it completely though.

"I want you to know, George, that your implication Duncan is a child molester was offensive and wrong and had nothing to do with this decision. I'm not worried about his relationship with Jessie and never have been."

He nodded. "I admit that was a bit…much."

"Good. I'd better go home and get Jessie moving."

"I'm about to leave. Staff meeting again before school." A smile switched on and off like a light.

"See you later." She started down the path.

"Poppy?"

She turned. He came down the steps.

"You must know how I feel about you. Is there a chance now that Duncan's not…that you've reconsidered…that we could give it a go? Get together?"

Poppy's heart almost stopped, and she had to gasp

for breath before the steady beat started up again. Her skin prickled and a bead of sweat ran down her side despite the cold morning air.

"I'm sorry, George, but no, there's no chance. I'm not interested in a relationship, not at the moment. You know that."

His expression hardened. "You were interested in one with him."

"That was a mistake."

"Give me a chance, at least."

"George, I'm sorry but…no."

"You'll change your mind. You've done it already with him."

"I won't, not this time."

"Why not?"

"Because I don't feel that way about you and I know I never will. I'm sorry."

"You will," he said. "In time. If you try."

"I have to go, and so do you."

Poppy turned and forced herself to walk rather than run for home. She glanced across as she reached her letterbox and caught a glimpse of him watching from the garden path.

Inside she went straight to the bathroom and closed the door. Her whole body shook. She leaned her hands against the vanity and stood with head bent taking deep breaths.

Duncan tapped on the door. "Are you okay?" he asked softly.

"I will be. Give me a minute."

Jessie was dressed and eating breakfast when Poppy went to the kitchen. Just on five to eight—a record for her now the novelty of school had worn off.

Duncan was drinking coffee and eating toast.

They both looked up as she joined them.

"Okay?" His eyes bored into hers.

"No problem." The steadiness of her voice amazed her.

"What's okay?" asked Jessie.

"Something I forgot to tell George yesterday. Anyone want a boiled egg?"

No one did so Poppy put one egg in a saucepan to boil, poured herself coffee, and sat down. "I can't believe you're ready so early. You were still in bed when I left."

"Duncan told me to get up and have breakfast with him so I can practice my uke before I go to school."

"Good idea. I'll have time to do your hair."

"I want it how it is."

"Unbrushed? You'll get knots in it—you know that."

"Brushing your hair makes it shiny," said Duncan. "My Mum used to say that."

"I want you to brush it," she said.

"I won't be very good at it."

"I don't mind. You'll get better if you practice."

No doubt something he'd told her in her music lesson.

"Can't argue with that," he said. "Have you finished your cereal?"

"Yes."

"Teeth and hair first," said Poppy.

Poppy lingered over her breakfast listening to the chatter from the bathroom as Duncan wrangled the curls into submission. He'd be furious when she told him what George had said and would be over there warning him off with God only knows what consequences. She couldn't tell him. She wouldn't tell him.

A burst of laughter came from the bathroom, but Poppy resisted the temptation to join them. It wasn't easy. All the mundane caring duties that were hers and hers alone for the first time weren't, and the thing that gave her a pang was how quickly Jessie asked Duncan to brush her hair. Her baby was growing up and away from her mother.

School was the first step in that process. There, her daughter had quickly become a person in her own right—Jessie French first, daughter of Poppy French second. It was all natural, but she knew exactly how other first time school mothers felt waving goodbye on that first day where previously she'd been confidently blasé in her belief Jessie would always turn to her mother ahead of all others. The two of them against the world.

The twanging of the ukulele strings sounded from the living room next, with Duncan's deep voice talking about tuning and reminding Jessie of the things they'd looked at yesterday. Jessie's bright voice asked questions and giggled and then the gentle and surprisingly musical notes sounded hesitantly but in a recognizable rhythmic pattern from the previous lesson.

"Not bad," said Duncan.

The pride in his voice made Poppy smile. She cleared her breakfast dishes and quickly wiped down the benches and table. She couldn't resent the fact that Duncan offered Jessie new things to explore and encouraged her to develop her creative side, because she certainly was creative. The musical aptitude must come from him, as well as her love of drawing. He had much to offer, and those things were a natural part of him.

She couldn't deny the feeling that another aspect of her closeness to Jessie had come to an end. It was as though a protective shell was breaking off little by little. A shell Jessie was unwittingly keen to discard but Poppy was clinging to, knowing it was a lost cause, and wrong to prevent her developing. If you love her, set her free.

She'd seen the paradox once before with a high school friend. Susie's mother had been the epitome of the helicopter parent, taking all autonomy away from her daughter and insisting on making decisions on her behalf, embarrassing her no end by coming to parties to check on the guests' behavior and generally stifling her. All in the name of love and protection.

Susie rapidly grew from a biddable thirteen-year-old to a secretive, deceitful wild child who detested her mother but played the good girl at home. It all came unstuck when at fifteen she was badly injured in a car crash involving four drunken teenagers.

Her mother, who thought she was at a study sleepover at a trusted friend's, was horrified but everyone at school knew it was inevitable. Poppy and her friends were as shocked as Susie's mother but felt no pity for the woman.

Her own mother wasn't like Susie's. She had her faults but over-protectiveness wasn't one of them. Her expectations were high, and Poppy always fell short but at the time her mother was surprisingly comforting and sad at the near loss of a friend, a girl she also knew. She commented that she trusted Poppy was sensible enough not to do what Susie did. And Poppy was but although she came close in recklessness later at times, the tragic consequence of driving drunk was indelibly imprinted on her brain and something she never did.

****

As soon as Poppy and Duncan began the walk back from taking Jessie to school and they were clear of the inquisitive looks from the other parents, he asked the inevitable question.

"What did George say to you this morning?"

"That I'd made the right decision not to marry you."

"Is that all? You were pretty shaken up when you came home."

"I wasn't. Aren't you cold?"

She pulled her beanie down over her ears against the biting wind. It had gained strength as they walked, and she'd forgotten to wear her scarf. Duncan had neither scarf nor beanie.

"No, and don't change the subject. Why go straight to the bathroom if you weren't upset?"

"I needed the loo."

Duncan snorted his disbelief. "Did he say anything else?"

"I told him off for implying you were a child molester and he agreed he'd gone too far with that comment."

"How nice of him, the bastard. Are you sure that's all?"

"Yes. Leave it. It's over."

The main street was relatively quiet with few people about in the cold. Poppy went into the bakery for fresh bread and a brief respite in the warm shop while Duncan waited outside.

"I should go home tomorrow," he said when she joined him.

"So soon?"

Judging by how he hadn't taken no for an answer this morning George wouldn't waste any time with Duncan gone. What would she say to him if he persisted? Threaten to call the police? She wanted Duncan to stay but he couldn't stay forever, and the George problem was something she'd have to deal with herself, sooner or later. She couldn't and wouldn't rely on Duncan to keep him at bay.

"I only came to bring Jessie the uke," he said. "I have gigs and things to do at home, Poppy. My life is there."

"Sure, fine. Of course. I meant Jessie will miss you."

"Likewise. She's a talented girl."

"Like her dad."

They waited at the pedestrian crossing as two cars went by. Duncan said nothing until they reached her street and started walking up the slow rise to the house.

"Thank you for letting me into her life, Poppy. I know now how hard it must have been to share her."

"It was but I don't regret it."

He slung an arm around her shoulders and pulled her closer as they walked. The warmth of his body seeped through the layers of clothing, and she wanted to stay there in the shelter he provided, not just from the cold wind but also the unwanted attention from the man next door. A man she'd thought was a friend but was revealing himself to be anything but.

"I think it's time to tell Jessie," she said.

"Tonight."

"Together?"

"Yes."

Chapter 24

Dinner was nearly over, and Poppy still hadn't taken the plunge. Duncan nudged her under the table with his foot. He was even more nervous than she was. She put her fork down.

"We have something to tell you, sweet pea," she said.

Jessie looked at her then Duncan. "Both of you together?"

"Yes," he said.

"Are you coming to live with us?" Jessie asked.

"No, not permanently but I'll visit as much as I can."

"Good because you have to give me my uke lessons."

Poppy drew a deep breath.

"Jessie, Duncan is your father. Your real father."

Jessie's eyes opened wide and for once she was rendered speechless for what seemed an eternity. Time hung suspended. Would she be pleased or cry? Poppy had no idea.

"Are you my real daddy?" It was a shy, wondering tone Poppy had never from her before, but she thought it might be infused with hope, and possibly delight.

"Yes, I am. What do you think about that?" His soft voice trembled ever so slightly. Hope tinged his tone, too.

She slid off her chair and came to Poppy, clinging to her side then climbing onto her lap. Poppy hugged her close.

"Why didn't you say you were my daddy before?" Jessie asked shyly.

"I wanted you to get to know me first. I hoped you'd like me so you'd be happy when you found out."

She gazed at him.

"Can I call still you Duncan?"

"Of course."

"Okay."

"Nothing will change, sweet pea," Poppy said. "It'll still be you and me living here and Duncan will come to visit us. Or sometimes we might even go to visit him in Sydney."

"But you said you had to be married or love someone for him to be my daddy."

"Well, yes, that was with someone new, not your real father...but it doesn't always work like that."

"We knew each other before you were born," Duncan said. "And then I had to go away but I am your real daddy and I won't go away again. Not like before."

"So can you still teach me music?"

"Yes, I can and I will."

"Good."

Poppy kissed her cheek. "Go and sit down and finish your dinner. We have a special treat dessert to celebrate."

"What is it?"

"A surprise."

Jessie clapped her hands. "Goody, goody, goody."

Poppy caught Duncan's gaze and he grinned, his eyes moist.

"Can I tell my friends I have a daddy?"

"Yes."

The normal level of chatter resumed during the course of which Jessie announced that George was sick and had to go home at lunchtime.

"He has the flu," she said. "Like Farah's mum and Bryony's daddy and her brother."

"He didn't look too good this morning," Poppy said. "Sounds like it's going around town."

"I had it, didn't I?"

"You had something."

"I hope I don't get it," said Duncan. "I have gigs then I'm in the studio recording."

"What's recording?" asked Jessie.

"That's when someone goes into a special room called a studio that has microphones and special machines that make a recording while the musicians play. Then people can buy the song or they can play it on the radio."

"Who are you recording with?" asked Poppy.

"Have you heard of Faith Kelly? This is for her new album."

"Sure. She's great. I have some of her songs. "Love Me Better" and "Harem" and maybe a couple more."

"She's recording one of my songs. We've already done three tracks for her new album. I played guitar on her last two albums and I'm touring with her in September. Promo tour all over the country for this new one."

"Wow. You kept that secret."

"Not really." He smiled. "I've known her for years."

"Who else do you play with that I might know?"

He rattled off a bunch of names, some familiar others not but impressive just the same.

"So you're not just a rock musician."

"No, I like studio work and that's picking up which is good. It means I don't have to do as many weddings and birthday parties." He smiled. "I actually really like writing songs, but it doesn't pay as much as playing. Not yet."

"Might it?"

"A couple of big hits and the royalties would be sweet."

"Faith might be the key."

"Could be."

"Are you famous?" asked Jessie.

"No."

"I don't mind," she said.

****

Duncan packed up and left after breakfast the following morning. He dropped Jessie at school because she asked him to and once more Poppy experienced the loss of another small piece of that protective shell she'd placed around her daughter.

Duncan held Poppy close and kissed her goodbye and said he'd let her know when he'd be back.

"I won't be able to for at least a couple of weeks," he said.

"No problem. We'll be here. Hope the recording goes well."

"Thanks."

She waved as he drove away with her daughter, watching until the car disappeared then turned to go inside, sniffing back a couple of wayward tears. A glance at George's house showed no signs of activity. How sick was he? She wasn't going over there to see. If he was in bed with a fever, he wouldn't be over at her house annoying her. The sicker the better.

She made sure the front and back doors were locked, telling herself she wasn't paranoid, just being security conscious, then settled down to do some preparation and organize the notes for her class at the Community Center. Maurice came to lie in a weak patch of sun on the floor but gave up and went away when a cloud came over.

At a quarter to ten Poppy drove to class in light drizzle and at twelve fifteen she drove home in rain. Duncan texted that he was home and that he'd seen Jessie safely into school, finishing with —*I'll miss you.*—

—*You too*— she replied.

The house felt empty for the first time she could remember. Even the day Jessie started school had been filled with activity. She'd relished the uninterrupted hours she could spend at the computer and school pick-up time had arrived in a flash.

Now the afternoon dragged. Maurice offered no help. He curled up in front of the heater and snored. Unable to concentrate she went to the spare room and stripped the bed. Next time Duncan came would they share her bed? He seemed reluctant and she didn't know why, not now they knew and trusted each other. She trusted him at least, and she suspected he trusted her too. There was an elemental attraction screaming to be addressed so why not act on it?

She stopped bundling sheets abruptly as the reason popped into her head. He wanted to make love in the true sense. He didn't want the type of sex they'd had all those years ago. In that respect he was the same as George. She'd told George that she wouldn't tell a man she loved him. Was that still true? At the time she'd been giving George a signal that she wasn't interested by pointing out the hopelessness of trying to woo her. That failed.

She didn't want the kind of relationship he wanted and thought she never would, but she hadn't experienced what Duncan had brought to her home. He didn't impose himself; he simply fitted. And it wasn't only because he and Jessie immediately clicked. It was because he was easy going, useful around the house, respected her work and her privacy. He was quietly independent, confident in his talent, but also emotionally vulnerable in a way that took her breath away.

She missed him. Was that true love? If not, it was a kind of love. It was a start.

****

Jessie was upset at how some of the children had taken her exciting news.

"They said I'm a liar," she said furiously. "But I'm not."

Poppy grimaced. She should have known that would happen. "I'll come in with you tomorrow morning and tell Mrs. Morton that it's true. I'm sorry. I should have done that today."

"Good."

"Are you happy that Duncan is your daddy?"

"Yes. I like him a lot."

"He likes you a lot, too."

"He said we can stay with him at his house near the

beach."

"We will."

"When?"

"We'll have to wait till the holidays."

"But that's ages."

"I know."

"We can ask him if we can come earlier."

"Yes, we can but he has his work to do. He's a busy musician."

"That's why he couldn't stay with us any longer. He has gigs."

Poppy smiled at the pride in her voice.

Sitting at the table having afternoon tea, Jessie said, "I miss Duncan. I wish he was here."

"I do too. When you've practiced your tunes enough we can do a video call and he can hear you play."

"Yes. I have to practice right now."

"Finish eating first."

She sat grudgingly chewing on a piece of muesli slice.

While Jessie plucked earnestly at the uke strings, Poppy prepared a casserole with Maurice hovering at her feet sniffing hopefully as the meat browned.

The afternoon dragged on. Dinnertime came and went and with Jessie in bed just after seven thirty a long evening stretched ahead. Duncan would be heading to his gig or already there. He hadn't said what it was. She'd like to hear him play with a band. She'd only heard snippets of the song he'd been writing and then the sing-along tunes he'd played so effortlessly. Despite what he said about his voice he sang well to her untrained ear. Admittedly Kyle was very good, but she hadn't heard Duncan sing with a band doing the style of music he liked best.

She turned the TV off and went through her playlist looking for Faith Kelly. Was Duncan on the tracks she had? She should have asked. This world of a professional musician was completely new to her. He worked all sorts of odd hours. Most of his work was at night but he had to be in the recording studio all day for three days and possible had nighttime gigs as well. He'd be exhausted. And then when he did have some spare time, he drove to Currong to visit them, a few times at her request.

He never said he was too tired. He just came when he could. How long would he be able to keep that up? He'd wear himself out trying to do the right thing by Jessie. She must never pressure him about the times when he couldn't be here. She'd have to organize to go to Sydney instead or perhaps they could even meet him somewhere when he was on that tour.

She pulled out her phone and did a search for Faith's tour dates and discovered she was going right around Australia over six weeks. If they had a couple of shows in one place it might be possible to catch him. Brisbane, for example. Three shows were listed there. That would a good place to visit. If he agreed. She wouldn't impose herself on him anywhere and either embarrass him in front of his colleagues or humiliate herself.

She might get to meet Faith Kelly. A frown crept across wiping out the little smile she'd had as she imagined the could be's. How well did he know Faith Kelly? Years he'd said but how close were they?

Stop it! She must never do the jealousy thing.

Duncan would have met and worked with lots and lots of musicians, male and female. Why assume he had affairs with all the women? Faith had two small children anyway, and that was something Poppy had always admired about her and her partner who she vaguely remembered was also a musician. She'd read that the family adapted their professional lives to fit around both their careers.

The phone startled her by ringing. George's name flashed onto the screen.

Her finger hovered over End Call, but he might be needing help in his illness.

"Hello."

"Poppy, sorry to bother you but do you have any paracetamol?" His voice rasped. He didn't sound good. "I've got this virus and my head is killing me."

"I'll see. I know I have the children's version. I haven't had a headache for years." Only him, the biggest of them all.

She went to the bathroom and checked the cabinet. An almost full box of twenty-four was there with a month left before expiry.

"Yes, I do."

"Would you mind dropping them in? I'm in no state to go out."

"Um…Jessie will be here alone, but I guess…okay."

"Thank you."

"I won't come in, George. I'll just knock and leave them."

"Fine. Thanks."

She disconnected, took the box, and went to check on Jessie. She wasn't asleep. She stirred in the dim glow of the night light.

"Who were you talking to?"

"I'm just going to take some headache pills to George. I'll be two minutes," Poppy said quietly.

Jessie sat up. "I don't want you to go. I'm scared by myself."

"What if you look out the front window and watch me?"

"But I can't see you at George's house."

"I'd only be out of sight for a few seconds. I promise I won't stay. I told George I'd knock on the door and leave the pills on the step. Then I'll run home."

"But it's raining."

"I know and I don't want to go but he's sick with a bad headache." Poppy pulled her phone from her pocket. "How about we call Duncan, and you can talk to him while I'm gone?"

"Yes." Her face brightened.

"He might be playing already but we can try."

He picked up almost immediately. "Hi there, everything okay?"

Poppy explained and he said, "Great, I have a couple of minutes before we start. Put her on, but are you sure he's really sick?"

"Why pretend?"

"I wouldn't put anything past him but if you're not back before I have to go, I'll tell Jessie to call the cops."

"You won't need to, but she knows what to do in an emergency. We've talked about it. Here she is."

Jessie grabbed the phone eagerly and began telling Duncan about how her friends didn't believe he was her father. Poppy blew her a kiss and hurried to find a plastic baggy to put the pill box in, get her keys, coat, and umbrella.

She carefully locked the door and swearing at George under her breath put the umbrella up and set off down the path in the sheeting rain, dodging puddles as well as she could but failing to avoid soaked shoes.

In the shelter of George's porch, she thumped on the door and put the little box of pills on the step. No lights showed from inside the house. She thought he'd put the outside one on at least, knowing she was coming. She banged again with no response.

Right, she'd done what he asked, and she wasn't leaving Jessie alone any longer. She smiled. Duncan would be calling the police if she lingered. Would he really follow through with that? She turned and splashed her way home.

Back inside she called to Jessie she was home, ditched her wet shoes and coat in the laundry, then went to check on her. She was asleep and didn't stir when Poppy kissed her warm cheek.

That was quick, and surprising given she was so keen to talk to Duncan until Poppy came home, but it was late for her, and she had been known to go to sleep mid-sentence. She retrieved the phone from under the doona. Jessie had disconnected the call so Duncan wasn't stuck on the other end wondering what was happening. She dialed his number but it went to voicemail so he was probably playing. Maybe that's why the call had ended—he'd had to deal with something at his end. She sent a text saying she was home, put the phone on the bedside table, straightened the bedclothes, and gazed at the cherubic face for a few moments.

In the kitchen she made a cup of tea, glanced at Maurice who was curled up in his bed, and went to the living room to resume her search for Faith Kelly tracks. Hadn't she left both the lights on in there? There were two ceiling lights because the room was large, but the light was unnecessarily bright, so she only ever used a vintage wooden standing lamp and a smaller one that stood on the bookshelf. Together they cast a softer yellower light which was much cozier and better for watching TV.

She was sure she hadn't turned them off because of Jessie and also because she was coming back into the room after the brief trip next door. Maybe the bulb had blown. She tried the switch on the standing lamp and the light came on.

"Hello, Poppy," George said.

The tea slopped over the edge of the mug and ran down the side as her hand jerked in surprise. Then fear took over and she fought to tamp it down.

"Gosh, you gave me a fright. What are you doing here? I've just been over...why... Aren't you sick?" Hand shaking, she put the mug on top of the bookcase and moved to face him.

"Thank you for rushing to my aid but as you can see it wasn't necessary."

"How did you get in?" She'd made sure the doors were locked. Had he deliberately asked her for help knowing she wouldn't let him in if he knocked? To get her out of the house?

He held up a key.

"Where did you get that?"

"From your kitchen drawer."

"What?" That's where she kept a spare and there

was one buried in the garden too for emergencies. He'd been poking around in her house. For how long? How often?

"When?"

"A while ago."

"You stole it, you mean. You've been in my house while I wasn't home?" She tried hard to keep the rising anger in check. He must have already been outside when he phoned. In the carport perhaps so he could slip inside without her seeing. She was only gone for five minutes.

"Yes, you don't lock up as well as you should."

"What do you want?"

"Sit down, Poppy." He patted the space next to him on the couch.

"No. Have you harmed Jessie?"

"No." That seemed to shock him. "I'd never hurt a child. She was asleep when I came in. I checked. She's so sweet when she's sleeping."

His tone made her skin crawl. She lowered her voice so as not to antagonize him. Somehow, she had to get him out of her house. Minus the key. "What do you want?"

"You know what I want."

"No, I don't."

He shook his head and sighed. "You do, Poppy. I want you and deep down you want me. You just won't admit it."

"You're wrong. I don't want you that way and I've told you that many times. I never pretended otherwise."

"You can't be serious about Duncan. Why would you prefer him over me? What's he got to offer you?"

"What makes you think I'm serious about him?"

"He's here all the time, Poppy. Everyone knows that and it's really humiliating for us both. It's also a terrible example for Jessie having her mother sharing her bed with some man she just met."

"I think you're imagining that, and I haven't slept with Duncan."

"Don't patronize me," he snapped. He was on his feet in an instant. Poppy took a step back.

"Duncan has gone home and as far as I know he won't be coming back. Unless something happens in his brother's case and…" Her voice trailed off as the expression on George's face altered.

"He thinks I murdered his brother," he hissed. "Do you think I did? He's poisoned you against me, hasn't he? We were getting along so well until he arrived. If bloody Kyle hadn't turned up, you never would have met him and we'd still be happy together."

"It wouldn't have made any difference, George," she said. "Please, can you go home now? I'm tired and I want my key back."

He held the key out. Poppy hesitated. If she went closer, he could easily grab hold of her and then…

"Put it on the coffee table," she said.

He did as she asked, with a weird little smile. "I will go home, Poppy but not yet. Perhaps we could have a glass of wine together and enjoy the evening now that we've got things straight between us."

What on earth was he talking about?

"Got what straight?"

"That Duncan means nothing to you, and we can go back to how we were before. We get on so well. Made for each other some would say."

Poppy stared at him. Had he always been mad or

had this delusion manifested itself in the last few months? She hadn't led him on, but had she done something to push him over the edge, or was it Duncan? Whatever the cause she had to keep him happy until she could get rid of him.

"Red or white wine?" she asked. "I have a nice bottle of red I've been saving. It's in the cupboard here."

"Perfect." He sat down again, and she forced herself to move casually across and remove the bottle along with two of her good wine glasses. The ones she saved for special occasions rather than the cheap ones in the kitchen. She poured and placed his glass on the coffee table, keeping well clear.

"What lovely glasses," he said.

"They're my best."

That pleased him.

"Thank you. Cheers," he said and raised the glass to her. "Here's to a happy future together."

Poppy raised hers. "Cheers."

The word sounded half strangled, but he smiled and sipped and nodded at the taste. "Very good," he said. "Is this local?"

"No. From a Canberra winery. I've had it a while."

"Saving it for a special occasion?"

She nodded and he smiled at the implication.

"Sit down, Poppy. Don't stand there like that. Relax."

She perched on the edge of the chair farthest from him, diagonally opposite across the little table where her key sat tantalizingly close.

"Isn't this nice? The two of us here enjoying being together." He smiled. "Your house is so cozy. After

319

we're married we'll stay here for sure."

Poppy clamped her mouth shut, letting his crazy talk wash over her.

"Were you very ill?" she asked. "Jessie said some bug has been going around the school."

"I wasn't too bad, but I kept away. After that pandemic we're all really conscious of not spreading germs, aren't we?"

She nodded. "That's true. It's probably the only good thing to come from it."

"You're not drinking, Poppy."

She obediently took a small sip. What a waste of a good shiraz, sharing it with a madman. She almost laughed at the insanity of the whole situation, but he was calmer now and with any luck would go home without a fuss if she humored him a bit longer.

"Mmm," she said. "It's as good as I thought it was."

"We should go away for a weekend. Leave Jessie here and do some wine tasting in the Canberra region."

"It's a possibility." About as possible as either of them becoming President of the US.

"I'll check out accommodation options."

"It would be better to go in spring, wouldn't it? The weather's pretty awful, and Canberra can get cold."

"You're right. We could take in Floriade as well."

"Jessie would like that."

"Yes, of course. I have to think like a family man now."

Poppy drank more wine then put the glass down firmly. "I'm sorry, George. I really must go to bed soon and so should you. You won't be completely recovered yet and you do look a little pale."

"Do I? It's so sweet that you care. I knew you would when you remembered how good we are together." To her relief he put the glass down. "We can finish the bottle tomorrow. Perhaps we can prepare dinner together?"

"Maybe."

"And we still haven't had the group dinner with Steph and her friend."

Poppy stood up, the relief pounding so fiercely through her body she could barely breathe. Only a few more minutes and he'd be gone.

George stood as well.

"Mummy, I didn't know where you were."

Poppy spun around. Jessie stood in the doorway, her teddy bear trailing from one hand, face flushed from sleep, hair tousled.

"You were asleep when I came home."

"I was talking to Duncan, but he had to go." She looked at George. "Hello, George. Are you better now?"

"Back to bed, sweet pea," Poppy put her hand firmly on Jessie's shoulder and turned her round before she said another word.

"Why were you talking to Duncan?" asked George.

"I was scared to be here all by myself when Mummy took your pills, so I talked to Duncan on Mummy's phone." She gave a cavernous yawn.

"Come on, off to bed," said Poppy but George was by her side, staring down at Jessie, his face twisted with anger.

Jessie cringed and clung to Poppy.

"Why did you want to talk to Duncan in particular?" he asked again.

"He's my Daddy," Jessie said, her voice barely audible.

Chapter 25

Poppy scooped Jessie into her arms.

"I'm taking her back to bed," she said, glaring at him, defying him to stop her.

He must have recognized the ferociousness in her voice because he nodded but still followed her to Jessie's room and watched from the doorway as she tucked her in. Her phone was still on the bedside table. Would he see it?

Poppy leaned down to kiss her, and Jessie grabbed her with both arms around her neck.

"Don't go," she said and burrowed her face into Poppy's shoulder.

Drawn tightly against her, Poppy whispered, "This is an emergency. Use my phone. It's a secret emergency. Understand? I'll close the door."

She kissed Jessie quickly and released herself from the embrace. "Goodnight, sweet pea."

"Sleep tight," said George from the doorway.

Jessie pulled her doona up over her head.

As soon as she'd closed Jessie's door George grabbed her wrist and dragged her back to the living room.

"You lying bitch."

He released her arm and gave her a blow to the face that sent her sprawling against the back of the couch. She sagged against it fighting to stay upright, incomprehension and shock swirling amidst the wave of pain and the blurring of tears. He strode forward and grabbed her jumper to haul her to her feet.

"You told me five minutes ago you never slept with that man."

He raised his fist again and she tried to block it with her arm at the same time kicking at his legs using the couch as support, but he was too strong, and his forearm connected with hers in a sickening thud.

Poppy yelped and scrambled around the end of the couch, panting with fear. Three strides and he caught her, dragged her across the carpet, then kicked her in the stomach, and again. Something cracked. She gasped at the searing pain and curled into a ball at his feet, covering her head with her arms, waiting for the next blow, incapable of moving.

It didn't come.

He'd backed off, breath rasping unevenly.

"Get up." His voice was unrecognizable.

Poppy struggled blindly, slowly onto hands and knees, pain stabbing through her with every small movement. She pushed herself to her feet and stood hunched over, swaying unsteadily. He was sitting on the couch with his head in his hands.

"I'm sorry." His voice was muffled. "I didn't want to hurt you. I love you more than anything, Poppy, but you lied to me about something so vital. So basic. You must never lie to me, or this is what happens. Understand?"

Poppy's tongue refused to move. Her brain couldn't organize words.

"Do you understand?" This time he raised his head and gave her a venomous look.

She nodded. Her head pounded. She touched fingers to her cheek and swollen lip and looked uncomprehendingly at the blood on them.

"Sit down."

He patted the seat next to her, but her legs wouldn't cooperate and a wave of nausea doubled her over with a groan. She clutched her stomach and staggered a few steps toward the nearest chair where she collapsed. The nausea subsided but every breath brought an agonizing stab in her chest. Broken ribs.

"You bastard," she muttered.

"I said I was sorry," he said.

"Not…good enough…you shitty…little… cowardly…worm." She gasped out the words.

"You have only yourself to blame." He stood up and edged around the table toward her, but Poppy heaved herself to her feet and lunged for the bottle still sitting on the table with the half full wine glasses.

As he reached her, her fingers closed over the smooth glass neck, and she swung the bottle with all her remaining strength. A cascade of deep red shiraz poured out, but the bottle connected with the side of his head, and he went down in a shower of broken glass and wine. Poppy scrambled for the door still holding the broken bottle. She turned but he lay unmoving where he fell.

She stumbled to Jessie's room and flung the door open.

"Mummy." Jessie's horrified face stared at her from the bed.

"I'm all right, I'm all right. Where's my phone?"

Jessie held it out. "I called Triple 0," she said. "Because you said it was an emergency. The lady is still there."

"Oh." Poppy burst into tears.

"Was that wrong?"

"No, no, no. It was perfect. Just perfect."

Poppy took the phone. "Hello."

"Hello, Poppy. The police will be there any minute. Are you in a safe place?"

"I…hit him. I…he's on the floor."

As she spoke heavy knocking sounded on the front door. "Police. Open up, please."

"They're here. Thank you, thank you. Stay here, Jessie." Poppy dropped the phone and stumbled down the hallway casting a quick glance into the living room as she went but the couch hid her view of him. Had he gone?

The two officers went into immediate action when Poppy gave a stuttering version of what happened. One sat her down in the kitchen and called an ambulance while the other went to the living room.

"Is there someone who can come to be with your child?" he asked.

Poppy's immediate thought was Duncan but that was stupid. Who else?

"Steph Wilcox," she said after a moment of blankness. "Her number is in my phone."

"Where's your phone, Poppy?" Such a kind, patient voice.

"With Jessie. I need to be with Jessie."

"I'll need to ask her a few questions about what happened."

"She's five, she's frightened. I need to be with her."

"I'll bring her to you. Don't worry. You need to

stay quiet. You're in shock."

Poppy sat at the table listening to the sounds of strangers taking charge in her home. More of them came through the front door. Her head ached and her chest hurt with every breath.

The policeman reappeared with Jessie in her dressing gown and slippers. He'd taken the rug off her bed, and he draped it around Poppy's shoulders.

"Mummy," Jessie wailed. "Your face is bleeding."

"I know but I'm okay. We're okay. You were so clever phoning the police." She hugged Jessie carefully, wincing as the pressure impacted on her battered body. "Steph is coming to look after you."

"Constable Jim said you have to go to hospital."

"Yes, but not for very long."

"You did extremely well, Jessie," said the constable. "You're a champion."

"I was scared because George was very, very angry. He hurt my Mummy."

"He won't do that again. You were very brave."

Poppy looked at the constable. "Where is he?"

"He'll need medical attention, but we'll take him to the Currong Medical Center. You need to go to Goulburn Hospital."

She drew in a shaky breath. "Thank you. I thought he…I thought…"

"He can't harm you now," he said. "But we will need to take a statement tomorrow."

Poppy remained sitting at the table with Jessie on her lap, drinking the hot sweet tea the kind constable made, until Steph came, all concern, warmth, and capability. Shortly afterward the ambulance arrived.

****

Duncan checked his messages when he arrived home at midnight after the gig but there was nothing new. Poppy had sent a text after she'd taken pills to that bastard. He would have let him suffer but she was too kind-hearted. He'd phone her tomorrow for no other reason than to hear her voice. Talking to Jessie had been a real treat. And she'd asked for him. Her daddy.

When the phone rang early the following morning, he half expected it to be Poppy but it wasn't. It was Al, the Currong policeman. The more he spoke the more horrified Duncan became. When Al hung up, he immediately made a call canceling his gig then threw some clothes into a bag and ran for the car.

He reached Goulburn Base Hospital in record time and just after ten walked into the room where Poppy lay in a bed by the window. A tall woman with copper colored hair stood next to her, and Jessie leaned on the bed. She saw Duncan first, let out a delighted cry, and ran to him. He hugged her tight.

"I'm Steph." The redhead held out her hand.

He shook it. "Duncan," he said but his eyes were on Poppy.

He leaned over and kissed her gently on the forehead, about the only unbruised part of her poor swollen face.

"I never dreamed he'd do this to you," he said softly. "I shouldn't have left you."

"No one thought he would," said Steph. "We're all stunned."

"Constable Jim said I saved Mummy," Jessie said.

"You did, and I'm extremely proud of you," murmured Poppy. She held out her hand to Duncan and he clutched it tightly. Her eyes drifted shut.

"She's a bit groggy," said Steph. "They've sedated her. They were worried about the blows to the stomach and the three broken ribs causing internal damage, but it turns out she's okay."

"So she'll be in here a while," Duncan said.

"A couple of days. I'll move in with Jessie and stay until Pop can cope on her own."

"Can't you come and look after me, Duncan?" asked Jessie.

"I'd love to, Jessie. I can stay tonight but I have to go back to Sydney for work." He drew Steph away a little. "I really want to be here with them, but I can't cancel out any more gigs at short notice. It's not fair to the guys."

Steph put her hand on his arm. "It's okay. Poppy understands and so does Jessie. We'll cope."

"Did she tell you about me?"

"A while ago, yes. She was a bit coy about you which immediately said way more than she thought it did." She grinned then put on a stern face. "But Jessie was the one who told me about her daddy. She's really excited, so you'd damn well better not bugger off and forget about her."

"I won't. I never thought I'd want the family thing but now…it's the most important part of my life. Being Jessie's father is extraordinary."

"Good answer." Steph kissed his cheek. "Just make sure you tell Poppy. I don't think she knows."

"What? She knows I love Jessie."

"Sure, but she doesn't know you love her."

"I don't know that she loves me," he said.

Steph shook her head. "What a pair of idiots."

She held out her hand to Jessie. "Come on, let's go

and find the cafeteria. We need chocolate."

Duncan pulled a chair up close so he could hold Poppy's hand. Her eyes opened and focused on him, and she managed a partial smile.

"I love you," he said and lifted her hand to his lips. "I want to be with you and our daughter forever."

"You're only saying that because I nearly got killed," she said slowly, the words punctuated by small gasps where she drew painful breaths.

He shook his head. "I should have said it ages ago, but I didn't realize until Steph pointed it out."

"She's a busybody."

"She's right."

Her eyes closed again. He didn't release her hand but a part of him was disappointed she hadn't said she loved him back.

A rotund gray-haired nurse came in to check Poppy's temperature and take her blood pressure. She gave Duncan a suspicious look as she straightened the pillows.

"It wasn't him," Poppy said.

"I've just driven from Sydney to be with her," he said. "She whacked the bastard with a bottle and floored him."

Poppy squeezed his hand and he smiled.

"Good for you," the nurse said to Poppy, then to Duncan, "We get a few women come in like this. Makes my blood boil." She produced a smile. "She's doing fine."

"How long will she be in?"

"You'd have to talk to the doctor about that, but I'd say a couple more days."

When she left, Poppy said, "Thank you for

coming."

"How could I not?"

"You're busy and…" A tear ran from the corner of her eye. "I so wanted you to be here."

"I'm here." He carefully dabbed away the moisture.

"George said something to me once…"

He hissed in air. "I don't even want to hear that name."

"No, listen." She paused and he waited knowing each word was painfully produced. "I said…I didn't want to get married…he was going on about…wanting fifty kids. I said I'd never tell…someone I loved them…he said that if I…did it would mean…I really meant it. I laughed…but I understand…now…he was right."

"He meant it would really mean something to you?"

"Yes. He was hoping…I'd say it to him…that was never…going to happen." She shuddered. "At the time I was…sure I wouldn't ever say…it to anyone except…Jessie but I didn't know…you then. Not properly."

"And now?" he asked hoarsely.

"I love you, Duncan." The last four words came out strongest and clearest of all.

****

Just over a week later, on Sunday afternoon, Rudy Dietrich and Portia Mason sat in Poppy's living room drinking coffee and eating fruit cake.

Poppy's face had regained most of its normal shape, but a deep purple bruise decorated her cheek and eye. The same color stained her stomach and chest, and

Elisabeth Rose

her ribs would be painful for weeks. Other bruises had appeared in places she hadn't realized were damaged, namely her hip, lower back, thigh, and forearm.

Duncan had arrived on Sunday and planned to go home early on Monday morning. He sat with Poppy on the couch while Rudy outlined the case against George. He was more relaxed than Poppy had ever seen him, and Portia had actually smiled several times already.

Rudy said, "From the extensive forensic analysis in the house we were able to determine that Kyle was hit and most likely killed in the living room. George had cleaned up but there's only so much that can be done in that regard by an amateur. We found small traces of blood on the lounge room carpet and bigger stains on the underlay where it had seeped through. It was Kyle's blood."

"Did you find what he was hit with?" asked Duncan.

"Not yet. He could easily have thrown whatever it was in the lake when he ditched the car."

"Was George driving the car I saw?" asked Poppy.

"Yes. After he'd hit Kyle, he packed everything into his car and drove it fast probably so anyone who saw would notice but not have time to see who was driving, and later would think he'd left in anger. It was quite dark with the rain starting. He left the car at the lake and came back home on foot."

"He came over that night to see if Jessie and I were okay after that fight. I remember now he was jittery, and his shoes were really wet, and he seemed surprised when I mentioned the power going off."

"That's because he wasn't at home and didn't know," said Rudy.

"I thought he was upset about Kyle."

"He was more upset about himself," said Duncan.

"After he'd dumped the car, he was able to take his time with disposing of the body. Kyle wasn't even reported as missing until late the following day. We found evidence that he wrapped him in plastic sheeting to transport him and then disposed of it later, which could have been anywhere, and I doubt it'll turn up now. But we found shreds in the boot of his car and matching fragments under Kyle's body where the plastic had caught and torn off."

"Did you find the ring?" asked Duncan.

"No, I'm sorry."

"But why did he do it?" asked Poppy.

Portia said, "When we looked into his past, we discovered George wasn't as squeaky clean as everyone here assumed. He'd been engaged once but his fiancée had an accident. She fell from her apartment balcony and died about two months before the wedding. Her family always maintained she'd called the engagement off and he'd killed her but they could never prove it. He had an alibi but, somehow, we think Kyle may have found out that it might not be true and taunted him with exposure. He would have lost everything. We also discovered he'd harassed a couple of women he'd been infatuated with, but they never reported it. One moved away and the other had a couple of brothers who confronted him."

"I heard Kyle threaten George," said Poppy suddenly. "When I was leaving after that fight. Ralph had gone already." She frowned. "He said something like 'I warned you, Georgie. When your boss finds out what I know your career will be in the garbage.' I can't remember exactly. And he also made some snide sort of remarks at the gig. About not telling tales about a tour they were on. Lismore seemed to mean something. George brushed it off as typical Kyle when I asked him."

"Why didn't you report the threat at the time Kyle went missing?" asked Rudy.

"I…don't know. It sounded like the sort of nasty thing Kyle would say when he was angry, but not mean anything. And I felt sorry for George."

"Hmmm. Okay."

He glanced at Portia, and she made a note.

"I'm sorry," she said.

"You couldn't know. Not then," Duncan said.

"Now," said Rudy, "I know this will be upsetting, Poppy, but in the house we found a room filled with photos of you. He was obsessed."

A shudder ran through her body and Duncan put his arm around her shoulders and held her close.

"Will you have enough evidence to lock him up?" she asked. The media was always reporting how terrible people were let off because of some mistake in the evidence, or insufficient evidence.

"Definitely. We have him on murder, a possible attempted murder, or at least an attempt to harm Duncan, and the attack on you."

Rudy took another piece of cake. "I'm sorry it took so long to nail him, and you had to suffer the way you did but we didn't know the full extent of his obsession and with Duncan in Sydney we thought you'd be all right."

"It's our fault. We told Jessie I was her father," said Duncan. "We shouldn't have because we knew she wouldn't be able to keep it secret."

"No," said Poppy. "We should have, and we did. I wanted us to live our lives the way we wanted to, not pander to his delusions. Not that I knew how mad he really is."

"So," said Portia. "When's the wedding and are we invited? I love a wedding."

"If we ever get around to marriage you will be, I promise," said Poppy.

"Will you stay here in Currong? From what I can tell it's a nice place to bring up a kid," said Rudy. "Won't have bad memories for you and Jessie?"

"We both love this house, but Jessie and I will probably spend quite a bit of time in Sydney. She seems to be fine. I think the excitement of Duncan has taken the edge off the fright and she didn't see anything bad, not really. She's proud of phoning for help."

"All I can say is good luck. You deserve it." Rudy smiled cheerfully and took another piece of cake.

"Whatever we end up doing," said Duncan. "We'll figure it out together because that's what we want most." He looked at Poppy as he spoke, his eyes, his voice, and his expression wrapping her in the best kind of love. "To be together. As a family."

****

By October the house next door had new tenants, this time a family who had relocated to Currong from Canberra seeking a quieter rural life for their three boisterous boys. A far cry from the previous occupant, they were, as far as Poppy and Duncan could tell, as normal as anyone. Whatever that meant. The father, Adam, was a writer and mother Lydia, a textile artist. The children went to the small catholic primary school rather than the Currong Primary but Jessie and their youngest, Harry, soon became good friends and were inseparable after school and at weekends.

Duncan spent as much time as possible in Currong and had graduated to Poppy's bedroom very quickly after her recovery. By the time the spring school holidays rolled around he was away on the Faith Kelly tour and Poppy and Jessie planned to fly up to Brisbane in the second week to meet him.

In the first week of the school break Poppy and Jessie set to work in the vegetable garden. They'd ridden their bikes to the nursery for spring seedlings to replace the exhausted winter crop and Poppy intended to prepare the area with compost for the tomatoes which she'd plant in a few weeks' time when the weather grew warmer.

The ground was wet after rain the previous week but today the sun shone, and she grew hot quickly. Jessie had her little shovel and helped dig out the spent plants and dump them in the wheelbarrow. Before long Harry appeared, and not long after that Poppy's two assistants lost interest and went off to play inside. Poppy continued digging and sifting roots and weeds from the soil enjoying the work and the sun on her back, humming one of Faith's songs and allowing her mind to wander freely to the trip to Brisbane where they'd be getting the star treatment according to Duncan. Apparently Faith was very keen to meet the woman who'd claimed his heart.

Poppy hummed and dug and sifted and suddenly a glint of silver caught her eye. She carefully lowered the shovel and its contents to the ground and poked her fingers into the mix of soil and roots.

A ring. The ring.

George had buried it after all. She took it to the laundry and washed away the soil, tears flooding her eyes as the elaborate, beautiful design came into view. She dried it carefully and pulled out her phone then stopped. No. She wouldn't call Duncan.

She wanted to be there with him when she gave him this precious memento of the little brother he'd loved and lost. She wanted him to know he wasn't alone and that he was loved and always would be.

A word about the author...

Elisabeth plays classical clarinet, tennis, practices tai chi and reads as much as possible.

www.elisabethrose.com.au

Thank you for purchasing
this publication of The Wild Rose Press, Inc.

For questions or more information
contact us at
info@thewildrosepress.com.

The Wild Rose Press, Inc.
www.thewildrosepress.com